Tarcadia

Tarcadia

A novel by *Jonathan Campbell*

Gaspereau Press ⁌ *Printers & Publishers* MMIV

For Lindee

Arcadia is perpetually being renewed because the longing for it is rooted in one of the deepest instincts of man; common to all people and all times, it will of necessity wear a different look in different times and places.

PETER V. MARINELLI

Bitter Constraint, and sad occasion dear,
Compels me to disturb your season due:
For *Lycidas* is dead, dead ere his prime,
Young *Lycidas,* and hath not left his peer.

JOHN MILTON, 1638

I

I MIGHT AS WELL TELL YOU RIGHT AWAY THAT MY brother drowned in Sydney Harbour. I don't want to spring that fact on you at the end and have you be completely surprised. I was with him at the time, too. You might as well know that. But it wasn't my fault in any way. I happened to be there and I saw him drown. Or at least I saw him disappear beneath the waves, as they say of ships that sink. We were coming back from the other side in the kayak and it was pretty rough. We shouldn't have tried crossing when it was so choppy. The wind and the tide were against us. But we just wanted to get across the harbour to Muggah's Creek as quickly as possible. Both Sid and I thought it was the only sensible thing to do after we saw those fruitcakes. But Sid didn't make it to Sydney. Halfway there he just slipped beneath the waves. He could still be alive for all I know. I didn't really witness his death like everyone says I did. No one's actually seen Sid dead. I was just the last person to see him alive.

A Coast Guard ship from Point Edward picked me up. I was clinging to the tower of a steel harbour buoy. My father went out on one of the search boats and helped dredge the little inlets around Sydney Harbour on the Point Edward side looking for Sid's body. The searchers didn't want my father on board because he was an aggrieved parent. It didn't matter. No one found Sid. He either made it safely to shore, or he was taken right out to sea with the ebb tide and was visiting the Hebrides by the time they even got ready to look for him. In case you didn't know, the Hebrides are a group of islands in the North Atlantic Ocean that we Scots are supposed to be able to behold in our dreams. That's what I've heard, anyway. I don't know. I've never seen them in my dreams.

The truth is that we weren't used to the swells in the harbour. That's the sorry truth. I wish I could say that we were used to them. We weren't sailors so much as we were paddlers. And a homemade kayak is not the kind of boat to cross Sydney Harbour in, especially when you have everything going against you. You learn these things.

I GUESS, WHEN I THINK OF IT, IT ALL STARTED TO GO wrong at Christmas.

We had the kitchen table set for Christmas dinner. We didn't have a dining room. But we had a kitchen big enough for a table that could seat the six of us and some cousins. At Christmas, we'd put in the middle section of the table because there was so much food. We had a white lace tablecloth on the table, too, and crystal goblets next to every plate. My father asked Sid to light the candles that were on the table while my father opened a bottle of wine. I understand that Europeans have wine every day, even the kids. But we were quite lucky to have wine even on such a special occasion. Everyone got a little bit of wine, even cousin Mandy got a little taste to shut her up. Our family had three boys and one girl. Sid was the oldest, then Heather, me, and Cosmo. My father had named the first three kids, my mother had named the last. Sid was fifteen, Heather was fourteen, I was thirteen, Cosmo was twelve. Our little cousin Mandy was five, and our cousin Daphne was ten. They stayed with us all the time because our uncle Bruce didn't live with them anymore and their mother was always working.

All of us were in our Sunday clothes. My mother took the turkey from the oven. It was an enormous turkey. Heather helped her by holding one side of the platter because it was so heavy. Then Sid helped Heather and my mother, and they placed the turkey in the middle of the table and we all looked at it for a moment. It was perfectly done, brown and crispy, and juices were bubbling out of the hole in the breast where the thermometer had been. And the smell was fantastic. Heather brought out a porcelain gravy train dish and filled it right up with her gravy. She could make gravy like you wouldn't believe. Usually, she just dunked it on your plate, but at Christmas we were allowed to help ourselves by using the special gravy train dish with the handle on the extreme end.

A pot of creamy mashed potatoes was put on the table. Heather could make the best mashed potatoes, too. Gravy and potatoes were her speciality. You'd think you'd died and gone to heaven. Some peas and mixed vegetables were in smaller bowls. Little dishes of other things like pickles and some gut stuff from the turkey were on the table, too. Cranberry sauce was taken from a can and put in a dish and we were all expected to help ourselves to cranberry sauce. I hate cranberry sauce. And stuffing was offered, too, in a deep dish. You could also have taken the stuffing from inside the turkey, but I wasn't planning on eating any oniony stuffing, either. Big hunks of onion all transparent and slippery? No thanks.

But it was quite a spread, all right. It was a rare sight.

The overhead light was turned off. Only the candles lit the room. The big kitchen window reflected the dark, murky gathering of people celebrating a special dinner. It was cold and snowing outside. The colours of red and green were everywhere, and the dull yellow light of the burning candles made Christmas mysterious.

"I wonder what the poor people are doing tonight?" my father said. He always said this when we had a good spread on the table. It was a good thing to say and we all smiled. I think it meant that no family with a spread like this could ever be called poor. And then, when we were about ready to dig in, we said grace. My father said it. We clutched our hands and bowed our heads.

"Bless us O Lord for these thy gifts which we are about to receive from thy bounty through Christ our Lord, Amen."

"Amen," we all repeated.

But before we could touch a single thing, the entire table collapsed. Starting with the big turkey, everything slid into the centre of the table and from there spilled out onto the floor. The white lace tablecloth pulled everything with it—bowls of hot food, empty plates, crystal goblets, wine bottles, stuffing, mashed potatoes, gravy containers, candles. Everything went smashing into the centre of the table and spilled and broke and rolled all over the floor. It was like somebody had pulled the plug on Christmas dinner and it went swirling around and vanished before our eyes. It all became a big heap of hot food and broken glass and chipped plates. In the second or two of silence after the disaster you could actually hear wine gurgling out of a bottle somewhere on the kitchen floor.

Sid jumped up and turned on the overhead light.

My mother and Heather were pretty upset. They were crying and wailing and that set Mandy and Daphne off and they were crying, too. Sid was trying to pick up the turkey but it was slipping all over the place because of the juices, and the plate underneath it had broken. My father was in shock. He had both his hands in the air, as if someone had a gun to his back, and he was looking at the spot where the feast had disappeared before his very eyes. Cosmo and I just sat there because we had our backs to the kitchen windows and couldn't get out easily. You don't often see your Christmas table breaking in two and spilling everything on it all over the floor and you don't often see half your family bawling their eyes out or your brother slipping all over the greasy kitchen floor trying to pick up a roasted Christmas turkey.

I'd say it's a safe bet that Christmas dinner was the start of the entire mess.

DESPITE THE DISASTROUS CHRISTMAS DAY DINNER, WE still had our annual Christmas night party. Forty-ounce bottles of rum, whiskey, vodka, gin—everything you could think of—were stockpiled in the back porch in thick cardboard boxes. The good room was opened up and the doors that separated it from the television room were removed altogether, which made most of the downstairs a huge area for dancing. We had an upright piano in the television room that nobody played. Sid sometimes tapped out a few one-finger tunes, and now and then someone tried "Chopsticks," but mostly the piano was used to hold our school books and other junk. Sometimes a cat would walk over the keys. Once a year, right before the party, our father drove over to Westmount on the other side of Sydney Harbour to get the piano tuner. The piano tuner was an old blind man who did an excellent job on the piano, but had to be driven to and from the job site. Cosmo, my younger brother, talked to him while he tuned our piano.

"Can't you see anything, sir?"

"No, son, not a thing. But I can hear like a fox, that's the truth."

"Why can't you see anything?"

"I was born blind, you see. I've never been able to see anything."

"Don't you miss not seeing anything?"

"No, son. Not like you would."

Irene, who was our neighbour and our babysitter and our housekeeper, would help us get ready for the party by making a thousand sandwiches and cookies and bread rolls and meat slices and olives with toothpicks through them. We weren't allowed to touch any of it. I wouldn't touch the toothpicks with olives, anyway. You'd have to be drunk to touch them.

The cars of the guests were parked up and down the street and all around the block. The MP for Sydney, several city aldermen, the entire staff of our father's union office—where our mother also worked—our aunts and uncles, a senator from Ottawa, and various businessmen from Charlotte Street, all were our parents' guests. We were allowed downstairs for the first hour of the party. We got to meet the early arrivals and were introduced to a lot of people.

"And who have we here?"

"Judge Sinclair, this is a trio of bad news, Sid, Michael, and Cosmo."

"Are these your boys, Rory?"

"I guess I'll take responsibility for them. But you'll have to ask the wife for a confirmation."

"Hello, boys!"

"Boys, say hello to Judge Sinclair."

"Hello, Judge Sinclair."

"How do you like the ceilidh, boys? Do you know what a ceilidh is?"

"It's a party," Sid said.

"We like it," said Cosmo.

"Okay, upstairs," our father said.

When we were little, we used to sit on the stairs leading up to the second floor and look at the guests through the pickets of the banister. Some people would walk right by us without noticing we were there. But other people would see us and say hello until we were noticed by our father again and told to get upstairs altogether.

A ceilidh was more than a party. A ceilidh had the same buildup as a tornado and followed the same laws of nature. Everybody got caught up in this thing that just happened, despite the planning, because sometimes it didn't happen even with planning and sometimes it happened without any planning or warning at all. The whole thing didn't get really rolling until Piper, the man who played the piano, took off his jacket. Then it would start. Some years there would be a fiddler, too. When there was a piano and a fiddle together the roof would almost come down on top of everyone. There was a fiddle that last Christmas. A man named Gordon played it. I don't know if that was his first name or his last name. The floor was pounding from the step-dancing and people were singing and clapping and laughing. While Piper was replenishing his drink, my mother accompanied herself on guitar and sang "The House of the Rising Sun" in a high stiletto voice. Everyone gave her lots of applause.

At around ten o'clock, Heather, along with the cats, Chipper and Cinder, was sent to her room on the second floor, and she stayed there with her door closed. Sid, Cosmo, Kerby and I went to the third floor, closing the third floor door behind us. Kerby was our dog. We heard the storm below as dull vibrations coming through the beams of the house.

2

A SMALL DOGLEG STAIRWELL LED TO THE THIRD FLOOR. Fourteen steps led up to the small landing where the stairway turned right for another ten or so steps. Wainscotting went halfway up the wall and lengths of rounded mouldings lay over the seam where the wainscotting met the wallpaper. If you were going down in the dark, and lots of times we would be going up or coming down in the dark, you put your hands on the moulding and followed it almost as you would a handrail. There was a light switch at the foot and also at the head of the stairwell, so you could turn the light on when going up and then turn it off once you got to the third floor. The door to the stairwell was almost always closed.

The only time anyone went to the third floor, except us boys, was to do a laundry. The washer and the dryer were in the hallway right outside our bedroom. The washer emptied into a deep porcelain sink which would fill with the dirty water of a spin. The dirty water would bubble up, threatening to overflow, but it never did.

Further to the left was a little door to a crawl space and further along still was the dryer. Near the dryer was a hallway window that looked out over the last houses in the north end, the tar pond, the steel plant, and Sydney Harbour. There was a little roof outside this window that we'd often sit on in the summer. Through a door next to this window was a big unheated room that wasn't used for anything. You got used to the washer and dryer going at night. A big wash would be the last thing our mother or Heather would do before going to bed.

The shunting of the CNR trains below us was also a comforting sound, although much more random than the thump-thumping of the washer. We often fell asleep to the shunting of the trains, which sounded like thunder. Our room was directly to the right as you reached the top of the stairs. A window separated the bunk beds from Sid's single bed. I slept on the top bunk. Cosmo slept below. The ceiling of our room slanted down from the peak of the roof.

The best way to fall asleep was by listening to one of Sid's stories.

"Tell us a story," Cosmo and I would say.

"What kind of story do you want to hear?"

Sid could tell all different kinds of stories. He could tell space stories or knight stories or any kind of story that you wanted. And they were good stories and long. They weren't short stories that ended before you fell asleep. The problem with the washer and dryer was that you sometimes couldn't fall asleep before they finished their cycles. But not so with Sid's stories. He told his stories flat out for an hour before he would allow a minute of quiet to elapse.

Sid would just stop the story cold. I knew he was

pausing to see if Cosmo and I were still awake. Cosmo would almost always be dead asleep, but not me. It got so that I learned how to say "Go on" in my sleep, just so I could hear the pleasurable monotony of Sid's voice, not even hearing individual words at that point, just a muffled sound that had no harm in it, like the washing machine or the shunting trains. There was nothing better than being in the top bunk in the third floor tower of a house that overlooked the rail yard, whose trains were bumping into each other in the night like restless cattle in a stockyard, those double locomotive eyes reflecting like false moons off the flat, black tar pond. If the upper branches of the linden tree were scratching the window during one of Sid's stories, that would be even better. Occasionally, Sid's stories were told just to frighten us.

Sometime after Christmas he came up with a beauty.

It was a story about a murderer who only killed people living in houses built on corner lots. Sid said this psycho had killed his own entire family very brutally—in their house on a corner lot. He was put in the Butterscotch Hotel for life as a result. We called the loony bin the Butterscotch Hotel because it was painted two shades of light brown. Anyway, this maniac, Sid explained, had escaped from the booby hatch just the previous night. As Sid was telling this story to Cosmo and me, who were very aware that we were living in a house situated on a corner lot, we somehow got the idea that this wasn't so much a story as it was a news bulletin.

"The city police and the RCMP are *still* looking for this maniac," Sid said.

Incredibly, there came a slamming from the other, empty room, on the third floor.

Bang!

We knew what made the sound: it was the crawl space door. If the window was left open, it would sometimes cause the crawl space door to slam. We all knew it was the crawl space door. But we also knew it might be the demented killer entering our house by a hole he had ripped in the eaves.

Bang!

Maybe that was his head slamming into the roofing nails as he stood upright. There would be blood streaming down his neck. That would make him even madder and more demented.

"If you're not going to hurt us," Sid said, in a voice remarkably controlled given the circumstances, "knock once. But if you're going to *kill* us, knock three times."

Bang!
Bang!
Bang!

Out of the top bunk landing on top of Cosmo who is already scrambling for the door which is opened blindly in the dark where thank god no murderer blocks our flight to the blackness that is down the stairwell two three steps both arms outstretched at a time to feel all the way down and kicking with bare feet the blocked door open even as the bastard's breath is on our necks and a bloody hand tightens on our shoulders—

And our father Rory wakes up from the terrible overhead stampede.

"What the *hell*—?"

"*Ahhhhhhhhhhhh!*"

His two youngest sons, who want so much to live, screaming for their lives and not stopping at the second floor but continuing all the way down to the kitchen while his nightgowned daughter appears in the second-floor hallway as if called from the stateroom of a quickly sinking ship, and all the kids crying as their father emerges stark raving naked from his bedroom with a mallet for a fist, bristling from the emergency filling his house which had been quiet and asleep only a moment before.

Sid really got it for that one.

Rory gave him a smack on the side of the head and told him that if he ever did something stupid like that again he'd get worse. And Sid said he was sorry, but he was still smirking, and Rory told him to wipe that smirk off his face. But Sid couldn't wipe away the smirk even after the smack. He couldn't because this was one of his greatest victories. His sister crying and his brothers bruised and suffering self-inflicted abrasions. How could he have done any better? Cosmo and I had to come back upstairs from the kitchen without sympathy, and Rory told us to get the blazes upstairs to the third floor and if he heard a peep from us, the smallest peep, he'd show us what for. So we had to go, without a whimper, because Rory's wrath was worse than being slaughtered in our beds by whatever weakling chickenshit was hiding like a rat in the third-floor crawl space.

Otherwise Rory and Sid got along like they were old pals. We called our parents by their first names. They felt that first names were more conducive to having a friendship with your parents rather than the traditional parent-child relationship. Sid was an identical copy of Rory, only a smaller version of the Big Fellow, as Rory was often called by friends. But Sid sure went in for practical jokes. Man, he scared me to death a half dozen times.

SID ALSO LISTENED TO MARCHING BAND MUSIC ALL THE time. When he wasn't listening to marching music, he'd be listening to Irish or Scottish music. He was learning how to play the chanter. The chanter is the piece of the bagpipe that sounds like a wheezing cat. Sid would have been happy to play the pipes in a marching band for the rest of his life. But you have to learn how to play the chanter before you can play the agony bags, as the bagpipes are sometimes called.

I thought the sound was terrible when Sid started to practise. It was just awful. And when he was learning, he was making all sorts of mistakes, which made it worse. He practised on the third floor at the window that overlooked Sydney Harbour. He would focus on a distant point in the harbour and play away. The only one in the entire house who liked Sid's music was Rory. He really liked the Irish and Scottish songs Sid was learning. He knew them, that's why. Sid would practise until Rory came home from the union office in the late evening, and then he would come downstairs to play his latest acquisition.

"All right, Bodach, what do you have for me?"

Rory always called his boys Bodach. It was a Gaelic word and it meant—I don't know what it meant. Son, I guess. Or boy. Whatever we were to him.

"Guess what this one is," Sid would say, and then the wailing would begin. Rory would have a beer after supper. He couldn't get to sleep without a beer.

"'Scotland the Brave'," Rory would guess.

"Right," Sid would say, stopping the tune immediately.

"Guess what this one is." And Sid would start playing again. He'd play and then he'd make a mistake and sort of shake his head to acknowledge that the last note, or the last two or three notes, were not a part of the song that Rory was supposed to be guessing. That made it kind of hard to guess, if you ask me.

"'Isle of Skye'?" Rory would guess.

Sid would shake his head and keep playing until Rory guessed right or gave up.

"It's 'The Canadian Boat Song'."

"Ah!"

And the playing would go on and if Rory had another beer he would encourage Sid to play some Irish songs of rebellion. As Sid improved, he could pick up the tune just from Rory's singing. Sid could play "Young Roddy M'Corley" and "The Rising of the Moon" pretty smoothly. Some of it was pretty good fighting music. The words were all fighting words. Other songs were really sad. Laments, they were called. One that Sid played all the time was a tune called "Dark Island." Ryan's Fancy sang it and Sid had their album. It was a song all about Cape Breton Island and how the singer longs to go back to its simplicity after living in the city. It describes the sea and the ships and hilltops high above the dark island. But at that time I only listened to Bachman-Turner Overdrive and April Wine, when I listened to music at all.

3

RORY AND SID WEREN'T OLD PALS ALL THE TIME. SID was terrifically pissed off with our parents for letting Heather and me smoke in the house. He didn't even like it when Rory and Gloria smoked in the TV room. He said the smoke choked him up. Said he couldn't breathe properly. Said he hated the room full of smoke and said the smoke stunk. It was unhealthy, he said. This was completely unreasonable, according to my parents. Sid would just have to get used to the smoke and stop complaining. But Sid didn't want to get used to it. Just because he got used to it, he said, didn't mean that it stopped harming him and everybody else. Sid thought getting used to something that everyone knew was harmful was just plain stupid. Every time they fired up a cigarette, he pulled up his shirt and covered his nose. Rory got so mad at Sid for doing this that he would order him out of the television room.

I started smoking when I was nine. There were dried reeds that grew wild in Victoria Park that could be lit and puffed and they were my first cigarettes. I remember puffing them and then rinsing my mouth out in the muddy puddle of Dave MacKinnon's driveway so my breath wouldn't smell. My sister and I both smoked. Heather smoked with her friends and I smoked with mine, and sometimes we'd smoke together out the bathroom window. We shared cigarettes, checked each other's breath, and kept each other's secret from our parents. I don't know when Heather started smoking, but we shared cigarettes all the time. And we also shared a vow to never tell on each other.

My father said to me one day in late February, "I want to talk with you. Go upstairs to my bedroom." The only time Rory invited you to talk in the bedroom was when you had done something wrong. And then it was heads-up ball, as Rocket MacDonald, my old baseball coach, used to say. Heather was already waiting in the bedroom and she looked like she had been crying. Before I could ask her a single question Rory came in the room. He told me to sit on the bed and I sat on the bed. I could see the shadows of the linden trees moving on the bedroom windows. Rory walked back and forth in front of the windows.

"Michael, how long have you been smoking?"

"I don't smoke, Rory."

"Tell him, Michael," Heather said.

"Heather, I don't smoke."

"Michael, just tell him."

"If I smoked, I would tell. But I don't smoke."

"How much do you smoke?" Rory asked.

"I don't smoke."

"A pack a day?" Rory looked at Heather.

"A pack a day," Heather agreed. "About a pack a day, same as me."

"I don't smoke."

"Just tell him, okay? Just tell him because he already knows."

"I don't smoke so why don't you keep your *big mouth shut*."

"Okay, that's enough," Rory ordered.

He looked out the bedroom window. A long time passed before he spoke again.

"Michael, do you use mescaline?"

"No."

"Do you use mescaline?"

"No."

"Do you know what mescaline is?"

"Yes."

"But you don't use it?"

"No."

"And you have never used it, or marijuana, or any of that other junk?"

"No."

"And you don't smoke cigarettes?"

"Yes."

"You *do* smoke cigarettes?"

"Yes."

"How much?"

"A pack a day, just like Heather said."

After a very long deliberation, Rory spoke.

"All right, Bodach, I'm going to allow you and Heather to smoke. But if I ever hear that you are using mescaline or anything else like it, I'll skin you alive. Is that clear?"

"Yes," I said.

"If you are allowed adult privileges, I expect you to behave like adults."

"Okay," I said.

My father also wanted me to understand that it was a privilege to smoke in the house, not a right. Did I understand the difference? Heather smiled and looked at me and wiped her eyes. I wiped my eyes, too.

"I understand," I said.

What a windfall. I was thirteen years old.

I lit my first cigarette in the house the next Friday night. We were just settling down to watch an episode of *Kojak* with Telly Savalas. Kojak smoked those long, thin cigars. They were okay, but kind of hard on the throat when you inhaled. I opened my package of cigarettes and lit one. My hands were shaking. My cousin Daphne was in the room. And so was Sid. Heather was out somewhere and I don't know where Cosmo was. Rory was still at the office and Gloria was reading in her bedroom upstairs. Daphne was sitting in one of the big lazy-boy armchairs. Sid was in the second lazy-boy, the one Rory liked to sit in. I was sitting next to the fireplace, I blew my first breath of smoke so that it went straight up the chimney.

"What do you think you're doing?" Sid asked.

"Having a smoke," I said.

"Put it out," Sid said.

"I'm allowed to smoke." I blew a blue cloud at the television screen.

"You're a kid."

"So?"

"Put it out," Sid repeated.

"No."

Sid got up and for a second I thought he was coming over to pound me. But he just got up and went out of the room. I heard him going upstairs to our parents' bedroom. Gloria read psychology books in their room at night while Rory stayed late at work.

"Can you make a circle, Michael?" Daphne asked.

I made a perfect smoke ring, a whole series of them. Daphne thought that was pretty cool. The smoke rings revolved around and around until they enlarged and finally distorted into the letter "L." Sid came stamping downstairs, through the hallway and kitchen, and into the TV room. He came right over to me. I had to lean back in the chair.

"If you blow any of that shit around me I'll punch your *face* in!"

And then he stamped right out of the room, through the kitchen and the hallway, and out the front door. He was steaming. Gloria had told him that I was allowed to smoke and I don't know who he was angrier with, me or her. Had my father been home that night, I bet Sid would have taken a swing at him. Man oh man, he was mad. Nobody's ever told me if Sid said anything to Rory about the whole matter. Sid was disgusted with all of us, that's all I know.

Sid wasn't the only one who objected.

I started taking my cigarette packages to school and wearing them in the top pocket of my denim jacket. The package made a big square outline and it was impossible not to know what it was. Sometimes I would prop up the cigarette package a little so the green part of the pack could be seen. I roamed the halls that way until I was taken by Sister Campion to see the principal, Sister MacGillivray.

"Tell Sister MacGillivray what you're carrying in your pocket, Michael."

"My cigarettes, Sister."

"Your cigarettes, Michael?"

"Yes, Sister."

"You smoke cigarettes, do you, Michael?"

"Yes, Sister."

"Listen to him," Sister Campion said to Sister MacGillivray. "As bold as brass."

"Do your parents know you smoke?"

"Yes, Sister. I'm allowed to smoke at home."

The two nuns looked at each other.

The Sisters of Notre-Dame ran both Sacred Heart and Holy Angels School. The girls of the north end went to school at Holy Angels, directly across the street from Sacred Heart. Holy Angels was a lot bigger than Sacred Heart. Not only was it a girls' school, it was a convent. It had pedways and courtyards and paved playgrounds and spiked fences. It also had a gym where we got to play floor hockey on Saturdays if we got permission first.

For three years, they allowed boys to attend Holy Angels for classes. We were the first boys to be allowed into the all girls school. We were pretty excited. Up to that time, all we'd done was shout insults to the girls of Holy Angels. And some of them had shouted insults back. And then one day we had to cross the street in September and begin grade seven in a class half filled with these same girls. I didn't date any girls in grade seven. But I played on the hockey team. There were always fights after the games because the other teams would find some amusement in the fact that we were the hockey team from Holy Angels.

"How old are you, Michael?"

"Almost fourteen, Sister."

"And you are allowed to smoke at home? In front of your parents?"

"Yes, Sister."

I sat there in Sister MacGillivray's office while she looked at me. And she looked at me with the strangest look. That was the first time I had seen that look, and I remembered it. Soon after, my aunts, uncles, and teachers all began looking at me in that same way.

"Where do you get your cigarettes, Michael?"

"Oh, I don't know. Anywhere."

My father smoked king size because the regular cigarettes were too small for his fingers. King size cigarettes looked in his hand like regular size cigarettes looked in everyone else's. Sometimes, he would leave his pack on the kitchen table or beside the lazy-boy in the television room and sometimes I'd take one or two if it was safe. If it was a new pack with only a few taken out, I could take a few more out and he would never know. But if there were only a few left on one side, or only a few left in the pack, I couldn't take any because he would know. The same was true with my mother. She sometimes had packs going upstairs and downstairs and taking a few cigarettes from either pack was easy. I got cigarettes from the grocery store, too. Or I could buy them loose. Or bum them from other boys. Someone always had a cigarette.

Sister MacGillivray looked at me with that look.

"Where are you going, young man? Do you know?" she asked.

"I don't know, Sister," I said.

"I know you don't," she said. "You may be allowed to smoke at home, but you will not smoke on school grounds. Do you understand, Michael?"

"Yes, Sister."

"And you will not be allowed to parade around the hallways of this school with cigarettes in your pockets. If I see any cigarettes at all, they will be taken from you. Do you understand, Michael?"

"Yes, Sister."

I knew I had won. Sister MacGillivray knew, too. She was no match for Rory. When Heather had been sent home from Holy Angels the year before for wearing jeans, Rory and Gloria both hit the roof, but Rory made the bigger hole. He phoned the convent and shouted, he marched up there and told them what for, and he wrote a letter to the editor that made them look like they were still living in the Dark Ages. Gloria emphasized to us the importance of having an "open mind." It ended up that Heather didn't have to wear a dress to school. She walked around the halls of Holy Angels as proudly in her skin-tight jeans as I did in my denim jacket with my cigarette package hanging out of my pocket. We were both advertisements for Free Thought, while the nuns and the other students were still struggling in slavery. It was the coolest thing.

4

I HAD ANOTHER INTERVIEW WITH SISTER MACGILLIVRAY before the school year ended. She called me from class one wintry day in March.

"Michael, your younger brother has fainted. I'm told he has revived and has run away from school."

"Okay," I said.

"Do you know where he might have gone?"

"Yes, I think so."

"Well, go find him and make sure he's okay. He should go to the hospital."

"Yes, Sister."

I knew exactly where he was because he and I had been there only a few days before. I walked right down York Street to Havelock and turned at the bottling company. It was a cold day. I had to draw my hands up into the arms of my jacket because I had lost my mitts. I went up to Ferry Street and walked across the Ferry Street causeway that led into the private property of the Sydney Steel Corporation, or Sysco, as it was called. The Ferry Street causeway was the dividing line between the north and south tar ponds. The causeway ended just before it reached steel plant property and a bridge jumped over the little strait connecting the north pond with the south. The two ponds looked like one of those long balloons that was twisted by a knot right in the middle. I walked out on the causeway, leaving the residential north end, and stopped at the bridge. A few cars went past in either direction. When there were no cars in sight, I scurried down the side of the embankment and slipped under the bridge. Cosmo was there, sitting like a little troll, under the bridge.

"What happened to you?"

"I don't know," Cosmo said. I could see he was pretty scared.

"What did you do? Just pass out or what?"

"I guess I did, I don't know."

"Why did you run away?"

"I don't know."

"Sister MacGillivray sent me to find you. She said that you should probably go to the hospital."

"I don't want to," Cosmo said. He was getting all worked up.

"Okay, we don't have to go to the hospital," I said.

"Do we have to go back to school?"

I thought about this before I answered.

"No," I said.

"What do you want to do, then?" Cosmo asked.

"I don't know," I said. "But it's freezing under this stupid bridge. Let's go down the CNR."

"All right," Cosmo agreed.

We left the bridge and walked back across the Ferry Street causeway. The wind was cold and my feet were sort of numb. We both wore blue parkas with white fake fur around the hoods. We both had blue jeans and Look-Like-Leather workboots and wool socks. I should have worn two pairs of socks because my feet were freezing. We turned off the causeway and walked down the Canadian National Railway road that followed the shore of the tar pond. We were safe and comfortable on CN property because it was nearby our house and because every single CN man was friendly. We walked right around the roundhouse and past a few dead-end sidings holding boxcars. We came to the narrowest part of the tar pond and looked over at the wreck of the *Bitiby*, frozen in tar-pond ice.

"Want to go over?"

"All right," Cosmo said.

We started over on the ice. It was slippery and had an off-yellow colour. We turned our faces against the wind as we shuffled over the ice toward the old hulk. There was nothing left of the *Bitiby*, just the outline of its hull and a little bit of the superstructure. It had burned completely and was hollow inside. But the steel parts, like the boiler chamber, were still in place. We knew from last winter that the boiler chamber got a "floor" when the water froze over.

"Jump in," I said. Cosmo went into the boiler and I followed.

"God, it's cold," Cosmo said.

"It's colder in here than it is outside."

"It was freezing under the bridge."

There was no wind in the boiler chamber. It was dark, too. I lit a match and cupped it with my hands and then lit half a cigarette that I had stubbed out before I went into school that morning. The chamber was simply a big old rusting iron box with an ice floor. There were no seats or metal protrusions to sit on. The match burned out and I threw it away. The plastic soles of my boots were frozen now and my feet were really starting to hurt. At least when we were outside we'd been moving.

"Let's explore the steel plant," I said.

"All right," Cosmo said.

"Want a puff?"

"Sure." Cosmo puffed on the cigarette and gave it back. I could tell he was pleased to share a cigarette with me.

"Want another puff?"

"Sure."

"Don't soak the filter," I said. I hated a soaked filter. A couple of my school friends put spit into the filter because they didn't know how to smoke. You could hear their spit bubbling as you drew hot smoke over it.

Cosmo went a little cross-eyed as he watched the smoke come out of his mouth.

"You're not inhaling."

"What's that?"

"Gimme," I said. Cosmo handed over the cigarette. I drew on it and showed him how I took the smoke into my lungs. I took a second draw, but the cigarette suddenly was blocked.

I looked at the lit end of the cigarette and saw that a stick or piece of a small branch was rolled up in the cigarette itself and made smoking impossible. The natural airway of the tube was blocked and all you were going to get sucking on that was a headache. I stubbed the cigarette out, removed the middle part where the blockage was, and relit the part with the filter. There was still lots left to smoke because this cigarette was king size.

"That's a weird thing to find in a cigarette," Cosmo said. He took up the disregarded piece and examined it.

"Maybe the tobacco warehouse got contaminated somehow," I said.

"It looks like some kind of small plant, or a stick, something like that."

Why some part of a plant would be mixed up with tobacco was a mystery to us.

We left the boiler chamber and walked around the

bow of the *Bitiby*. The wreck ran parallel to the plant shore road, but the ice between the ship and the road was broken and unsafe to walk on. We had to walk a couple of hundred feet toward the harbour in order to find a place where solid ice came right up to the shore. We helped each other over the pushed-up ice chunks and then we were on steel plant property. We walked back down toward the *Bitiby* and were almost parallel with it when a steel-plant police car suddenly appeared on the horizon, a great cloud of dust and dirty snow behind it.

"Run for it!" I said.

We took off toward Slag Mountain. It was the only place to go. We were too far away from where the ice met the shoreline road to make a run back. The crumbly slag poured down the steep face of the mountain as we climbed. It was like trying to run up a gravel pile. We weren't getting anywhere. The big Chevy Impala came to a skidding halt down below us and a man got out of the car.

"All right—*down*," he said, as if he were talking to a couple of mutts. I looked back and he was standing there with his hands on his hips. His winter coat was open. He had a big gut that burst out of his blue shirt. Sideburns came halfway down the sides of his face and he was smoking. His hair was very black and he had it swirling around in some sort of ducktail hairdo. We didn't stop climbing.

"*I said down!*" he shouted.

He was buttoning up his coat now because it was cold. Cosmo and I just kept climbing. It was obvious that he wasn't going to follow us. If he tried climbing up the loose slag, he'd have brought the whole mountain down on top of himself.

"You little bastards!" the man shouted.

"Fat pig!" Cosmo shouted back.

We were almost at the top of the mountain when we heard the car door slam. I turned around and saw the Impala go back the way it had come.

"He's going to come around up top," I said to Cosmo. As soon as we got to the top of Slag Mountain, we ran like hell and hid behind some dumped piles of loose black dirt. I tried to breathe regularly out of my mouth so my ears would work. We listened, but he never followed.

This was the first time we'd actually been on top of Slag Mountain. We'd only seen the stacks of the steel plant from our neighbourhood before. Now we could see everything that Slag Mountain had hidden from us. We found an abandoned stretch of rail track with an abandoned line of train cars on it. There was an engine, a few flat cars, a coal car, and a caboose. The train cars were just sitting there on a track that went nowhere. We stayed there for quite some time. We went in and out of the cars, pulled a few broken levers on the locomotive, and climbed up the top of the caboose roof. We could see all around so no fat bastards in over-heated Impalas could sneak up on us. And we were out of the wind but still moving around and keeping warm. It was just great.

We saw oil storage tanks at the steel plant that made the oil company tanks down the north end look puny. These were the biggest tanks I'd ever seen in my life. Four of them. And we found a small box of Sysco security passes in an abandoned security shed. They were blue cards that each had a blank space for someone's name.

"If we showed these passes to the steel plant police, we'd be allowed to stay," Cosmo said.

"Let's take a few home anyway," I said.

We stuffed the passes in our pockets. In a drawer of the security shed, Cosmo found a dozen asbestos mitts. They were way too big for us, but we put them on anyway. I was happy to have them because my hands were bare. They came right up to my elbows. They had a space for the thumb and forefinger and a space that the other fingers had to share. Cosmo wore his asbestos gloves over his wool mitts.

When we were leaving the security shack we almost ran into a crew of steelworkers. They were walking along the road, five or six men, slowly trudging by with their winter jackets on. Their hard hats had earflaps covering their ears. Their heads were down against the cold wind. They carried their lunch pails under their arms like metal footballs. We dove behind a sand pile.

"They saw us," Cosmo whispered.

"No, they didn't," I said. I was right. The men just walked right by. They didn't talk, or make any sound at all. They just walked with their heads down and their shoulders turned into the wind. We watched them walk along between the dumped piles of slag until they disappeared.

5

"WE SHOULD GET BACK," I SAID.

"Okay," Cosmo said.

We stood on the top of Slag Mountain, at the same place where we had climbed up, and looked across the tar pond to the north end of Sydney. We could see our big white house on the corner of Meadow and Brook.

We could see our third-floor windows. I thought of how often we had stood at those windows and looked out across the tar pond to where we now stood. The wind was freezing the tip of my nose.

"Here goes," I said.

"Geronimo!" Cosmo said.

I began running down the crumbly side of Slag Mountain. The drop was almost one hundred feet. The loose slag moved with me like an avalanche as I rode it to the bottom, where I fell. I got up and looked for Cosmo. He was coming down the side of Slag Mountain like a California surfer. He slid right down to the flat ground, a smile pasted on his face. He didn't fall once.

We were so close to the *Bitiby* that I could have hit it with a rock. But we had to go back the way we had come, to the place where the ice met the road. That meant leaving the cover of the mountain and running out in the open.

"Ready?"

"You go first," Cosmo said.

I began running. Cosmo was right behind me. The sound of the car came almost as soon as we hit the packed-down ice and dirt of the steel plant road. The bastard must have been just sitting there with his heater on, listening to the radio and smoking cigarettes. I could hear the engine straining and getting closer. He was speeding down the sloping hill that was built into Slag Mountain. There were no speed restrictions here and I could hear him *lifting* it down that dirt road after us.

"You with me, Cosmo?" I shouted, not looking back.

"Yeah!" Cosmo said, running right behind me. The car had hit the straightaway and was really racing now. We were still a hundred feet away from the ice. That bastard better be able to stop his stupid car, I thought. He'd better not run over us by mistake. He'd better not. The ice pans along the shore were like the landing obstacles at Normandy beach that I'd seen in a movie. These obstacles are holding us to the shoreline where we'll get killed, I thought. The car's engine whined down as the driver took his foot off the gas. The tires were skidding to a stop. He was almost on top of us when I saw our earlier tracks. I scrambled down the embankment and ran out onto the yellowy ice of the tar pond. I heard the door of the car open as I slid to a stop and turned around. The steel plant cop was only a few feet away from Cosmo, but that might have been a mile. Cosmo had reached the ice and was slipping and sliding out toward me. The cop stood with his door open, looking at us. He was way too heavy to follow us out onto the ice, way too heavy.

"Ha, ha! Fat pig!" Cosmo shouted.

"Shut up," I said, under my breath.

"Almost had us, Tubby!"

"Cosmo, shut up!" I said. But Cosmo was twitching with adrenaline and he couldn't shut up. He was too excited.

"Nice try, Fatso!"

The cop silently watched us walking across the ice, away from him and his jurisdiction and authority. Cosmo shouted insults to him the whole time until the cop finally got back in his car, turned around, and slowly drove back the way he had come. I thought about this later and remembered that the cop had called us "bastards." He deserved everything he got from Cosmo. Police are supposed to have better manners.

I went out on the ice of Sydney Harbour by myself the following week. The whole harbour had frozen over and the ice was a foot thick. Families skated on a large area cleared by the city between the government wharf and the Robin Hood warehouse. Snowmobiles and cars raced on the Westmount side. You couldn't really see them from the Sydney side, but you could hear the sound of their throttling engines coming over the ice. I started walking across the harbour from the tar pond and I didn't stop until I reached the path cleared by the *Louis St. Laurent* a few days before. The ice breaker had opened a route for the little coastal tankers that came up to the Sydney River oil facility. It was there, a half mile from shore, that I heard the sound of ice cracking and felt the first step give out from under my weight. The ice pan I had stepped on dipped slightly and harbour water came up around my foot. I turned back immediately. Walking on the frozen tar pond was a lot safer than walking on the harbour.

When I remembered about nearly choking to death on the cigarette I had shared with Cosmo, I wrote this letter to the tobacco company on the typewriter that my father kept at the house:

> DEAR SIR OR MADAM,
> THERE WAS A STICK IN ONE OF YOUR CIGARETTES.
> I DON'T KNOW WHAT IT WAS BUT MAYBE IT WAS
> NOT SUPPOSE TO BE THERE. HERE IS THE STICK SO
> YOU CAN MAYBE IDENTIFY IT. →
> I HOPE YOU HAVE GOOD LUCK. GOOD BYE.
> —MICHAEL CHISHOLM

And I took the little piece of the stick and taped it to the letter right after the arrow. And then I got the tobacco company's address from the side of Rory's king size cigarette package and got an envelope and mailed it the next day. You never know about things like that. Maybe somebody like me would be just enjoying a cigarette on a nice day and all of a sudden they would inhale a little stick that would choke them. Those things happen. What about the man who worked in the turkey factory and lost his thumb and then a family roasted their turkey and this guy's thumb fell out of the turkey right on the kitchen table. I guess it was a gross out all around. But those things happen. Somebody could have choked to death on that man's thumb. You have to think safety all the time.

6

WHEN THE ICE BROKE UP IN THE HARBOUR & DRIFTED out of the tar pond, the air around the shore didn't feel any warmer. But we had good shelter from the wind a few hundred feet inland, behind the trains. Cosmo and I used to go there a lot after school and flatten pennies.

We were using a long line of empty coal trains to flatten pennies when this stranger walked down Brook Street leading his dog on a leash. Our dog, Kerby, didn't like it when we took him for a walk. He liked to go on his own. He didn't even have a leash. Anyway, this guy suddenly began yelling at us all the way from the Brook Street sidewalk. The tracks were built on landfill down on a marshy area, so you had to look up at the houses which were built on real land. "Hey!" he was yelling. Can you imagine doing that to two people you didn't even know? He and his dog came running down the path at the back of French's house as if it were an emergency. Cosmo and I were amazed. It was a red-headed dog.

When the trains were shunting back and forth, all you had to do was put a coin down on the rail and wait for the train to run over it. The result was an oblong penny or nickel, or an elongated dime that was a scream to look at. You had to look real hard to see the Bluenose schooner because its sails were stretched as far as they would go and the line of the hull was very faint. The Queen's head looked as if a train had rolled over it. She had the longest jaw you ever saw and her forehead was as big as Frankenstein's and her hair was in a style like Elvis Presley's. We flattened pennies, mostly. Nickels, dimes, and quarters were expensive.

"You children shouldn't be playing here," the stranger said. "This is very dangerous."

"We always play here," I said. I didn't like him calling us children and I didn't like it that he made me say that we were *playing*. We weren't playing, we were flattening pennies. The stranger was wearing a white sweater that had a little alligator on the chest.

"Where do you live?" he demanded.

"Right there." I pointed to the big white corner house up above us on the raised ground of our neighbourhood. Somewhere at the front of the line, the engine pulled and snapped each train in the line to attention. You could hear the clicking of the couplings as the trains were pulled snug right down the line until it reached our train. The stranger took a step back and pulled his dog with him. We leaned closer to the train as it lugged ahead and rolled over our pennies. The train came to a stop only after a few feet. Cosmo and I picked up our flattened pennies. They were hot to the touch.

"Do your parents know you're here?"

"Do yours?" Cosmo asked. Cosmo cracked me up. He was just like our father. He wasn't afraid of anyone, even these nosy adults from who knows where. Where did this guy come from? I never saw him before in my life.

"You can be seriously maimed or even killed playing around trains," the stranger said. He was trying to be very serious and authoritative. "I know of a boy in Ontario who lost both arms playing around train tracks."

"Whoopee," Cosmo said.

"This is Nova *Scotia*," I pointed out. They were always trying to make you do something by telling you somebody else did it somewhere else.

"Trains are dangerous anywhere," the man said.

"Go to hell!" Cosmo shouted and he took off around the end of the train.

"Why don't you clear outta here and go back to Ontario," I said.

"You may be too young to understand this," the man said, "but I am morally obligated to do something when I see children playing in an environment that is so obviously dangerous."

DANGEROUS? WE KNEW ALL ABOUT TRAINS. WE WALKED the tracks all the time.

Sometimes we could walk the length of ten steel rails without falling off. If you think that's easy, you try it. It wasn't easy but it wasn't dangerous. I guess maybe you could trip on the rail easily enough. Or you could stumble on the ties. And near the switches you might get your foot jammed. But that's not really dangerous, not the way that man was trying to make it seem. Only someone who was never around trains would say they were unsafe. We were all over them. Rolling stock is what they were called. Rolling stock. There were trains from all over the world right below our house in the north end marshalling yards.

A Devco coal hopper had a sloping shape, like a V if you looked at it straight on. And if you climbed up the side ladder and looked inside, you'd see that the hopper was divided in the middle by big sheets of metal. The sloped insides made it so the coal was directed toward the chutes that ran along the side of the train. These dumping chutes were not always perfectly sealed, and the trains were sometimes overfilled, so coal was scattered on both sides of the tracks and was there for the picking if anyone needed coal.

Devco was the Cape Breton Development Corporation, a federal government department that was formed to encourage and oversee industry on the island. Devco operated the coal mines at Glace Bay, New Waterford, and Sydney Mines.

The gypsum cars were just like the coal cars, designed to dump their cargo. But you hardly ever saw gypsum cars in the north end. And when you did, they weren't full. The grain trains used on the prairies were dump cars, too. Sometimes you would see the big emblem of a head of grain stencilled on the side of a car and you would know it was feed for farmers' livestock. But it wouldn't be a dump car, you could bet on that. When they shipped wheat from the prairies to the Maritimes it was always in a closed boxcar. Occasionally, you could see an American car in the yards, from North Dakota or California or someplace else. I remember one from Louisiana. You could read the rail cars on the tracks below our house like you could read tourist licence plates in any Cape Breton provincial park. It was interesting. It sort of brought the world to you.

Now and then you'd see a flatbed carrying something under a tarp. And you just had to see what was under the tarp. You imagined that it was a piece of war machinery, a gun, like a big piece of field artillery, a howitzer, maybe. But when you squeezed your way under the tarp, and couldn't even stand up inside, you wouldn't recognize the weird machinery, if you could even see it. It was very dark under the tarps even in the middle of the day. You'd see lots of trains carrying new cars and trucks for the dealerships on Welton Street. These trains were made up of ramps, which left the cars and trucks they were carrying tilting either upward or downward. You saw brand new Buick Skyhawks, Pontiac Astres, Ford Pintos and Granadas, and big Lincoln Monarchs. You saw a lot of Dodge Darts and Plymouth Valiants. Maybe a Volvo here and there. Some Japanese cars, too, but not many. Montreal was starting to ship used cars to Cape Breton by rail because there was a good used-car market in Sydney.

Trains carrying acids and bleach for the pulp-and-paper industry looked like ships designed to carry liquid. They had a large skeleton on the outside with lots of crosswise beams and metal struts. These cars were usually painted white, which made them very conspicuous among the red-brown Canadian National boxcars and the black Devco coal cars. The boxcars were the most common cars on the track. They had ladders on the ends and you could climb right up on them if you wanted because there was a little catwalk on top that led right across to a ladder at the other end. They were almost all made from metal and painted a red-brown to make them look like wood. Every Canadian National boxcar had the huge initials CN painted on the sides in white. Very rarely did you ever see an all-wood boxcar. They were considered antiques. Sometimes a caboose would be all wood. But most of the cabooses were made of metal, too.

Sometimes, in a whole line of trains, you could hear the hum of a refrigerated car. I guess they were carrying frozen fruits or vegetables or meats. A big puddle of water would form below the refrigerator and the water would become oily from the rail ties. Maybe somewhere there were also trains that hauled livestock, like cows, sheep, and pigs, but I never saw cattle trucks down the north end. The slaughterhouse was on the harbour side, down by Wentworth Park, nowhere near the train tracks.

There was lots of piggybacking, too. This was for containers that may have first come here by ship, and then were transferred to train, and might later be put on trucks. The piggyback flatbed cars that carried the containers weren't anything special. They had sprockets and wheels and chains to keep the containers in place. The heavy-duty flatbeds had two sets of four wheels each, on both ends, making thirty-six wheels per car. The wheels were big, four feet, I guess, and had a flange on one side that kept the wheel from slipping off the track. When the wheel rolled over your penny, the penny would flip and curl up. The pennies always curled. None of them were perfectly flat because they took the shape of the wheel that was flattening them, not the rail they were being flattened on.

Don't get me talking about trains because I could go on about them all day.

And they weren't dangerous.

If they were so dangerous, why did the engineer of

one of the diesel engines allow us to ride in the cab with him for about two full hours? We went all the way up to Prince Street on his train and we saw how the whole thing was done. I didn't hear the engineer asking us if our parents knew where we were. If we didn't play near the tracks, we never would have gotten to ride in the diesel engine. They have little miniature water coolers on those engines that dispense cold water. The engineer invited us both to have a drink because it was a very hot day and he said we could have as much water as we liked. Mister Ontario Smart Aleck.

7

ON THE LAST DAY OF SCHOOL, JUST LIKE ALL THE DAYS before, my mother was shouting up the third floor steps.

"Sid, Michael, Cosmo! Get up! Get up! Get up!"

"We're up!" Sid shouted back. Sid was already up and half dressed. In fact, he had already been down to the second-floor bathroom.

"Michael, Cosmo, get up! Get up!"

"We're up!" we yelled back. Gloria wanted to hear our voices before she left us alone. I knew I had ten minutes before she would remember to come looking for me so I flopped over and put my head under the pillow.

Cosmo got up and tramped down the third floor stairs to the bathroom. Heather was in the bathroom and I could hear him pounding at the bathroom door. Six people using one bathroom meant there was always waiting. If you just stayed in bed and listened, you could sometimes time it so you got downstairs when the bathroom was free, just when you needed it most.

Sid said, "Get up, Michael."

"I will."

"Mom's already asked you twice."

"I will."

Heather was already in the bathroom so there was no sense rushing. It was the last day of school anyway so what was the rush? I just closed my eyes again. Sid went downstairs to the second floor and I could hear him continuing all the way down to the first floor. I heard him greet Kerby and I heard Kerby barking.

Kerby was a mutt, but he was the best-looking dog you ever saw. He was a cross between a collie and a German shepherd. He had the shaggy hair of a collie but the marking of a shepherd. Sid was the only one in our family who did anything with Kerby. He took him for walks, fed him his food, brushed his coat, took burdocks out of his fur, and got him to chase me and Cosmo in the house.

Sid would say, *"Goooooo git him, Kerb!"* And Kerby would be off after you. You'd run upstairs as fast as you could and Kerby would be right behind you. You could hear his nails clicking on the steps, and you'd have to run like hell. He'd be whimpering with frustration because he was so close to biting your heels. And you'd turn at the second-floor landing and hope that the third-floor door was open and then you'd fly up the third-floor stairs with Kerby barking and yowling behind you, because he'd almost had you a couple of times. By the time you got to the third floor you would be out of breath and desperate for someplace to turn around. You'd run into the empty storage room with Kerby right behind you and you'd fall on the floor and put up your feet in self-defence and Kerby would grab your pant cuff and begin tugging backwards, snarling and growling, tugging backwards.

You'd have to hold onto your pants at the waist because Kerby would tug them right off you. Sid was Kerby's best friend, more or less.

On that last morning of school, Kerby wouldn't stop barking downstairs. Sid had left the door to the third floor open and the sound of Kerby's barking came right up the stairwell. I crushed the pillow against my ears and that helped a little. I just wanted to finish my dream. Sid was in my dream. We were sailing a small schooner on a huge ocean. She was a beautiful vessel, with a curl of white at her bow as she shouldered into the swells. Her sails were full and white, her hull was black and glossy.

Sid took up a sextant and used it to determine our course and position. We were dressed in immaculate Sea-Cadet uniforms—white blouses, blue pants, flat-top white caps, white gaiters, black boots—all spit and polish. I was at the wheel. I even had my hair cut short. Sid was standing at my side, scanning the horizon now with a pair of binoculars. Even in my dream Sid was older, taller, stronger, a natural leader. It was an ideal day on an ideal boat and we were a pair of ideal brothers.

"Starboard five degrees, Michael," Sid ordered. "By my calculations, Australia's only a few days' sailing."

"Aye aye, Sid. Starboard, five degrees! I always wanted to go to Australia!"

"Australians are seafarers, Michael, just like Canadians. Looks like we're in for some weather. Let's batten down the hatches and put our life gear on!"

"Aye aye, Skipper. Sid, a ship is the best thing in the world!"

Suddenly there was the sound of my mother's slippers coming up the third-floor stairway. They made this little flapping sound when the back of the slipper hit the bottom of her foot. By the way they were coming up the stairs, I could tell she was sick and tired of calling for me. My mother became very hysterical when she blew a gasket. Her footsteps sounded like she was mad as hell. In a second I rolled over onto the edge of the bunk and dropped to the floor. She was practically *running* up the stairs. She wanted to catch me still in bed so she could scream: "I told you to get up out of that bed!" But I was out of bed and into my jeans before the sound of her feet made the top landing.

"I'm up, Ma! I'm up! I'm up!" I said as I frantically put on my shirt.

The door to our room flew open and ... it wasn't my mother at all. It was Sid, wearing my mother's slippers.

"Did I get you?"

"*Shut the hell up!*" I shouted at him.

"Got you, didn't I?"

"Get the hell outta here!"

"I got you! Ha, ha, ha!"

"No you didn't! I was getting up anyway!"

"Ha, ha, ha! I got you!"

BY THE TIME I GOT DOWNSTAIRS BREAKFAST WAS ALmost over. "You're going to be late, Michael," Heather said.

"I know."

Heather went out the door and I watched her through the kitchen window as she walked up the street. My mother had already left for the union office. Sid and Cosmo went out the door. Irene, our housekeeper, was starting the morning cleanup. "You're running a bit slow this morning, Michael," she said.

"I know."

"Do you want a bowl of porridge?"

"No, thanks. I better get going."

What I wanted was to have a cigarette.

When my mother left the house, sometimes I'd get a ride with her to the school. Our father left the house at around seven o'clock or earlier. He always left early and came home late. That last summer I didn't even know he wasn't coming home at all, because I never used to see him in the morning anyway.

I left the house and got as far as Louie V's store when I saw Cosmo already coming back from school. I was a year and three months older than Cosmo and he was twelve and a half years old that spring. My birthday was in August, so I'd be fourteen soon. Cosmo was coming back from school with his marks. I could see the brown envelope he was carrying.

"You got your marks."

"Yeah." He handed me the envelope and I opened it. He'd gotten B's and C's.

I could see a whole stream of kids walking down York Street and onto George, all of them holding these little brown envelopes. They looked like a line of black ants carrying brown leaves. We went into Louie V's store. The V stood for Van something or other.

"Well, if it's not the young men with the big silver," Mr. V said. Louie V was a tall man with grey hair and glasses. His store was built right into his house. You went in by the side steps and that was the store. A pop cooler was the first thing you saw coming in the door. The bottles were sitting in ice cold water. The walls of the store were crammed with every sort of cereal box and cleaner and canned food. One long counter blocked off the end of the room, and Mr. V stood behind it. A doorway that led to the rest of the house was behind the counter. The pipe from the upstairs toilet ran right through the counter, near the cash register. It was painted yellow so it fit right in with the room. Sometimes you'd be buying something and all of a sudden water would rush through the pipe.

The other end of the counter was glassed in and there were chocolates and gummies and jujube balls and sweet-and-sours and anything else you could think of. On the wall behind the counter were all the varieties of cigarettes. The green packages were Export A; the red, Craven Filter; the blue, Player's Filter; the black and red, Du Maurier; the black and gold, Benson and Hedges; the yellow, Matinee; the lime-green, Cameo, a menthol. One time we were in a grocery store, me and a few boys from school, and we accidentally stole a carton of menthol. They were *terrible*. You couldn't give them away they were so bad. What a mistake!

I put twenty-five cents on the counter.

"I'll have ten cigarettes, Mr. V, and two books of matches."

"Ten cigarettes, the young man said." Mr. V counted out ten cigarettes from an open package of regular Export A Filter. It was good that Mr. V sold loose cigarettes. Lots of times I didn't have the seventy-five cents for a full pack and if you had a nickel, you could get two cigarettes and a book of matches at Louie V's.

He gave me ten loose cigarettes and two books of matches. I carefully put the cigarettes in the chest pocket of my denim jacket.

"And what will you have?" Mr. V asked Cosmo, who was down at the other end of the counter looking at the candies through the glass.

"I'll have two jawbreakers, and two bubble gums, and the rest in niggle balls," Cosmo said.

"How much are you spending, young man?"

"A dime."

Louie V collected the candies and put them in a little brown paper bag. Cosmo gave him the dime and Mr. V handed over the bag. Cosmo immediately opened the bag and began to take an inventory, even though he had carefully watched Louie V put the candies in the bag.

"Is that all, boys?"

"Yes."

"The men with the big silver," Mr. V said. "Go home and get more silver. Come back and buy lots more stuff." He wanted us to leave the store so he could go back into the house to eat chips and watch television.

"Thank you," I said.

I don't know what I would've done if Louie V didn't sell loose cigarettes.

Rosemary Hawthorn was outside the store when we came out. She lived right next to the school and she was in my class. It was a very lucky coincidence that we met.

"You didn't get to school again, Michael Chisholm, on the last day of school."

"I know," I said. I lit a cigarette.

"And you're smoking all the time! You'll die before you're thirty, I swear!"

Rosemary scolded me all the time like that. It was kind of nice that she did.

"Why weren't you at school to get your marks?" she demanded.

"I slept in," I said.

"You slept in!" Rosemary laughed.

I had a whole range of excuses for missing school or arriving late: The alarm didn't go off in my parents' room. I had to help get the garbage out. My mother made lumpy oatmeal and it took twice as long to make up a new batch. These were real reasons for being late. I never once told a lie about what made me late. The last time I explained to Sister MacGillivray the reason why I was late, she smiled. I said the cat had followed me to school. And that was true. I had to turn around and walk the cat all the way home. You can't concentrate on school work when you know your cat is walking around in a strange neighbourhood.

"Well, *I* got your marks *for* you," Rosemary said. She handed me a brown envelope. "I told Sister that I could give them to you."

"Thanks a lot," I said. That was very thoughtful of Rosemary. It saved me from going back to school on the last day. I opened the envelope. C's and D's.

"I hope you didn't fail anything?"

"No," I said. I handed her my report which I knew she wanted to see. She handed me hers and I saw that she had A's and B's.

"At least you made it into grade nine," she said.

Rosemary smelled nice, like warm candy.

"Want to go down the CN?" Cosmo asked.

"Okay," I said. I didn't ask Rosemary if she wanted to go down the CN. It was no place for a girl. I folded my school grades into a square and put them in the back pocket of my jeans.

"Goodbye, Rosemary."

"Goodbye, Michael Chisholm."

CANADIAN NATIONAL HAD A FENCED-OFF TRUCKING yard right down by the tracks. There were all sorts of pallets strewn all over the place. Pallets were used for transporting barrels or packets of flour or anything that could be lifted with a forklift. The pallets had double bottoms that allowed the forklifts to get their prongs underneath. Once they got their merchandise from the truck to the train, a lot of pallets were thrown away. Some of the wood was exceptional. Some of it was groove-and-tongue, as a matter of fact. The freight taken from the trains was placed directly into the big CN tractor-trailers. Cosmo and I stopped and sat on the back steps of a warehouse that overlooked the CN yard. The trailers were parked back against the cyclone fence.

"Wanna smoke?"

"Sure," Cosmo said.

I gave him a cigarette. We smoked with great pleasure. And then I said we ought to see what was in one of those CN trucks. Cosmo thought that was an excellent idea. We climbed the cyclone fence and walked to a trailer. I gave Cosmo a leg up and he removed the little metal pin that held the door in place, by just pulling down on the lever. Just like that, the back of the truck was open. I don't know why they don't have more secure locks.

Merchandise was packed almost right to the ceiling. There were various boxes in all shapes and sizes piled up with the product names stencilled on the sides of the boxes. Cosmo climbed up over the front boxes, which we couldn't inspect anyway because they were too big, and he disappeared for a minute.

"Oh man!"

"What?"

"Oh *man!*"

"What? *What?*"

"*Games!*"

A long, slender box came inching up over the larger boxes. It was about four inches high by a foot wide by, oh, three feet long, or thereabouts. I put my hands on it and dropped it down to the ground. It was heavy as hell. The stencilled name on the box was "Cooey." Cosmo said that was the name of a company that made games. He said "Fun For Everyone" was their motto.

"All *right!*"

Cosmo slid out another box. I lost my grip on it because it was so heavy and the box sort of slammed down to the ground, crushing the cardboard on one end. I heard a metal sound. If these games had metal in them, we had quality games, all right. Most games were made with plastic.

Cosmo appeared from behind the large boxes and he used my shoulder to steady himself as he jumped to the ground. We swung the big door closed and replaced the pin.

"Let's take them over to Louisa Gardens," Cosmo suggested.

"Let's open them under the loading dock," I said. Cosmo took one box and I took the other and we crawled under the loading dock of the wooden CN warehouse. The warehouse was about five hundred feet long with loading bays on one side for the trains and on the other side for the trucks. We went right underneath the truck side. We had to hunch down because there wasn't much room. It was dirty and filled with pop cans and paper and plastic wrappers and dead weeds and lots of dust and faded cigarette packages. The sun filtered down through the wooden slats above us.

"Let's open it up," I said.

I took out my pocket knife and began slitting the sides of the box. I had a damn fine pocket knife. The handle was made of wood and the blade curved right into the handle. It was razor sharp, too. It's good to have a knife with you, just to carry it around in your pocket. You never know when you're going to use it. I wish I had one now.

The lid came off the box and I removed the wrapping. The game was broken in two and the parts were sunken in styrofoam. It was like we were looking at some sort of fossil. It took a moment for us to assemble the parts in our heads.

"Shotgun," Cosmo whispered.

A funny twisting feeling started in my stomach.

I opened the second box and removed the wrapping. The shotguns looked identical. The long single barrel was one piece, the wooden stock another. The stock had a rubber shock-absorber on the butt and a fern design etched into the wood. We began assembling our guns. Cosmo could barely hold the gun steady as he looked down the barrel and pulled the trigger. It made a "click" sound. My gun did the same. The guns were way too top-heavy. We could barely hold them up because the metal barrels made the fronts of the guns droop down.

"Let's take these up to the schoolyard," Cosmo said.

The idea of showing the shotguns to our friends was a good idea. But to do that, we had to walk up Amelia Street and take the shortcut over to York. We'd be walking right through the middle of the north end with these shotguns in cardboard boxes that we could hardly lift properly.

"We can't walk around with these things," I said.

"Yes we can." Cosmo was still aiming the gun around, but there wasn't much to aim at under the loading dock.

"We have to hide them."

"I'm not hiding mine, no way."

"What're you going to do with it then? Walk around with it in the open?"

"I'm going to get some bullets and shoot it."

"Where are you going to shoot it at?"

"I don't know. Someplace. Down the B&D Cement factory." He was still tilting his head almost completely sideways and clicking the trigger. But he finally put the gun down because it was heavy. We were both cradling the shotguns on our laps. They were very fine instruments, excellent combinations of wood and metal. And they had a nice smell of wax and oil.

Suddenly, a warehouse door above us opened and several men and a forklift came out onto the loading dock. Cosmo and I froze as we looked at the shadows above us.

We decided to put one gun back and to keep one. That was fair enough. We put Cosmo's gun back after we had wiped it completely clean with our shirts. Our dirty fingerprints were all over the white box, but smudges didn't count as fingerprints. When the coast was clear, we went back to the truck and opened up the door again. Cosmo jumped up and I hoisted the heavy box up to him. He took it and pushed it in back. We closed the door and put the pin back in the lock. I carried the shotgun back along the rail lines, being careful to walk behind the trains that shielded us from the houses, until we were at the bamboo jungle at the back of the oil company. We burrowed a hole among the bamboo plants and stuffed in the white cardboard box. Then we covered it completely with grass.

"If you shoot it, you have to let me shoot it, too," Cosmo said.

"I know."

"Or I'll tell," he added.

"You keep your mouth shut. You're the one who stole it, too."

"All I'm sayin' is that I want to shoot it if you get some bullets."

"I know, I heard you. But if you tell anybody about this, any of your friends or anybody, you'll be in deep trouble. You'll go to Shelburne."

Shelburne wasn't even on Cape Breton Island. It was all the way down the tail end of Nova Scotia. Shelburne was where the provincial reform school was located. Any time you did something wrong, somebody would be sure to mention Shelburne. Shelburne this, Shelburne that. The floorwalker at the Metropolitan store, when he took me to the office and made me hand over the miniature dump truck that I had slid into my pocket, said, "You're going to be in Shelburne if you keep it up." If you missed a couple of days at school, the guidance counsellor said, "Do you want to go to Shelburne? Is that where you want to go?" And the manager of the grocery store said that Shelburne wasn't good enough for the little thieves that were stealing cartons of cigarettes from his display, as if somebody taking a carton of cigarettes deserved to be sent right off the island. As if a carton of cigarettes was Holy Communion or something.

"I know you want to shoot it," I said to Cosmo, "but if you tell anybody else about this you'll *never* get to shoot it. Promise that you won't tell anyone."

"Promise. You promise me that you'll let me shoot it if you shoot it."

"Okay. But there's no place to shoot it around here and

I'll probably put it back in the truck tomorrow. I don't know what else I'm going to do with the stupid thing."

"I get to use yours 'cause we put mine back—"

"Will you shut the hell up about that? I know what we did. I'm not deaf."

Cosmo could explore Slag Mountain with you and climb up on the oil company tanks and help you take a look inside a transport truck and ride with you on the diesel engine and then sometimes out of the blue he could act like a little child. The only thing I was glad about was that he'd forget all about this gun in no time. I came back down to the bamboo grove after dinner and re-hid the box under a cement slab in the army hospital just to be safe. Boy, little brothers.

8

COSMO AND I BOTH KNEW OUR FATHER COULDN'T ever find out about the gun. If he found out about the gun, he would kill us. Rory was very impatient about certain things. He hated lying and cheating. He didn't like complaining, either. And taking a shotgun from a CN transport truck would definitely be something he would have no patience with. Guaranteed.

People mistook Rory for a prize fighter because his hands were so large. He sure had the attitude of a prize fighter. He was six foot two, two hundred and twenty pounds, fit and trim. He could float like a butterfly and sting like a bee and was as powerful as Muhammad Ali. Our father could have clobbered Mr. Ontario Smart

Aleck. And strangled his dog, too. He could have clobbered the guy, and then, if the dog gave him any trouble, he could have given the dog one smack with the back of his hand and it would have been good night ladies for the dog.

Our father was a fighter. We were told our father could fight by a man we didn't even know. It was when Rory was in a dunk tank during Sydney Days and people paid a dollar to try to dunk him. They had to hit a little target that would collapse the seat above the dunk tank. Sid and I stood by holding a towel.

"Your father was quite the scrapper when he was younger," this stranger told us. I didn't know who he was or why he wanted to tell us anything, except that he admired our father for being a fighter.

"Really?" Sid asked. "He fought?"

"Oh, yeah. He liked to mix it up."

ONE TIME WE WERE ALL IN OUR BIG LIGHT BLUE STATion wagon waiting for the light at Dorchester and George to change. We were going to the country for the weekend. The wagon was jam-packed with supplies like hot dogs and beer. We were the first car at the light and other cars lined up behind us. The light changed from red to green, and before Rory could even take his foot off the brake, before he could even put his foot on the gas, the car behind us was laying on the horn. Instead of going forward, instead of obeying the horn behind him by speeding up, Rory suddenly put the car in park and kicked open his door. I still remember the big heavy door of the station wagon opening up, swinging on its hinges and recoiling with enough force to close. By then Rory was walking to the car behind us. The car behind us couldn't go anywhere because it was stuck in the lineup.

We all crowded to the back windows and watched Rory walk up to the car, lean on the driver's-side door and say, "Do you have a problem?" We couldn't hear what the driver of the car said. And Rory said something in a lower voice and then he walked slowly back to our car.

That was the bravest thing I'd ever seen in my life.

What if the guy in the car behind us had said, "Yeah, I've got a problem. You're too goddamn slow at green lights, you poky bastard." He could have said that. He could have said something meaner. What if he kicked *his* door open and went toe to toe with Rory? He could have. He could have been another George Foreman in the driver's seat, just driving around Sydney after a workout in the ring, and maybe he had to get back quickly to the gym and he was impatient with this big old station wagon ahead of him loaded down with kids. When it didn't pull away as quickly as he'd liked, he maybe just gave it a blast of the horn to hurry it up. It could have happened like that. Rory didn't know who was back there.

Our father was always getting in fights with people. And he never once backed down. He was a union organizer. Before that, he had worked at the daily newspaper in Sydney, which had a list on the wall of prominent people that the reporters were never allowed to criticize or question, despite the fact that some of these people were the biggest bastards in Cape Breton. So now Rory criticized them through the union. He had to because he was the most honest man in Sydney and he was fighting a lot of ignorance and corruption.

IT WAS GLORIA'S IDEA THAT WE CALL OUR PARENTS BY their first names. They were always having discussions about such things. They would sit in the kitchen when Rory was home at night or sometimes on the weekends and smoke up the kitchen with cigarettes and drink instant coffee and discuss. They had been discussing ever since I could remember. At first I thought they were arguing, but they weren't. They were discussing and debating and we were always welcome to listen and sometimes to contribute to the discussion if we had something to say. Thus we learned to have open minds. We were never ordered outside or told that we couldn't hear something being discussed, which would have constituted closed-mindedness.

Mostly I remember my mother getting excited about something and my father trying to interrupt her enthusiasm by calmly repeating, "Gloria ... Gloria ... Gloria," in order to get her attention about some important first fact that she had overlooked. It was fun to listen to their discussions. I learned a lot from my parents just by being in the same room with them.

The discussions held in the good room were different. That room was kept closed and off limits for all but special visitors. When the president of the steel plant visited, he sat in the good room. When the president of the local chapter of the United Mine Workers of America visited, he sat in the good room. When the senators and MP's and MLA's visited, they sat in the good room. After their departure, the room was cleaned up and aired out and then resealed until the next important visit.

There was a good chesterfield in the good room, and two good chairs, and a good rug on the hardwood floor. There was a stout coffee table with a blown glass ashtray with bubbles trapped in the blue glass. The drapes were a brown and orange floral pattern and the colour of the rug matched. A portrait of my father that my mother had painted hung above the bookcase. The bookcase was the best thing about the good room.

The books were divided equally between my father's books and my mother's books. I could almost tell whose book was whose by the title. *Rules for Radicals, The Prince, Unions, Management and the Public,* and all the war books were my father's. There was *The Rise and Fall of the Third Reich,* which didn't have one single picture, and *The Last Days of Hitler,* which didn't have a single picture, either. But *World War II Encyclopedia* had some great pictures of tanks and Stukas and Spitfires and the living skeletons in the concentration camps and the big mushroom cloud that was the last picture in the book. And there was *The Bismarck Episode.* The *Bismarck* was my favourite ship of all time, more favourite even than the *Titanic.* Sid, as a Sea Cadet, knew more about the *Bismarck* than the *Titanic,* and he told me about the *Bismarck.*

"The *Titanic* wouldn't stand a chance against the *Bismarck,*" he said.

"Wasn't the *Titanic* faster?" I asked.

"Nope."

"Was it bigger?"

"Yeah, okay, it was bigger. It was longer than the *Bismarck,* but the *Bismarck* was wider by thirty feet and displaced more water. The *Titanic* was slower and didn't have any guns. The *Bismarck* had eight fifteen-inch guns!" Fifteen inches didn't seem like such a big gun to me. It seemed sort of tiny. But Sid said these guns could sink the *Titanic* from fifteen miles away, just like they sank the HMS *Hood.*

Sid knew that Sydney Harbour was used in wartime as a gathering place for ships that joined the huge convoys setting out from Halifax to cross the Atlantic Ocean. The Atlantic was infested with German U-boats. I knew already that the *Caribou,* the Newfoundland ferry that ran between Port-aux-Basques and North Sydney, was torpedoed and sunk by a German U-boat during World War Two. Everybody knew that.

I also knew the chorus of Johnny Horton's song "Sink the Bismarck," but Sid knew the entire song by heart. I thought that Johnny Horton himself had something to do with sinking the *Bismarck* by swinging her guns around. But Sid said Johnny Horton only sang the song, he wasn't actually there when they sank the *Bismarck*. And then I thought that the Americans had sunk the *Bismarck* because Johnny Horton was an American. But Sid told me that the British sank the *Bismarck* after the *Bismarck* had sunk the HMS *Hood* with one shot. Johnny Horton was in Alaska at the time.

The books that my mother collected were in the middle shelves. They were mostly brand new paperbacks. Some of them were as interesting as the World War Two picture books. *Chariots of the Gods* had some really thought-provoking pictures that proved that mankind had come from outer space. There was a picture of an ancient Egyptian wearing a space suit, just like the one Neil Armstrong had worn on the moon five years before. There was a photograph of the earth taken from hundreds of miles in space that showed the image of an insect. How could anyone living thousands of years ago know to draw a huge insect that was only visible from space unless they were drawing it *from* space? No one has been able to answer that one.

Worlds in Collision was a book in my mother's collection about how the planet Venus was once a comet that had passed close to the earth. All of the disasters written in the Bible were completely explained in this book. And Christianity could be understood by reading *The Cult of the Mushroom*. The writer had proven that the early Christians were actually drug users, so you had to interpret Christianity first as a drug-using cult before all its mysteries became clear. It had plenty of pictures, but most of them were boring. *Pyramid Power* showed by interesting graphs and charts how pyramids channelled "cosmic energy" into a beam and how, by following a simple cut-out design, readers could make Pyramid Power work for them. Gloria had already put a red cardboard pyramid under our bunk beds to help improve our school marks. I don't know what *People of the Mountain* was about.

On the bottom shelf there was a complete set of the *Encyclopedia Britannica* which I only opened to see the transparent pictures that showed the guts and sex organs of men and women. Every volume in the encyclopedia set smelled like a Bible when you opened it up. They must have been made at the same place.

IRENE NOT ONLY KEPT OUR HOUSE, SHE MADE LUNCH and started supper, too. When Gloria came home at five o'clock from the union office, Irene would be ready to walk out the door to get supper ready for Tim, her husband, who would be coming home from his job at the school a few minutes later. It was a good arrangement for Irene because she could dash back and forth from house to house working on two suppers and have both done when the time came. Tim often came over to our house to see Irene, and we often went across the driveway to the Carsons' just to talk to Tim. Tim was the boiler man for our school and he knew all about anything of importance. He always had a simple explanation for things that everyone else tried to make complicated. And all his explanations made sense.

At first I wanted to tell Tim about the shotgun because he would know how to go about fixing the situation. For example, he had known exactly what to do the time we found the torpedo.

The first place the railroad tracks ran past, when they left the CN Roundhouse below our house, was the old army hospital. We called it the army hospital, but I don't actually know what it used to be. It was an abandoned tract of overgrown land. Huge slabs of cement jutted out of the sod as if from an explosion, and twisted wires and metal made the army hospital a very good spot to explore. To tell you the truth, since the discovery of the torpedo, nothing much has happened in the army hospital.

But that torpedo was something.

It was as long as a canoe, or longer. It was as long as Mr. MacPhee's car with his Trailways trailer hooked up. When we found the torpedo, it was just a little bit of a metal tube sticking out of the earth. We pulled back the sod and dug around the tube and exposed a fin welded on the side of it. We cleared away more and more earth, and there was no disputing that it was a torpedo, all right. We didn't know what to do at first. There was Sid, Sid's best friends Alex Gunther and Rene Dumont, and me. Alex was in Sea Cadets with Sid. He was shorter than Sid, but stocky, and had curly hair. Rene lived near us on George Street. He was tall and thin and always had a fresh brush cut. Sid, Alex, and Rene went around a lot together because they were older boys. I went with them sometimes.

We took turns standing on the overhanging slab of cement dropping boulders on the torpedo head. As the boulder struck the tip of the torpedo, all of us would "hit the dirt," just like the soldiers in World War Two.

"Bombs away!" Sid said, as he let the first huge stone fall on the torpedo.

"Hit the dirt!" Alex shouted.

We all hit the dirt. But nothing happened. Only a metallic bong and an echo that returned to us from the steel plant across the water. After we did this about ten times, it was clear that the torpedo wasn't going to explode, and there isn't much you can do with a torpedo except explode it.

"We should tell somebody about this," Rene suggested.

We left the army hospital by sliding under the chain-link fence, which was the same way we had gotten in, and ran down along Brook Street. Tim was washing his Chevrolet. Tim would know what to do about unexploded torpedoes. At first, he didn't believe our breathless chatter about there being a torpedo in the old army hospital grounds. But he came with us anyway to have a look.

"For the love of Mike! Get away from that thing boys!" he said when he saw the torpedo.

The old rusty gates of the army hospital were opened and a stream of tractors and police and army trucks and hoists and cranes and jeeps came into the field. An army bulldozer had to make a road to the torpedo so the other equipment could get near it. We weren't allowed to watch up close. We were the ones who *found* it and they wouldn't let us watch. We climbed up the cyclone fence of the army hospital and hung there, like flies on a web, trying to watch the entire operation. Tim was right. We could have blown up the north end with that torpedo.

I didn't tell Tim about the shotgun. I should have, but I didn't. Sid and I visited him all the time simply by walking out our back door and in through his back door. Irene and Tim had kids of their own but they were grown up. The last son had just moved out of the house. But now there was something wrong with Tim. He wasn't eating properly.

"Something's wrong with me guts," he told us.

"What's wrong, Tim?" Sid asked.

"Ah, everything hurts to eat, boys," Tim said. "A potatee feels like I'm passing a lump of coal, know what I mean?"

I had no idea what he meant.

"Didn't the doctor know what it was?" Sid asked.

"Doctor didn't know his head from his hole, if you'll excuse the expression, boys. And the *counsellor*, what they call the counsellor, was just as bad. She was saying something about the nu*trition*, boys. Something about the nu*trition*. She said, 'Mr. Carson, did your mother feed you well when you was a baby?' I said, 'Very well, thank you very much. And did your mother feed *you*?' 'And Mr. Carson,' she says, 'did your mother eat right during her preg*nasty*?' Her preg*nasty*, boys! I said, 'Well, Doctor, me mother drank coffee and smoked cigarettes all through her pregnasty with me'—which is the truth, boys."

"Is that why there's something wrong with your guts, Tim?" I asked. I thought this story had something to do with his guts.

"No, boys, nothing to do with me guts. But it explained why I cried for three weeks after I was calved. Baby Tim's hollering was a big mystery, boys. They thought I had the colic, but it wasn't that. They thought I couldn't suck me own dear mother's teat, but it wasn't that, neither, boys. They just couldn't figure out ol' Tim. Well, it turns out this *counsellor*"—Tim could not say certain words without pain— "it turns out that she knew the reason why I bawled like a bull when I was born. It turns out that little Timothy Carson was addicted to *drugs*, boys! They kept feeding me mother's milk and penicillin to stop me yelling when all I wanted was a cup of coffee and a cigarette! Ha, ha! That's me, ain't it, boys? Addicted to me vices before I'm even out of the room! What? God help us all, boys!"

"What about your guts, Tim?" Sid asked. "Are you going to have an operation?"

"No—thank Jesus, Mary, and Joseph," Tim crossed himself. "No operation. But they want to give me some sort of test to look at me insides, some sort of goddamn test called a *barium* test. Ever hear of it, boys? I've got to drink this transmission fluid and they X-ray me as it runs through me guts and a nurse catches it in a bottle at the other end."

"Will you be able to eat again after that?" Sid asked.

"Not bloody likely, boys. Not bloody likely. I'm on a restricted diet as it is and the doctor said I'd better get use to it."

"That's too bad, Tim," I said.

And it was, too, because Irene was an excellent cook. She made pork chops with potatoes and carrots and gravy, and casseroles and meat loaf and shepherd's pie. She made Scotch broth from scratch (Tim told us that Scotch broth was just Irish stew watered down) and she made fish cakes from scratch and they were delicious with ketchup. Sometimes Irene made open-faced sandwiches with roast beef and vegetables, and thick gravy poured over them. And all kinds of goulashes and Swiss steak and beans and wieners and fried baloney and eggs. I'm telling you, there was just nothing like it.

I loved mashed potatoes myself. I liked making a hill

with them and plopping a big hunk of butter on top. I'd build a sluiceway in the potatoes for the butter as it melted. Sometimes, I'd rake my fork across the potatoes and the butter would melt into the furrows, like water on a farmer's field. Then I'd carefully score the flattened potatoes with a knife and eat them block by block. When we had chicken, I'd put a little mashed potato under a slice of chicken on my fork, and then touch the bottom of my fork to the peas in order to pick up a few. Man! Irene made pancakes now and then. I once ate twenty-nine pancakes in a row. Irene couldn't believe it.

But some foods I didn't like. Fried liver was horrible. And Brussels sprouts with fried liver was hideous and horrible. How can people eat that? And then sometimes Irene would fry up *onions* and put them *over the liver* and expect you to eat it! Can you believe it? I couldn't believe it. Anything an onion touched I considered polluted. And occasionally you'd come in the house after school and smell something really *off*. And Irene would say hello as she was cooking and tell you not to walk on the scrubbed floor. She would not seem to notice that there was this *stink* in the house. Later, we'd have a big boiled dinner of brisket and turnips and sauerkraut and that would explain everything. I would nearly puke. I ate the roasts, the ham and the beef, but when they were drenched with onions and celery and god knows what else, then they weren't worth eating.

Everybody else ate everything Irene cooked. Cosmo just inhaled it all. Irene could boil an old shoe and pour gravy over it and Cosmo would tell her it was delicious. Man, that guy just ate anything. We were watching a television news broadcast one time and it showed a continuous miner, the kind they use underground in the collieries. A continuous miner is just that, a huge conveyor belt with teeth. That's all it was. Anyway, Sid said that Cosmo was just like a continuous miner when he opened the fridge. And that was the funniest thing to say! Sid could bring up an image every now and then and put it in your head as easy as pie. But it was terrible for Tim to not be able to eat Irene's cooking. And we just felt terribly for Tim because he was such a good guy. We grew up with him being our uncle, sort of, and we always went to him with problems that we couldn't take to anyone else. I wanted to tell Tim about the shotgun but it was a lot different than telling him about the torpedo. So I didn't tell him anything about the gun. But it was frustrating carrying around a secret like that.

9

WE HAD A TWO-DAY STORM AT THE START OF THE SUMmer. We found the raft on the tar pond shore on the first day of the storm, and we found the kayak on the Sydney Harbour shore the next day. Actually, Rene and Sid found the kayak and Alex found the raft. I had nothing to do with finding either of them. They brought the kayak back to our place and set it up on two sawhorses that Sid borrowed from Tim. It was still raining and cold outside. I saw them bringing it into the yard from the kitchen window. I loved the look of the kayak as soon as I saw it. I put on a jacket and went outside.

"Where'd you get it?"

"We found it washed up by the dry docks," Sid said.

"Probably came from the other side of the harbour," Rene said.

"Westmount," Sid said. Rene was carefully examining every inch of the kayak.

"It looks pretty good," I said.

"It's not seaworthy." Sid pointed to where the fibreglass was punctured in several places and the red paint faded and shattered near the ribs. There was a long slash on the bottom that Rene put his finger through.

"All damage is easily fixable," Rene said. His head was inside the cavity of the boat and his words had a strange echo to them. "This damage was probably done by ice. I bet this boat was under the ice all winter."

"But you think it's fixable, Ren?" Sid sounded like a man asking a doctor about a certain risky operation.

"Oh, it's fixable. No problem at all. All we do is get a strip of fibreglass and some fibreglass paint, maybe replace a rib or two, and it's ready."

"Want me to go to the hardware store for the stuff?" I asked.

I was trying to invite myself into the group so I could use the kayak. Volunteer work was the only way in. Of course, being Sid's younger brother helped, too.

"How old are you, Michael?" Rene asked.

"Fourteen," I said.

"You're not fourteen," Alex said. "You're only thirteen."

"I'll be fourteen next month," I said.

I wasn't mad at Alex for pointing out my age. I was just disappointed that I was too young for just about anything, like driving. Next summer, Rene and Alex would be fixing up cars, not kayaks. Sid wasn't interested very much in cars. He liked ships. But I was interested in cars, all right. I was already looking at magazines filled with pictures of souped-up cars, and I had pictures of hot rods on the wall of our bedroom.

"We don't need anybody else," Alex said. "So what can Michael do? There's nothing for him to do, that's all."

"He could be the official tender," Sid said.

Alex and Rene both thought about this for a minute.

"What's a tender?" I asked.

"See?" Alex said. "He doesn't even know what a tender is."

"What *is* a tender?" Rene said. Rene wasn't a Sea Cadet either.

"Oh, great!" said Alex.

"It's the boat that takes people back and forth to the ship when the ship is at anchor and can't tie up at a dock," Sid explained.

"A taxi, you mean?"

"That's right, a taxi."

"I could be that," I said.

And as soon as Sid said it, I knew that I had seen tenders every summer when the passenger ships anchored just off Sydney because the government pier wasn't deep enough for them to dock. They sent their passengers in on a *tender*.

"Someone has to be the tender, otherwise how will we get back and forth to the raft?"

Rene and Alex thought some more about this, visualizing going back and forth to the raft in the kayak. It made sense for there to be an official tender.

"Then we have to make the kayak fit two people," Rene said.

"That's right," Sid agreed.

"Do you know what side starboard is?" Alex asked me.
"Right side."
"And what side is the left side?"
"Port."
"I'll think up more questions for you later. Are you going to get a haircut?"
"No."
"How can you see with that hair in your face? You look like Donny Osmond. It's like girls' hair. Are you going to get a ponytail?"
"No."
"Pigtails?"
"No."
"There's no smoking on the raft," Sid told me.
"Okay," I said.

And that's how my involvement with the kayak and the raft came about. One minute I was doing nothing, and the next I was doing a lot. For example, besides being the official tender, I was also the quartermaster. I was in charge of supplies, which meant that I had to go buy them when they were needed. I guess I was a gopher.

"We need you to go to the hardware store and find out how much paddles cost," Sid said.

"No problem," I said.

"If they cost more than ten dollars, don't buy any."

Sid gave me ten dollars in bills and quarters.

I walked all the way to the hardware store. It was at the very end of Charlotte Street, at the corner of Charlotte and Falmouth. Charlotte Street started in the north end, right at the gate of the army barracks, and it ran straight through to the Wentworth duck pond. As soon as you crossed Dorchester Street, you were out of the north end. There were three banks on the corner of Charlotte and Dorchester, and the big post-office building was on the fourth corner. All the shops and stores started from this point and continued on both sides of Charlotte Street until the big Baptist church stopped them at Douglas. As soon as I entered the hardware store, the clerk asked if he could help me because he thought I was there to shoplift. But this time I was there on business.

"Do you have any kayak paddles?"

"No," the clerk said. "But we have canoe paddles." He was a weird-looking clerk. He had thinning hair and pasty white skin and was as skinny as a rail. His Adam's apple was very large and it went up and down when he spoke. He had a package of cigarettes in his shirt pocket along with a plastic shield for two or three pens. The first two fingers on his right hand were orange from holding lit cigarettes. Player's Plain, no filter, same kind Tim smoked.

"No kayak paddles at all?"

"No, son. But canoe paddles are just as good."

"But we have a kayak," I explained.

"Canoe paddles are good for kayaks, too. Every bit as good."

He told me how much for two canoe paddles and he smiled when I asked how much for just one. But I bought both paddles. They were bright orange and cost four something apiece. I had just enough money. I almost didn't have enough because of the tax, but I had enough. After every purchase at the hardware store they gave you fake store money that you could put toward another purchase. I suddenly saw the value in this currency and knew where there was a big wad of it at home in the junk drawer.

I walked all the way back to the north end. It would

only have taken me a second to go back and forth if I still had my bike, but somebody had stolen it the summer before. It was a second-hand, girl's bike anyway, only one speed. Everyone was riding ten-speed bikes. So I walked back to the north end.

I GUESS I SHOULD EXPLAIN ALEX. ALEX STARTED LIVING at our house that summer. He slept in the big, unheated room on the third floor. The only room that had heat on the third floor was our own room. It was heated by a single radiator. The pipes rattled like hell when hot water was trying to climb up from the furnace in the basement to the radiator in our room. That was quite a climb and often the water didn't make it. It just gave up after turning the radiator lukewarm. Alex's room didn't have any radiator at all so it was cold even in the summer. Summers in Cape Breton aren't all that hot, though they aren't freezing, either. The days are nice and warm and the nights are cold.

Alex had been staying over at our house more and more and it just became normal to have him at the house all the time. Alex and his father didn't get along very well. I don't know what it was, but it had something to do with his father's second marriage. Alex's mother wasn't his real mother. His parents had divorced and his father had remarried when Alex was still a kid. I didn't know whether his real mother was dead or alive and I didn't ask. All I knew was that Alex and his second mother didn't get along at all, and Alex's father was angry with him for not liking his new mother.

Alex went with Sid every Friday night to Sea Cadets. They had their uniforms in the closet in our room. That was about the only thing the closet in our room was used for. Their tunics and pants were hanging on hangers and their white flat-top hats were on two nails at the back of the closet. Sid had hammered the nails there for that purpose. They would get dressed up in their uniforms, and look quite smart in them, too. Sid was very conscientious about dressing up for any important occasion.

"Come on to Sea Cadets with us, Michael," Sid said almost every Friday night. If Sid wasn't trying to get me to go to Sea Cadets, he was trying to get me to go to the Gaelic Society meetings on Thursday nights, or trying to get me to go with him to church on Sunday mornings.

"No, thanks," I said.

One part of me wanted to go with Sid to Sea Cadets, but I think that was just to be with Sid. I liked the uniforms, but I didn't want to wear a uniform or get a haircut. I wanted to go with Sid to the Gaelic Society meetings, but I wouldn't have known what anyone was saying.

Allan Noonan, Ronnie Ferguson, Joe MacKenzie, and Mike MacMullin were all Boy Scouts. They were in my class at school. I joined Scouts on the night they had pellet rifles to shoot and then I quit going because the next meeting we had to salute and obey orders and always be prepared and I just wasn't interested. I wish I had stayed in Scouts, though. Mike and Joe and Ronnie and Allan had gone to Newfoundland that spring for two weeks on a Scout trip. They'd boarded the Newfoundland ferry at North Sydney and sailed to Port-aux-Basques. Allan said that as soon as he had gotten off the boat, a Newfoundland girl had acted like she would go all the way with him. Apparently, the girls who would go all the way waited for the boat to come in from North Sydney. When a Boy Scout got off the ferry, they would make an offer to go all the way. I wouldn't have believed this at all if Mike and Joe hadn't backed Allan up. They'd been there and they said it was just the way Allan told it. Allan said he would have gone all the way with her but he had been sick as a dog on the ferry. The trip over to Newfoundland, I understand, isn't a bowl of cherries.

"If you come to Sea Cadets you can learn navigation," Sid said.

"I don't care," I said.

"I'm learning it. Alex is learning it."

"I know."

"Why don't you want to go?"

"Because I don't want to learn navigation," I said.

"You can learn something else, like seamanship. Or precision drill. You'd like precision drill. You like watching the team practice on the parade square, don't you?"

"What else can you do?"

"I don't know. Semaphore. Everything. Secret codes. I'm going to get my swimming certification at the radar base swimming pool. You can join the band, too. Alex is learning to play the trumpet and I'm learning to play the pipes. And we're going to camp for two weeks this summer. If you join now, you can come with us to camp."

"I don't want to."

"Okay, then. See you later."

"See you later," I said.

I was a little bit nervous about turning down Sid's offer to go to Sea Cadets, because Sid and Alex had allowed me to join them in fixing up the kayak, but I just didn't know what to think about Sea Cadets. So I didn't think about it at all, except to feel sorry for myself that I couldn't make a decision about it. I guess I just didn't want to be called a "dory cork." That's what the Sea Cadets were called; that, and "flat tops."

When I got back home to Meadow Street from the hardware store, with the orange paddles, there was no sign of Sid, Alex, or Rene. I found out later they had taken the kayak up to Rene's so he could cut a bigger opening in the frame of the kayak, so two people could fit. Our father's sky-blue station wagon was in the driveway, and there was an unfamiliar car on the street in front of our house. It was a sports car, and a nice one.

It was a bright Competition Orange 1967 Mercury Cougar hardtop. I could tell the date by reading it on the tail light. It had a three-speed transmission and a 289 v-8 engine. Monster power. I hadn't seen anything like it on the rail cars. A true muscle car. They made them this way right off the line. You didn't have to do a thing to them. They'd just fly. But it was classy, too. The front headlights were concealed. The bucket seats were black, carpets were black, floor mats were black. It had a tachometer. I leaned my head right in the open window and read the mileage: forty-eight thousand. That was nothing for a seven-year-old car. The steering wheel had a leather racing grip. The windshield was tinted. The interior smelled of cigarettes and perfume and there was a girl's sweater draped over the driver's seat.

I stashed the paddles behind the bushes in our yard. I went directly to the kitchen and opened the fridge door because I was starving. My mother came out from the good room.

"Where have you been?" she asked.

"Out," I said.

"Come in the good room and meet Miss Taylor."

I closed the fridge door and followed my mother to the good room.

"Here he is," my father said when he saw me. "Michael, say hello to Miss Taylor."

"Hello, Miss Taylor."

"Hello, Michael. You're a busy boy to track down. I've been here twice and have talked to everyone in the family but you."

Miss Taylor was tanned and had remarkable red-orange hair almost the colour of her car. She was very small, smaller than me. Her frame was slight and her shoulders pointed inward. That was probably because her bosoms were very pointed and big for such a slight woman. It's surprising that she didn't keel right over and fall flat on her face from carrying that load. When I was younger, I thought women had only one breast because when they were dressed you only saw one long protrusion on their chests. Breasts, I imagined, were a long horizontal flap that went from one armpit to the other without separation. Nipples were at either end. But I soon learned from my sister and the *Encyclopedia Britannica* that breasts came in pairs. It was certainly true of Miss Taylor's breasts. They were very well defined and very individual. Miss Taylor was sitting on the chesterfield between my parents.

"What do you want to talk to me about?"

"Nothing, really. I just wanted to meet you," Miss Taylor said.

"Oh."

"You must be glad school is out for the summer?"

"I sure am."

"Do you like school, Michael?"

"Michael, tell Miss Taylor about your reading," my mother said.

"I've read *The Call of the Wild* by Jack London. That was the first book I ever read. And I read *The Old Man and the Sea* by Ernest Hemingway, which my father just gave me to read. And I read *The Synthetic Man* by Theodore Sturgeon. He's science fiction. And I read *The Illustrated Man* by Ray Bradbury. And I just read a book called *Hot Rod* because I like cars. Right now, I'm reading *The Shore Road Mystery* by the Hardy Boys. And I've already read *The Case of the Crooked Claw, Footprints Under the Window,* and *The Missing Chums,* which are all Hardy Boys."

"You like the Hardy Boys books?"

"Yes, I do. They're very exciting."

"Have you ever read any Nancy Drew books?"

"No! And I won't ever read them, either."

"You don't like Nancy Drew? I like Nancy Drew."

"You're a girl."

"Glad you noticed, Michael," Miss Taylor said. "One last question. What is your favourite book, and why is it your favourite?"

"That's two questions."

My father laughed with approval.

"Treat it as one question, Michael," Miss Taylor said.

"Okay. My favourite book. It was *The Call of the Wild,* because I didn't think Buck would survive up north because of the cold. But he did survive, only he turned wild and went back to nature and lived with the wolves."

"I'll have to read that book, Michael."

"I'll loan it to you, if you want," I said.

"Yes, please."

I glanced at my parents and they were both smiling. Whatever I had said to Miss Taylor was the right thing to have said. When I had left the room I heard Miss Taylor say something like, "This obviously has been a false report." I ran upstairs to the second floor and then up the narrow staircase to the third floor. I found the book under the bunk beds next to the dusty red pyramid, which was lying upturned on its side. That explains my report card, I thought. I put the pyramid back on its base. I wiped *The Call of the Wild* on Cosmo's blanket to get all the dust and hairballs off. When I came back downstairs, Miss Taylor was at the front door, preparing to leave. I presented the book to her.

"Thank you, Michael. I'll read it and return it as soon as I can."

"Is that your car, Miss Taylor?" I asked.

"Yes, it is. Do you like it?"

"You bet. It's a 1967, isn't it?"

"Yes, it is. Goodbye, Mrs. Chisholm. You certainly have remarkable children."

"Goodbye," my mother said.

"I'll see you to your car, Miss Taylor," my father said.

I stood at the front door watching Rory accompany Miss Taylor to her car. He held the car door open for her. She placed one foot on the running board as she and Rory exchanged a few words. Then she slid in behind the wheel and looked up at Rory and smiled. Rory firmly closed the door with both hands. He said something to Miss Taylor as he looked down upon her and she said something as she looked up at him. Rory must have said something funny because she laughed.

My mother had returned to the good room to straighten it up.

"Why did Miss Taylor want to see me, Gloria?"

"Oh, some busybody reported that you children were being neglected," she said as she cleared away the empty coffee cups. "But that's what your father can expect when he's so outspoken in the community."

10

THERE ARE TWO ARMS TO SYDNEY HARBOUR. TO TELL the truth, they don't look like arms at all. Each arm looks more like the root of a molar. The city of Sydney and the steel plant are located on one of these roots. Muggah's Creek is a little sliver of black cavity that runs between the north end of Sydney and the steel plant. The creek, a tidal estuary, makes the north end of Sydney into a peninsula. If you have a map of Sydney, you'll see exactly what I mean.

Sydney has always been called the Steel City. I don't know too much about the making of steel. Coke is needed, I know that. Coke is coal that was once-burned and afterwards could be burned again in a blast furnace. Don't ask me how they could burn something that was already burned, but they did it.

The raw coal is baked at ferocious temperatures and then doused with water. When the water falls on those hot coals—man! The huge plume of steam that rises in the air is the purest white you can imagine. Whiter than snow. And it rises hundreds of feet in a great billowing mushroom cloud. It is seen easily from every neighbourhood in Sydney—the Shipyard, the south end, Boulderwood, the Pier, Sydney River, Hardwood Hill, Ashby, Welton and Alexander Streets. I was in the north end and I saw it all the time.

They take this coke and mix it with the limestone and iron ore that they convey from the ships at the deepwater pier and they put it all in a blast furnace and blast it. What results from all this stuff being blasted is molten iron.

The impurity made in the process is called slag. The slag is skimmed off and put in twenty-two-ton trucks and dumped on Slag Mountain, which faces the north end. The iron, meanwhile, goes to the open hearth furnace where it is mixed with scrap metal and more limestone. Something else happens to it in the open hearth, I'm not exactly sure what, and after a while the metal is poured off as steel. But that is only the beginning, because the plant is filled with mills that roll, press, stamp, bend, stretch, and punch the steel into all kinds of shapes—including rails for the railroad. The Sydney steel plant makes the best steel rails in the world.

My father had worked in one of the mills when he was younger. His job involved taking the raw steel from the open hearth and refining it into something useful. But he left the mill job to attend university, Saint Francis Xavier. I don't know which mill it was. The blooming mill, or the billet mill, maybe. Maybe it was the wire or nail mill. I'm not sure.

Anyway, you need coke to make steel. And the first runoff or extract or throwaway from making coke is called coal tar. And this coal tar ran through Coke Oven Brook into a series of sluiceways and a giant reservoir and finally into Muggah's Creek. Over eighty years, the tar fluids had turned the estuary of Muggah's Creek into the tar ponds. That's about as simple a description of the tar ponds as you're ever likely to find. Most other descriptions use the names of chemicals that you can't even pronounce.

There are two ponds. The south pond, which you can easily see from the north end, is farthest from the harbour and is empty at low tide. The north pond is hidden by Slag Mountain, and gets deeper near the steel-plant pier. The bottom of the north pond drops off where it opens into Sydney Harbour. The Ferry Street causeway leading to the steel plant crosses over where the north and the south ponds meet. The CNIB canteen is at the steel-plant-end of the causeway.

Houses along Intercolonial Street face the south pond and the steel plant administrative building. The only interesting thing about the south pond is the huge wooden holding tank next to the steel-plant office building, and the long wooden channel next to the holding tank that carries black coal-tar water. It looks like the aqueducts that had carried drinking water for the Romans. I'd seen pictures of them in our encyclopedia. Everyone knows about the south pond because it is surrounded by public roads and houses. The north pond is something else all together.

Slag Mountain is a treeless, shrubless, grey blind that blocks the city's view of the steel-plant. It is one hundred feet high, a mile long, and nearly sheer in its angle of ascent. The train marshalling yard, including the CNR roundhouse, is directly across from Slag Mountain. The roundhouse and marshalling yard are on private industrial property built on a landfill. The landfill bulges out toward the steel-plant side and hides the biggest part of the north pond from anyone looking toward it from the Ferry Street causeway. There is no commercial or residential traffic near the pond, no access road, and very little CN activity on the back lines of the yards. With Slag Mountain on one side, and the industrial buffer of the rail yards on the other, the north tar pond is very private. Very few people ever saw it or even knew it existed.

If you told people who had lived in Sydney all their lives that four north-end boys had built a raft with a door and a stove and two sliding windows and floated it on the north tar pond and used a flat-bottomed boat and a homemade kayak to get to it at its mooring in the deepest part of the north pond, they wouldn't believe you. That's because most people in Sydney, and even most people in the north end, had never seen the north pond. There are wrecked ships and parts of ships in this part of the tar pond. The water is deep and never drains at low tide. There is an old dock, still usable. There is the wreck of the *Bitiby*, where Cosmo and I had gone the day he'd fainted in school. There is a barge stuck in the pond halfway across between the rail yard and the steel plant. Old wooden ship ribs are visible above the oily water. The pond is open to Sydney Harbour but is almost always calm because of the thickness of tar and oil in the water, and because of the huge backdrop that is Slag Mountain. This was a tar pond that would have been an eyesore if it was anywhere else. Here, it was a secret enclosure. This tar pond was our home port.

The only other people we saw near the tar pond were the linemen of the railroad. They would jump off a train, switch tracks, and jump back on again. There was a road that ran along the shore at the base of Slag Mountain, but very rarely did a truck or a security car pass by. Sometimes we'd see some movement at the B&D Cement factory but the trucks never stayed long. A screen of scrub trees and bulrushes, in addition to the series of train tracks, separated the tar pond from our homes in the north end. Sometimes, if the wind was right, you could hear someone blaring a car horn on Brook Street, or sometimes you might be able to hear a fire siren if it was coming down the north end of George.

But most always it was perfectly quiet. We were almost always alone.

When the kayak was repaired, we carried it from our backyard on Meadow Street through the bulrushes at the very end of Oak Street and across the tracks of the CNR down to the little forgotten dock. The dock had once faced the sea water of Sydney Harbour, but Slag Mountain had grown and moved toward the north end, and it had made Muggah's Creek narrower and narrower. And as the tar had accumulated from so much steel making, Muggah's Creek became shallower and shallower, too, and the dock had become isolated from the harbour over the years to the point that it could no longer be used for ships and it belonged only to the tar pond. And that was fine by us.

There were a few scattered boulders in the oily water near the dock. Some of them were covered with water at high tide, others weren't. You couldn't step on the ones that were covered at high tide, because they were too slick with tar. It was high tide when we brought the kayak down to the tar pond dock and dropped it in the water for the first time. Rene examined it carefully for leaks. There were none.

"There's the raft, Michael," Sid said.

Sid pointed across the tar pond. I couldn't see the raft. There was just the black pond stretching off for about a quarter of a mile, with various large marine obstacles stuck fast in the bed of tar: the barge, the ribs, the *Bitiby*. Slag Mountain and the six gigantic smoking smokestacks of the steel plant filled the background.

"I can't see any raft," I said, looking over toward the steel-plant shore.

"Because it's flat. You'll see it when you get over there. We have it tied up to the old barge."

Alex steadied the kayak and carefully got in from the boulder he was standing on.

"Okay, Michael. Get in," he said.

I jumped from the top tier of the dock down to a boulder and then I got in the kayak in front of Alex. I sat down on a little plywood square that Rene had nailed over the lengthwise-running ribs. I was actually sitting below the water line. The orange paddles were put in the tar pond for the first time.

"Ready?" Alex asked.

"Yes," I answered.

Alex manoeuvred us backwards past the boulders into open water.

"Give it to 'er," Alex said. And we started out for the barge. I looked back at Sid and Rene. They were both standing on the dock. Sid was grinning. Only then did I notice that I was smiling, too. It was as fun as hell to be riding on the water. My legs were stretched right out in front of me, under the canvas bow of the kayak. I could feel Alex's feet at my hips. I suppose no more than two inches separated us from the water—a thin piece of plywood, a few pine slats, and a skin of painted fibreglass. When I paddled, it felt like I actually was a kayak because my legs were wrapped in the canvas that was the front of the boat. It was nothing like a canoe. A canoe was like paddling a huge sofa or a lazy-boy armchair through the water. The kayak felt like being in a sleeping bag. I touched the flat, black water with my hand every third time I dipped my paddle. About halfway across, Alex soaked me by accidentally splashing his paddle against the water.

"Sorry," he said.
"That's okay," I said.
When he did it again, he laughed.
"I'm sorry, Michael. I'm forgetting to bring the paddle up high enough after I bring it out of the water."

The water had pasted the shirt to my back and I could feel a trickle running down my spine. But I didn't care. Being on the tar pond was so much goddamn *fun*.

When we approached the barge, Alex brought the kayak in by using his paddle as a rudder. The barge was stuck fast in the tar. It had two enormous holds, both open now and filled with a cargo of tar pond sludge and black water. The deck was really a deck. It had bollards for tie-up and gangways that were almost entirely intact. In fact, the entire barge was in surprisingly good shape. I think the tar in the water must have acted as a preservative. The starboard side of the barge was the leeward side, but it might have been the port side that was leeward, I couldn't tell. I don't think anyone knew which end of the barge was which. It had no superstructure whatsoever so who could tell?

We had to turn the corner on the barge before I got my first sight of the raft. It consisted of seven very large unmilled logs with bark still on some of the ends. It was about fifteen feet long by seven feet wide. Long spikes fastened one log to the next. Cement was blobbed in some places and splattered in others. The raft rode deep in the water. No wonder I hadn't been able to see it from shore.

"We'll bring her right alongside the raft," Alex said.

He leaned out for the side of the raft at the same time I did. The kayak capsized instantly. We both went under. I didn't even have time to take a breath. My whole body was shocked by the coldness of the water. I reached out blindly and felt nothing. My eyes were tightly shut and I wasn't opening them. I had to right myself under water before I could feel anything above me. I felt my fingers and palms being cut. I was under the raft. I kept feeling along until I put my hand above water and Alex clasped it and pulled me aboard. He hauled me right up onto the raft. I just flopped where he had landed me and breathed in gasps, like a big tuna fish gasping on a dock. Alex didn't say anything for a while. We could hear Sid shouting something from the CN shore.

"I thought you were gone ..." Alex said finally.

"No ... no ... no problem," I said.

Alex retrieved the water-filled kayak and hauled it up on board next to me. We were both soaked. The water didn't taste good.

"Don't capsize us like that again," Alex said.

"Me?!"

And he laughed at the way I had rebuked him. And I laughed at his reaction, laughed lying with my back on the raft looking up at the summer sky in Sydney.

When I'd caught my breath, Alex and I turned the kayak upside down to empty it. We couldn't get all the water out, but we got out enough so that I wasn't sitting in water when I got back in the kayak. Alex stayed on the raft as I set out to return to the CN shore on my first official tendering duty. I sat down in the back position and felt the uncomfortable coldness of my shirt and pants touching my skin. The cold shirt hung off my shoulders and I tried to cave in my chest so the fabric wouldn't touch me. That's when I realized that my cigarettes were completely ruined. I took the cigarette package out of my pocket and opened it. Three soaked cigarettes were on the right side, and the left side, the larger side, which didn't even have the foil removed, was ruined too. It took twice as long paddling back to the dock because my hand hurt like hell and I had to keep switching the paddle from side to side.

"What happened over there?" Sid shouted when I came within earshot.

"Alex capsized the kayak," I shouted back.

"Is the kayak okay?" Rene shouted.

"Yes, it just tips easy!"

I had thrown away my sodden cigarettes at the halfway point on the return trip. Almost a full pack. What a waste.

11

WHEN THERE WAS ANY WIND ON THE TAR POND, VOICES were carried away. You could shout yourself hoarse from the CN dock and still not be heard from the raft when it was tied up to the barge. Even without a wind, the tar pond did deceptive things with sounds. Slag Mountain returned a very rich echo that tricked you if you were shouting from the shore. It meant listening carefully and speaking in pauses; otherwise, the echo would run over the next word in your sentence and whoever you were shouting to wouldn't be able to make anything out of it.

Seagulls in a loose flock flying overhead, on their way to the city dump off Welton Street, made a ruckus. Individually, the gulls called, "Hey! Hey!" More than once I was fooled by an accusing call from a seagull hanging around up above. Other than that, there weren't many living sounds at the tar pond. In fact, the sound of water at the sewer outfall was the only other sound the tar pond made. There were no grasses, or insects, birds, dogs or cats. There was never a blackfly or a mosquito, even in the dead of summer. You'd know what a blessing that was, too, every time you went out of the city and into the country and had to be swatting horseflies all day. Once when I was swimming in the Bras d'Or Lakes, I got stung across the stomach by a jellyfish. Getting stung by jellyfish wasn't a concern in the tar pond. But the sun was a problem. Sid got a bad sunburn in early July and had to wear his long-sleeved shirt for the rest of the summer. Sid burned very, very easily.

THE BOTTOM OF THE TAR POND CONSISTED OF TAR. With the kayak paddle or the raft pole, or with any stick on hand if you wanted to try it, you could gouge the bottom and bring up big, gooey lumps of tar. You could make colourful designs in the black water by simply swirling the kayak paddle, and you'd see the iridescent circles spread out, their rainbow hues becoming dissipated as the circles widened. The smell that came up with the tar was the same old smell of the tar pond, only much more intense. Sometimes I didn't want to smell it, especially if I had an empty stomach. And unless you got a big solid clump, most times what you brought up was just goo and it dissolved and dropped off your stick as you looked at it.

You could touch the bottom at any time in most places with a ten-foot pole. At high tide in some places you might have to drop the pole down a foot under water to reach the bottom, but you could still reach it. You were all right as long as you didn't pole too near the harbour or the steel plant pier, where the tar pond dropped off into deep water. The north pond was always at least five or six feet deep at low tide, so there was never any danger of grounding.

We only left the tar pond once with the raft. Alex said he had seen a buoy washed up on shore near the dry docks, and if we moved fast we could claim it as salvage and sell it back to the Coast Guard, who were in charge of setting and maintaining buoys.

"Loosearm will have a fit," Sid said.

"It's not his," Alex insisted. "It's not even on his property."

"Where is it?" Rene asked.

"It's right next to the dry docks."

"That's his," Rene said.

"No, it isn't."

"Let's go see," Sid said.

Loosearm was the only person we knew who worked at the dry dock company. I had heard that he'd lost his arm when a ship fell on it. Or he'd lost it in a fight with a sailor. Or he'd had it blown off in the war when he was throwing a grenade. He was a very angry and dangerous man because of his lost arm. He could also rip your head off with the remaining arm, too. How? Simple. His only arm was superhuman in strength because it had to do the work of two arms. It had muscles in it like Popeye's, but the rest of him looked normal. He was a completely normal man otherwise. If you saw him in church, you wouldn't ever know that you were looking at Loosearm—except for the huge scars on his face and the lost portion of his nose. The scars criss-crossed his eyebrows and the hair grew up in weird sprouts in the furrows of the scars. And his nose was all mangled with one of the nostrils missing because he'd gotten it caught in some machinery. Part of his lip was scarred, too, and this permanently exposed his crooked teeth. He ran with a limp and made a barking sound when he was angry or out of breath. His lungs were ruined on account of being gassed in the war.

I had never actually seen Loosearm. It was difficult to get a clear look at him because of all the metal ribbing and other camouflage he had put up around the dry docks, but he was there. Sid had said that if you couldn't see him, he could still see you, which gave us the almighty creeps. We didn't want to have anything to do with Loosearm. So we stayed away from the harbour side of the north end and stuck to the Muggah's Creek side, which was closer to our homes anyway. But getting a buoy to salvage was too much of a temptation. A big steel buoy like that was worth hundreds if not thousands of dollars.

We left the tar pond by poling and paddling around Battery Point. The raft had to hug the shore because of the drop-off. Once we had cleared the point, we were in the harbour proper. Because it was low tide, we had to navigate out past an old pier and then come back to the shoreline. We went past the cement company property, the oil company's huge holding tanks, and the military buildings that overlooked the harbour. A single rail line ran along the edge of the embankment, and parallel to that was a road. But not many cars used the road on any given day. Most people driving along would not have been able to see two boys in a kayak towing a raft carrying two other boys, who were poling.

The "Rockies" began after we cleared the old pier. The Rockies were so called for the huge sandstone blocks that had been dumped along the harbour road to shore up the crumbling shale bank. Between the place where the Rockies ended and the place where the dry docks began was a small beach. Resting above the high-water mark on this little beach was an enormous steel buoy.

"There it is!" Alex said. "What did I tell you? What did I tell you?"

We brought the raft and the kayak onto the beach and stood around the huge marine object. It was about ten feet in diameter with a circumference of thirty feet, easily ten feet high, impossible to see over. It used to be painted two colours, but the paint was so faded and the rust in places so prodigious that it was hard to say what the original colours had been. Barnacles clung to the bottom half in great profusion. To me, the sheer size of the thing was awesome, but nobody else seemed to be very impressed.

"Let's put it on the raft," Alex said.

"You can't put that thing on the raft," Rene said. "It'll sink!"

Sid agreed with Rene. "Allie, that buoy weighs a ton."

"Let's float it out and tow it back to the tar pond," I suggested. "It's got a rope on the top."

Rene was filled with doubt. "What if it sinks? Maybe it's on shore because it's got a hole in it."

"If it sinks, we leave it," Sid said. And his was the last word.

The four of us took hold of the buoy's frayed rope, itself three inches in diameter, and rolled and cajoled the reluctant buoy down to the water. With great effort, we managed to float it next to the shore. Once it was in the water, it became much easier to handle and followed the raft like a huge steel balloon. We kept the same seating arrangements for the trip back to the tar pond: Sid poling, Alex spelling him off while holding the buoy's tow line, and Rene and me "towing" the raft from the kayak. To tell you the truth, I thought our contribution in the kayak wasn't very much. The two pollers did most of the work. That changed when Sid altered course.

"Let's take it out into deeper water," he said. "We don't want to get hung up on any boulders."

The kayak duly headed out into deeper water. Sid put aside his two-by-four pole when he could no longer find the bottom and took up a plank that he used for a paddle. I guess paddling counted for something because we made excellent progress. The buoy bobbed behind the raft like some sort of obedient steel pet on a leash. We were at the point of leaving the Rockies and the shoreline road when a white police cruiser appeared on the cliff overlooking our position. Sydney police cars were painted white. We called them ghost cars. Two men got out of the car. One was a cop with a bullhorn. The other figure was Loosearm himself. He was jumping up and down, pointing at us, cursing and swearing. What a madman.

"*Bring everything in to shore, boys,*" the cop said through the bullhorn.

"But this is our buoy!" Alex shouted back.

"*Come on,*" the cop said, "*we haven't got all day.*"

We had to bring everything back into shore. Loosearm came scrambling down the embankment to the beach, holding his one good arm up in the air for balance. He looked to me like a normal guy with only one arm.

"Dirty punk thieves!" he screamed.

"We're not thieves," Alex said. "That buoy was washed up on the shore! We took it by salvage rights, fair and square!" Loosearm snatched the rope from Alex.

"It belongs to the dry dock!" he shouted.

"But we found it washed up on government land," Sid said. "That makes it salvage."

"You little bastards go to hell!"

Loosearm began to walk down the beach, tugging on the rope, in clear violation of the law of the sea. The huge steel buoy followed him, bumping along the shoreline.

"But officer, *he's* stealing from *us!*" Alex said to the cop.

"That's his buoy," the cop said. He was looking at us and smiling.

"But the law of the sea says that if anything is washed away during a storm and if it's found by anybody else, the finders have the salvage rights," Alex explained.

"That means the original owners have to buy it back from the salvagers if they want to have it again," said Sid.

"Is that right?" the cop said. "Is that raft yours, too?" the cop asked.

"Yes, it's ours!" Alex said.

"We found another raft two weeks ago," Sid explained. "McAlpine is expanding the pier at the steel plant and they're using rafts for the workmen who have to weld on the harbour side." McAlpine had a big green sign facing the water that said, "McAlpine." I don't know who they were advertising to. Ships, I guess.

"We sold the raft back to them for thirty-five dollars," Alex said.

"That's the law of the sea," Sid said. It seemed like an open-and-shut case and the real villain was the one-armed bandit, pulling on the steel buoy, getting farther and farther away from justice. We could still hear him curse whenever the buoy hung up on a rock. We just had to sit there and watch him go with our salvage rights.

The radio crackled inside the police car and the officer leaned in to answer a call.

Rene, who hadn't said a word to the cop or to Loosearm, finally whispered something to us. He said, "We don't have any life jackets."

"So what?" Alex asked.

"We don't have any life jackets," Rene repeated.

"You're right," Sid said. "None of us have life jackets on. That's illegal."

"Stop arguing with the cop," Rene whispered, "or he'll take the raft and the kayak and we'll be left with nothing."

"Okay," said Alex.

The officer finished his radio transmission.

"Look, boys, the buoy belongs to the dry dock company. They built it, they've used it for twenty years, and it wasn't washed up on the beach. It was placed there deliberately."

"Oh! We thought it was a-*ban*doned!" Alex said. Alex had completely changed his tune, but the cop didn't notice. I wanted to laugh my head off.

"No, it wasn't abandoned. And nothing else along here is abandoned, either. Just be careful what you pick up."

"Okay, officer," Sid said. The cop jumped back into his cruiser and skidded away on the loose stones. We waved to him like he was our best friend in the world.

"That was a close one," I said from the kayak.

"Okay, no more bringing the raft out into the harbour, agreed?"

We all agreed to Rene's proposal. And Sid had a good rule that we also agreed with.

"We always wear a life jacket if we ever come out into the harbour in the kayak. If we're seen in the kayak without a life jacket, they'll take the kayak from us."

"Agreed," we all said. We poled and paddled the raft and the kayak back to our home port. It took over an hour. After that exhausting expedition, we were happy to keep the raft in the tar pond forever. I bought a fifteen-pound waterproof anchor, bright orange, from the hardware store the next week with enough line to anchor the raft anywhere in the tar pond, but not enough line to go any deeper. The raft never left the tar pond again.

It was just as well that the raft was restricted to the tar pond because beyond a certain depth, there was no real way to propel it. The only effective propulsion available, not counting being towed by the kayak, was by pole. Sid was the biggest and strongest so he could really get the raft going using the pole. Great slimy gobs of oily tar hung from the end of the pole when he extracted it from the bottom of the tar pond. He hoisted the pole like a caber-tossing competitor at the Highland Games, and walked to the front of the raft where he splashed it in the water and let the forward current bring it alongside the raft once again. Iridescent circles bobbed into sight moments after one of his momentous pushes, like multicoloured depth charges following a destroyer. You could tell just how much strength he exerted by the quantity of muck that came up on the pole. His face would be red with effort when, at the end of the raft, he pulled the pole from the water with a jerk. Sid got this procedure down cold. He did it smoothly and mechanically as if he and the pole had become one.

And that was another thing about the tar pond. When Sid drove that pole down into that tar, the tar was naturally resistant to letting go of the pole. And because Sid and the pole had become one, Sid was naturally resistant to letting go of the pole, too. It was in that split second at the end of the raft, when the pole had to be pulled from the clinging bottom with as much force as had been used to drive it in, that moment when the raft was speeding away from the very tool that had provided it with motion, that the strength of the boy would be tested against the strength of the tar pond. We watched once as Sid's arms stretched out further and further with a death-grip on the pole, his legs stiffening, his feet becoming rigid on the ends of his legs, hoping to hook something to prevent what now was inevitable, stretching in vain to remain with the raft that was moving onward now at a great clip, his body almost horizontal, hands strangling a pole in the water with iron determination, feet up on tiptoes until there came the unthinkable *splash!*

We doubled over with laughter.

We laughed just as hard the time Rene tried to jump from the raft to the barge. Sid and Alex had hooked the raft on a loose tether so it could rise and fall with the tides without getting hung up on the barge. All Rene accomplished when he tried to jump from the raft was to send the raft out behind him while he fell straight down. To see it, you'd think he'd wilfully stepped right into the water because he hadn't actually gone forward one inch. With Rene's full immersion, we had all come to be baptized as legitimate children of the tar pond, proudly sponsored by our extended family: the coal miners, the steelworkers, the railmen, the deepwater pier workers, and the dry dockers.

"WE HAVE TO MAKE A CHART OF THE TAR POND," ALEX said. Everyone thought this was an excellent idea. Most of the north pond could be sketched easily enough since there were very few shallow spots or what you would call reefs. But further up toward the causeway, past the *Bitiby* and through the narrows, it was a different tar pond altogether. Alex and I got in the kayak, Alex in front with a sketch pad, me in back, paddling. I had learned to pass the paddle behind my back, from one side to the other, instead of passing it in front. Passing the paddle in front meant dripping water from the paddle onto the person in front of me, my passenger. We set out when the tide was falling and the south pond was emptying into the north pond through the little strait under the Ferry Street bridge. The upper reaches of the north pond were also draining and we could see a shallow area developing. I threw the anchor overboard and we waited until it caught and held us in the ebbing stream. Alex started sketching away. He was a pretty good artist. I took out a smoke and fired it up. I was halfway through my cigarette before I interrupted Alex's drawing.

"You don't like your stepmother, do you, Alex."

"No, she's a bitch. I hate her guts," Alex said, not looking up from his sketching.

"Why?"

"Because she's always doing things behind my back and she thinks I don't know about it."

"Like what?"

"Like she'll say I don't have to pay my rent if I clean up the basement and when I don't do it the next thing I know she's said to my father that maybe it's a good idea for me to clean up the basement. And so he yells at me to clean up the basement with her standing right behind him smiling like a hyena. I have to clean up the basement and I still have to pay rent. I hate her guts."

"You pay rent at your own house?"

"She told my father that it will teach me a valuable lesson," Alex said. "I can either pay it, or I can do extra work around the house, like cleaning the basement."

"Paying rent, holy mackerel, Alex. You're not even out of school."

"I know," Alex said, still sketching.

"Why don't you tell your father about what she did?"

"I can't."

"Why not?"

"Because he's a dickhead." Alex sketched more and a few minutes passed before he thought of a question to ask me. "Why do you call your parents by their first names?"

"Because they want us to," I said.

"Nobody else in your family calls them by their first names."

"Sometimes they do."

"Only you do it all the time."

Alex drew a very detailed chart of the whole area showing where the main channel was and where the submerged pieces of rebar and cement were. He drew the old drum barrel nearly under the bridge and he drew the sewer outfall coming out of the pipe on the CN shore.

The south pond was good for nothing because it was too shallow for anything. Even the south end of the north pond was no good where it approached the Ferry Street bridge. It looked like it was deep when the tide was up. But when the tide went out you could see that, aside from a few channels, there was no place to bring the raft without getting stuck. There was hardly any water for the kayak. This was just as well because Ferry Street was used by hundreds of plant workers and we didn't want them to see us poling a raft around in the tar pond or paddling a kayak. First thing you know someone would be on the phone and that would be that.

I spent a lot of time paddling around the north pond. Many times I slowly drifted by the wreck of the *Bitiby* and examined the hull, the bow, and the stern—burnt to a crisp. Although you could see rivets and steel plating here and there, it was predominantly a wooden ship, or had been. Portholes were now just eroded circles on its side. The ribs still stood in places where the hull planking had given way. The main boiler where Cosmo and I had huddled a few months before on an ice floor was now filled with flat black water. From the kayak you could look right in the boiler door and see the black water inside.

I always thought the *Bitiby* had been a transport ship for the army hospital. I don't know why I thought that. I think I just made it up for want of any other information. And I always thought it had run aground on tar and then caught fire when slag was dumped on it. That just made sense. But I never learned the real history of the *Bitiby*, and as far as I knew it had always been sitting there, scuttled in the shallows of the tar pond.

Besides the barge where we tied the raft, and the *Bitiby*, the ribs were prominently displayed on Alex's chart. They looked like the rib cage of an animal. As the tide fell, you could see they were ribs because the rows drew in toward each other and formed a perfect "V." You could paddle through them if you wanted to be smart, but you took your chances. Rusty spikes were jutting out from the boards. As the tide fell, the bottom of the kayak got closer to the centre where the ribs converged, presumably upon a keel. But this you couldn't see. The *Bitiby* you could look at and respect because it was a wreck, and all wrecks deserve respect. But the ribs weren't really anything. It could have been that the ribs and the barge were both once part of the *Bitiby*. But I couldn't really tell you where they came from. They were just there, and they were all marked as separate marine obstacles on our chart, as they should have been.

12

OF COURSE WE DIDN'T SPEND ALL OUR TIME DOWN AT the tar pond. We spent a lot of time at our house, too. From the third-floor windows we could look out and see the tar pond and the steel plant and Sydney Harbour. We could even see North Sydney across the harbour. Sid pointed out that it would be perfect to have a walkie-talkie on the third floor and another one on the raft. It was an excellent idea, too. But we couldn't afford to buy walkie-talkies and he only mentioned it once. Besides, someone would have had to stay behind at the house in order to talk to the raft and no one wanted to stay behind at the house.

We all liked to meet at the house. Rory and Gloria were both working all summer and Irene was at her house next door in the afternoons. We had the house to ourselves, mostly. If Heather and her girlfriends were there, we'd go into the television room and set up with tea all around. Sid and Alex would break out the chess board and play a few games.

Sid was a nut for chess, and he taught Alex how to play. I didn't play, but I sat in on the games. They all began the same way. Sid would put a different colour pawn in each fist and ask Alex to choose. Alex would tap one of Sid's hands and Sid would open his fist to reveal either a black or a white pawn. Alex drew the white pawn on this particular Saturday and they set up the board to play: Sid black, Alex white.

"Where's my bishop?" Alex asked.

"I don't know," Sid said. They looked around the table and the floor and couldn't find it.

"Michael, have you seen the white bishop?"

"No," I said. But I helped them look for it. We didn't find it, so Alex used a salt shaker instead.

"I guess the question is, are we going to keep the raft," Sid said, moving out a pawn.

"What do we want to keep it for?" Alex said, slurping his hot tea. "They gave us thirty-five bucks for returning the first one."

He moved his salt shaker out on the board right away. I noticed that about Alex. He liked getting the big pieces into the game immediately.

"I say we sell them this one too, and we'll be thirty-five bucks richer."

"It's worth more than thirty-five dollars," Sid said. "I know that just those logs alone are worth maybe a hundred dollars. You can't make a raft like that for under a hundred dollars."

Sid moved his queen out into the centre of the board.

"Rene thinks those logs are from British Columbia," I said.

"He *thinks* they are," Sid said.

"No, they're not from British Columbia," Alex said. "They're just pine trees, that's all. Why would anyone build a raft of logs from British Columbia when there are plenty of trees in Cape Breton?"

"They're too big for trees here," I said, repeating what Rene had said.

"I've seen trees twice that big on Boularderie Island," Alex claimed.

"I don't know one way or the other. I was just repeating what Rene said. He said they were Douglas fir."

"How much would it cost to get some logs from British Columbia? A little more than thirty-five dollars, I'd say."

Sid said this without looking up from the board. Alex had already put his salt shaker in the same row as Sid's king.

"McAlpine isn't going to give us a hundred dollars for the raft," Alex said. He pushed himself back a little from the table and took another big slurp of tea. "I say we sell it for thirty-five dollars."

"If we keep the raft," Sid said, "we can build a cabin on it."

As soon as Sid said this, I could see a cabin on the raft.

Alex looked at Sid as the same vision settled in his mind's eye. "That's a good idea," Alex said.

It was an *excellent* idea. I could see a cabin already built.

"Let's build it, then," Sid said. And to me he said, "Go phone Rene and tell him."

Alex tipped up his cup to drink the remaining tea. As he did, his eyes opened wide and he stared into the bottom of the cup. Sid burst out laughing. Alex put the cup down and looked at Sid. Sid was almost in hysterics with laughter. Alex put his fingers into the cup and pulled up his missing bishop.

"Good one," Alex said. "Good one. I'm going to get you for that one."

Sid and Alex were always playing practical jokes on each other. I think it was something they learned in Sea Cadets. They were filled with practical jokes. We had a whole month of pushing a door open and having a plastic cup of water fall on us. You'd come into the house and Alex would be putting Kerby's dog kibble into Sid's spaghetti, or Sid would be taking some rancid chicken stock that went bad at the back of the fridge and hiding it under Alex's bed. And if you saw this, Sid would say, "Don't tell Alex." Or Alex would say, "Don't tell Sid."

And if you told, one or the other would then consider you fair game and short-sheet your bed or black-ball you during the night. Sid and Alex short-sheeted Cosmo's bed one night and Cosmo was so tired that he just huddled up in a fetal position and slept without being able to stretch out his legs. And one time I was awakened in the middle of the night, it was four o'clock in the morning, by Sid applying black shoe polish to my face. The stink made me sick, but Sid and Alex thought it was hilarious. They had this sort of barracks mentality. I'd bet if I had thrown a bucket of piss on them to retaliate they would have doubled over with laughter and thought that I had "got them good."

But their ongoing gag was with tea and coffee. You had to be careful about leaving your tea or coffee alone when Sid was in the room because Sid knew which herbs and spices in our mother's spice rack would sink when sprinkled on tea or coffee. This was very specialized knowledge, I always thought. He must have experimented when everyone was out of the house. Sometimes he didn't get it right. I remember dumping my instant coffee in the kitchen sink when I saw some crushed bay leaves floating around in the cup. Anything that floated was a giveaway. But Sid could salt your tea in two seconds flat if you weren't looking. He salted my cup lots of times before I learned not to leave it alone. I learned to never make a cup of coffee and go upstairs, or outside, or into another room. I learned to always take the cup with me. Sid got a kick out of watching me discover that the coffee tasted weird. And then he would start laughing and I would know that he had salted my cup. He and Alex did those things to each other all the time. He and Alex used semaphore, too, as a secret way to communicate, and the

Alpha, Bravo, Charlie method of talking. They even had special code words that meant the opposite of their ordinary meaning. They had learned all this in Sea Cadets.

I watched while Sid and Alex continued their chess game. I couldn't stop thinking about building a cabin on the raft. I phoned Rene, but his phone line was busy so I just ran up to his house. It was on George Street and I was there in three minutes. Rene lived in a big three-storey house, as big as ours. Rene's father taught industrial arts at the high school. He had a workshop down in his basement and power machines in his garage and every tool you could think of in his back porch. And there was a nice green lawn that Rene had to mow and a little flower bed that his mother tended. The house was painted white. The garage was painted white, too. I rang the doorbell. They had a doorbell.

The door opened and Rene's older sister looked at me. She was talking on the phone.

"I don't *care!* Honestly, I don't care! Jenny can go out with him for all I care! I don't care *one single bit!* I think he's a jerk anyway! And I never thought much of her—" Her name was Deborah and she was black-haired, angry-looking all the time, and she wore thick glasses with thick rims. Big tits. She motioned for me to come in. She took the phone and went around a corner and into another room, without saying a word to me, but never ceasing to talk to her friend on the phone.

"Come in, come in," Rene's mother said. Her voice was tiny, like a mouse squeak. I came into the hallway. It was polished hardwood and led straight into the kitchen. I could see chrome reflecting in the kitchen as it caught the sun. The house smelled like lemons.

"Is Rene in, Mrs. Dumont?"

"Yes, he is." Mrs. Dumont looked at me like she wanted to scrub behind my ears.

"*Rene!*" she squeaked. Rene appeared at the top of the stair.

"Come on up," he said. And then he returned to his room.

I started to move toward the stairs. It was the first time I had been allowed upstairs.

"Take your shoes off," Mrs. Dumont said.

"Okay," I said.

Mrs. Dumont stood next to me as I untied my sneakers. They were rubber-soled sneakers with black canvas tops. They had little rubber circles where my ankle bones were. I slowly untied both sneakers while Mrs. Dumont stood right over me. She didn't move off, or go back into her kitchen. She stood right over me and watched me untie my sneakers and of course that meant that I had to take off my sneakers and when I did she saw that I had holes in my socks. That's why I *hated* going places where they wanted you to take your shoes off. I bent down and poked most of my socks between my big toes and second big toes and held onto the socks with my toes. Mrs. Dumont just looked at me like she wanted to swat me for having socks with holes in them. But the joke was on her because they were Sid's old socks.

I went up to Rene's room and found him sitting at a little table, looking like a mad scientist working on a harebrained scheme.

"What are you doing?"

"Drawing plans for another kayak," Rene said, hardly looking up. Rene liked to build things and was very industrious. Drawing up plans for a kayak was just the sort of pastime that you could expect from Rene. We thought he could have been the son of Thor Heyerdahl, the man who sailed the *Kon-Tiki* across the Pacific.

"You're going to make another kayak?"

"It's a very simple design," Rene said. "We're only talking about a few plywood braces to give it a superstructure, a few lengthwise slats for support and a couple of yards of canvas that we paint with fibreglass paint. I'm also working on plans for a flat-bottomed boat." He showed me his sketches. The kayak on paper looked like an Indian teepee to me.

"Oh," I said. I was distracted because of this grinding noise I was hearing. It was right in the room with us and it was this grinding noise, like a rat eating something in the wall. Rene didn't have any music in his room, no posters, or anything like that. He had a set of *Popular Mechanics* and some other Do-It-Yourself books in a small bookcase. He had a chest of drawers with separate drawers for pants, shirts, and socks. He had a jacket for each season hanging in his closet. But I kept hearing this grinding noise, as he was talking about the light plywood frame and the long slats for reinforcement and the fibreglass paint. That's how simple it was to build another kayak, Rene explained. And he could do it because his father had an entire workshop in his basement. But I couldn't stand it anymore.

"Rene, what the hell's that *grinding* noise?"

"The rock tumbler," Rene said.

"Rock tumbler?"

Rene got up from the desk and showed me this little motor that was turning this little drum that was full of these little rocks. It was turning away right there on the top of his dresser.

"Are you interested in lapidary?" he said.

"*Lap*idary?"

"Making gems," Rene said. He stopped the motor and opened the drum. He emptied the drum out onto a dish and all these stones came out in a mucky fluid. He took one rock and wiped it with a cloth and showed it to me. It looked like it had a coating of glass on it.

"Agate," Rene said. "It's a stone. I got it at the store, but I'm going to look for some amethyst up at Little Narrows. I'd heard there was some near Lewis Mountain."

"Oh."

And that's the sort of guy Rene was. While he was working away on one hobby, he'd have another hobby grinding away on the top of his dresser.

"Sid had a great idea for the raft," I said.

"What?"

"Build a cabin on it."

Rene looked at me for a moment before he spoke.

"That is a perfect idea," he said. He left his sketch and walked with me back to Meadow Street. Sid and Alex were playing another game of chess.

"The raft needs a raised deck, first thing," Rene said.

"Agreed," Sid said.

When the wind and the tide were high, the greasy swells in the tar pond slobbered up over the raft and left a slippery film on the deck. Any time you walked on the raft afterwards you'd nearly break your stupid neck because it was so slippery.

"It needs a deck that will let water escape underneath it," Rene said.

"Right," Alex said.

"What's that kind of deck called Sid?" I asked.

"I'm not sure. It has a name, though. It's not freeboard ..."

"Tumblehome," Alex said.

"No, it's not called tumblehome," Sid said. "Tumblehome is the angle of deflection on a deck."

"No it's not," said Alex. "Tumblehome is how the water is taken off the boat deck and that's done by the false deck that Rene's talking about."

"No, it's not."

"Yes, it is."

Rene laughed. "I thought you two would know something like that."

"Sea Cadets learn about motorized boats like whalers and launches. We don't study sailing terms for pleasure yachts," Alex said defensively.

"A raised deck is a good thing to call it for now. I know where we can get the planking we need," Rene said.

"Okay, that's settled," Sid said. "Anymore questions?"

"Do we have to carry the kayak all the way back home every time we leave the raft?" I asked. Every time we went to or from the tar pond, we put the kayak on our shoulders and walked through the bulrushes at the dead end of Oak Street and down Brook Street to the corner of Meadow. It was a pain in the neck.

"Let's hide it in the bamboo grove next to the oil company," Alex said. And that's what we did. It was ten times better than carrying the stupid thing back and forth every time we left the tar pond.

13

MY MOTHER'S PARENTS WERE FROM HALIFAX. THEY weren't Cape Bretoners at all. Her father was a retired history professor at Dalhousie University. My grandmother was a thin woman whose hair was a blond-white colour. She always wore slacks with colourful vests. She was a constant smoker and always had to tilt her head back a certain way in order to see past the cloud of smoke she had created in front of her. On her knuckly fingers she had silver and gold rings. Sometimes she wore bracelets that had precious gems in them. My mainland grandparents never ate or stayed at our house. They only sat for coffee and cigarettes and then they returned to their room at the Isle Royale Hotel, the most expensive hotel in Sydney. We had to clean up the house before they visited us, which was every couple of years, and we were supposed to wear good clothes. We used to be formally introduced to them every time they visited, as if we were expected to have forgotten who they were.

When Sid and I came into the house from the tar pond on this day, however, no formal introductions were necessary. Sid hugged our grandmother and lifted her right off the floor. He shook hands vigorously with our grandfather and was genuinely surprised and happy to see them both. Both of Gloria's parents liked Sid, probably because he was the first-born. Meanwhile, Gloria moved over to me and deftly tapped down a cigarette package that was showing in my denim jacket pocket. She whispered, "No smoking while Mum is here." I nodded and took my jacket off before I welcomed my grandparents. My grandmother gave me a polite little hug.

"You have certainly grown since we last met, Michael."

"So have you," I said. Gloria's mother laughed, and so did Gloria. I was glad to see my grandmother laugh. She always looked depressed.

"Is that Sheba in the back of your station wagon, Grandpa?" Sid asked.

"That's Sheba. She's almost a year old."

"Can I see her?"

"Take my keys, Sidney. Don't let her off the leash."

"Now Gerald," our grandmother said, "Sheba's still a very young dog."

"I'll be careful, Grandma. I promise."

"Don't call me Grandma! Everyone has a proper name, including me. My name is Uma and yours is Sidney."

"Go on, Sid," my grandfather said, passing him the keys to the station wagon. Sid took the keys and dashed out the door. I couldn't go with him because I still hadn't officially said hello to my grandfather.

"Michael, come here and say hello to your grandfather," my mother said.

"Hello, young man." We shook hands and his handshake was firm and professional. He smoked a pipe that had an intelligent smell.

"Are you staying at the Isle Royale Hotel?"

"No. Because of the dog, we're staying at a campsite."

"Do you have your tent?"

"No," my grandfather said, "we have a trailer."

"A trailer? Can I see it? Do you mean a trailer with a sink and a little bathroom?"

"Well, yes, it has all that. And a little shower, too."

"No way!" It would have been just fantastic to have gotten a look at a trailer like that. But my grandmother stopped her conversation with Gloria and interrupted.

"We cannot show you the trailer, Michael, because it is simply too much trouble. Come here young man. How are your studies?"

"Okay, I guess."

"Okay, I guess, doesn't sound very promising. You know that your father is too busy to help you and your mother can barely help herself—"

"Mother!"

"—but that's still no reason to neglect your children's education, is it, Michael?"

"Mother! Nobody is being neglected!"

"If people have children, they are responsible for those children. I made sure I gave your mother an education. She and your father went to the same university. Do you know which university you want to go to, Michael?"

"I don't know."

"Mother—"

Gloria was going to say more, but the sound of dogs barking outside stopped her.

"Is that Sheba?" I asked.

"Sheba?" My grandmother stood up and looked through the kitchen window.

"Oh, Sid, no! No, Sid! No, no—"

Sid had Sheba and Kerby both on leashes, but Kerby was going around in a circle trying to jump up on Sheba. My grandmother came down the front stairs in a panic.

"You will not with our Sheba!" she said. I didn't know whether she was talking to Sid or to Kerby. Sid was laughing.

"He's a little bit excited," he told our grandmother. Sid was getting all tied up in Sheba's leather leash and in the length of yellow nylon rope that we used as a leash for Kerby on special occasions. "No, you ruffian," my grandmother said to Kerby. She snatched the leash from Sid and dragged Sheba to the car. "Gerald, please open the back!" Our grandfather calmly unlocked the back of the station wagon and ordered Sheba to jump in. She immediately obeyed. Kerby was pulling against his rope and standing on his back legs trying to get a look at Sheba. He kept going in circles and looking up at Sid. He was pretty excited. It was pitiful, actually.

Sid took Kerby in the house because we didn't want

him jumping up on the car and scratching the paint. Sheba just turned around a couple of times and flopped down on her blanket in the back of the car and went to sleep.

"Well, at least that misalliance was prevented," my mother said.

My grandfather chuckled.

"What's that peculiar smell?" my grandmother asked.

Most of the time the prevailing wind kept the tar pond smell away from the north end. But, of course, the day my grandparents visited that wasn't the case and the smell was all through the neighbourhood. And it was impossible to open your eyes and not see the CN rail cars below the neighbourhood and Slag Mountain and the smokestacks of Sysco.

"I imagine that smell would be the steel plant," my grandfather said.

"Yes," my mother said. It was actually the tar pond. Actually, I suppose it was the steel plant. Well, okay, to be accurate, it was ultimately the coal mines, because without the coal mines there would have been no tar pond or steel plant.

"Let's go inside," my grandmother said.

The smell of the tar pond would occasionally fill the neighbourhood the way the smell of spread manure blew through a farming district. And sometimes the smoke from the plant covered the neighbourhood like an orange wool blanket. Baseball games being played down at the Louisa Gardens were sometimes delayed because the smoke was so thick. The smoke from the plant had its own dry, chalky smell that you could taste in the back of your throat. But the tar pond smell was aromatic, especially if the wind was blowing this way right at low tide. Some complained that the smell of the tar was sour or tart. Some said it was sulphur that made the tar pond smell of rotten eggs. I liked the smell. I thought it was a very simple, very good chemical smell. Everything that's simple is at first thought of as bad.

My mother had been an only child. She was raised outside Halifax in an isolated and pretty house situated between a paved road and a quiet dirt road. We went there once a long time ago. It was before we got Kerby so I couldn't have been more than eight years old. Heather slept in the big white frame house and Sid, Cosmo, and I got to sleep in the tent under the pine trees. It was very, very quiet. No trains and not much traffic. That was the first time I had seen pine trees and I used the long pine needles as cigarettes to "smoke."

In front of the house, the highway carried commuters into Halifax each morning and brought them back each afternoon. Gloria's father had two cars, the station wagon and a Chevy sedan. Across a dirt road at the back of the house was a fresh water lake that we swam in. There were several little houses built along the dirt road and we were told not to walk too far down the road because it intersected with the highway. I remember walking down that dirt road with Cosmo. I took his hand because I was the older brother. There was a man leaning on the door frame of his house near the end of the road. He saw us coming and he just leaned there, looking at us.

"Hello," I said, very politely. Cosmo said hello, too.

But this man didn't say a thing. He just looked at us, his eyes never wavering. I stopped looking at him but when I looked at him again he was still looking at us. I thought that maybe he didn't hear us, so I said hello again, louder. But he didn't respond. He just continued staring at us.

That was it. I clutched a handful of gravel and *fired* it at the bastard. I was starting to play a lot of baseball at that time so I had a good arm. I threw the gravel sidearm and that bastard moved then. Cosmo picked up some gravel, too. When I threw the handful of rocks the man sort of jolted away and went into his house. We didn't know it then, but he was calling our grandmother behind our backs.

My grandmother made me walk back with her to where this man lived. Apparently, she knew this man by name. I cried because I didn't want to go back. It was his fault for not saying hello. But I had to say to this bastard that I was sorry for telling him to go to hell and for throwing rocks. You could see that he thought he was smart, getting a little kid to apologize for mistakes that he had made. Afterwards, I never liked where my mother grew up and where my grandparents lived on the mainland.

My father came home from his office in the middle of the day to see Gloria's parents. They drank coffee and smoked cigarettes in the good room. Rory and Gerald talked mainly about Sydney's economy and the political and industrial position of Cape Breton and the wisdom of the province to assume ownership of the steel plant. It was a lot of yackety-yack.

I didn't know who owned the tar ponds, if anyone did. I thought that Hawker-Siddeley bestowed them on the public, in the same way that Mr. Carnegie, the American steel baron, bestowed libraries. But there were other companies who had run the steel plant before Hawker-Siddeley. There was the British Empire Steel and Coal Corporation, which was known as Besco. They started the plant way back in 1901. In 1928 they sold out to the

Dominion Steel and Coal Corporation, Dosco. Hawker-Siddeley bought the plant in 1957. (A hawker to us was a spit with a lot of snot in it.) And then came October 13, 1967, Black Friday, as it was called afterwards. I was six years old. Out of the blue, Hawker-Siddeley announced they were closing the plant and ending over three thousand jobs. In other words, they were shutting down the city of Sydney.

My father had been furious. He called it a double-cross and a sellout and called Hawker-Siddeley bloodsuckers and parasites. Somebody organized a great Parade of Concern and twenty-five thousand people marched through Sydney holding posters and placards saying "Uprooted Industry—Uprooted Families," and "Human Values over Material Values," and "We are All Responsible." A priest who addressed the crowd asked for "God's blessing in this great time of need." There was singing and shouting, and the clapping of hands. I dimly remember walking in the Parade of Concern with a sign around my neck that said "Save Our Steel," or something like that. To tell the truth, I've forgotten what the sign said.

"For all the wealth you have here, Cape Breton's still poor," my grandfather said.

"That's because wealth has never stayed in Cape Breton," Rory explained. "Look at fishermen on the south shore, or farmers in the Annapolis Valley. They work the land or the sea and they keep what they make. You see it in the homes they've built and in the prosperity of their communities. But coal miners don't get to keep profits. Steelworkers don't. All the profits from the mines and the plant went overseas to England, like it goes to the mainland now. In the Scottish Highlands we called them absentee landlords. The wealth was taken away from us. It still is."

"Why didn't the migration from the Scottish Highlands to Cape Breton solve any of these problems?" my grandfather asked.

"Highlanders didn't migrate from their lands, we were cleared."

"Some must have wanted to come voluntarily. Economic necessity," my grandmother said.

"Economic expediency," my father argued. "My people came with nothing. The landlords wanted us gone."

"In either case, migration occurred. If the parallel between the Scotland of a hundred years ago and the Cape Breton of today is valid—"

"Do I think clearing industrial Cape Breton will solve the problem of the absentee shareholder?" my father asked, laughing.

"It could just solve the problem *for* the shareholder," my grandfather replied, puffing on his pipe.

"You make it sound as if we're stuck in a cycle of history."

"Well?" My grandmother demanded. "Are you?"

"Maybe we are," my father shrugged. "I'll say this, that it's always easier to clear than to keep. It's always easier to kill than to nurture. But Cape Bretoners are like family. And when there's a problem we solve it because we all have to live together. A problem won't solve itself. A problem will only get worse."

When my father mentioned family, I automatically thought of the clan. Back in Scotland, large extended families of uncles, aunts, and cousins all pledged allegiance to the Laird. There's a name for you—Laird. To me it sounded like *Lard*. We pledge allegiance to the *Lard*. Portraits of these Lards showed sickly, inbred weaklings wearing long, dainty wigs and possessing thin, powdered noses. But that's the clan system for you. Whoever is the Lard gets the say. Whoever pays the piper calls the tune, as my father used to say.

Rory couldn't stay long. He had to get back to the office. He shook hands with my grandfather and gave my grandmother a little hug. My grandmother had perked up for the time that Rory was there. But she got bored again after he left. She looked around the house and sighed. When she went outside she looked around the neighbourhood and sighed. I thought there was something the matter with her lungs. She was a pretty heavy smoker and the tar pond smell might have bothered her. Some people can't take it at all.

As my grandparents were preparing to leave Sydney an hour later, I saw my mother trying to refuse something that her mother was trying to put in her hand.

"Just take it," my grandmother was saying.

"Mum, I don't *need* it," my mother said.

"I don't want to hear anymore about it."

"You don't have to do this at all," my mother said.

"I'll take it, Grandma!" Cosmo said. Cosmo was a laugh and a half. He was right there on the sidewalk with his hand out. My grandmother looked down at Cosmo and said, "Your poor mother."

"Mum, I'm perfectly all right!"

My grandmother angrily thrust what she was holding into my mother's hand and refused to take it back. "Take it," she said. "Take it, take it."

"Good night, what a racket," my grandfather said from behind the wheel.

"Okay, well *thanks* Mum. It's been so nice to see you both."

After they were gone everything returned to normal.

RENE'S FATHER HAD A DOZEN TWO-BY-SIX PLANKS THAT were splattered with cement on one side. They worked perfectly. We just put a couple of crossways boards down and nailed the planks into them. That was our raised deck, and that meant no more wet feet. The discarded pallets down the CN yard had all the rough boards we needed to begin work on the cabin. Before we began construction proper, Sid and Alex started talking about building a mast with a boom on the deck of the raft. Rene objected.

"Why do we need that?"

"So we can put up a sail in an emergency."

"Okay," Rene said.

"Michael, we need two long poles," Sid explained. "We're going to lash them together to make a mast."

"Two long poles?"

"They can't be two-by-fours. They have to be poles, round poles. Think you can find them?"

"I think so."

I knew of two poles that I could get that were perfect for the job. They'd been just lying in our backyard for a couple of weeks. I got them and helped paint them white. Sid then joined the pieces by an elaborate arrangement of coiled rope, no nails at all. It made a mast of fifteen feet straight up. Alex was building a two-by-four support column right on the deck and the mast was to be placed in that. While he was re-lashing the joint, Sid asked me something out of the blue.

"Did you talk to Miss Taylor yet?"

"Yeah. Who is she?"

"Heather says she's from some child welfare office."

"What's that?"

"Alex says it's a spy agency. What did she ask you?"

"She asked me my favourite books and if I liked school."

"Did she ask if you smoked?"

"No."

"Good thing."

Sid picked up both parts of the mast in one hand and passed a length of cord underneath. Watching his expert and meticulous lashing was mesmerizing me.

"I like her," I said. "She's nice."

"You just like her car."

Sid finished the re-lashing and I helped him hold up the mast to see if the two pieces were tight. They looked securely bound to me. Sid ran his eye up the mast as if he was taking aim at something.

14

WE DID ALMOST ALL OUR WORK ON THE RAFT RIGHT ON site. For those few times when we worked into the night, we had a little hidden place on the CN shore where we lit fires to keep warm. The firepit was right near the railway pier, facing the tar pond, so it made a good beacon for me as I paddled back and forth from the raft to the shore. There were no street lights around the tar pond on the CN or the steel-plant side. If the moon was not out, the tar pond was the pitchest black you could imagine.

"Let's get some gasoline," Rene said.

"Do you have the mayonnaise jar?"

"Yes."

Night was falling when Rene and I started up the

tracks for the B&D Cement company. Sid and Alex were on the raft, which was anchored about one hundred feet out in the tar pond.

"Hey, you guys!" I shouted.

"What?" Sid shouted back.

"Rene and I—are going to the B&D—to get some gas!"

"Okay," Sid shouted.

The dried bulrushes that had grown and died along the train tracks were perfect for torches. I snapped a few off as we walked.

"We won't use them," Rene said.

"You never know," I said.

There was no one at the B&D, as usual. They kept their gas pumps locked, of course, but they didn't lock the hoses. There was always enough gas for our purposes just resting in the curve of the hose. I put the empty mayonnaise jar under the nozzle and Rene lifted the hose up as far as he could. The gas ran out of the hose and into the glass jar.

I put one of the dried bulrushes into the jar and it soaked up the gas.

"Watch this," I said.

I lit the match and touched the bulrush. The bulrush whooshed into a flame, burned brilliantly for a minute, and then went out.

"They don't work so well," Rene said. "And we don't want to be carrying torches around here at night. Somebody'd call the police. Let's go."

I screwed the lid back on the jar of gasoline and we followed the train tracks out of the B&D and down alongside the CN dock. We could see Sid and Alex on the raft the entire time. It was getting dark fast.

Rene constructed a little teepee of sticks in the small

firepit and gave it a sprinkle of gas. He had a tidy little fire going in no time. I warmed my hands as I smoked a cigarette. The pond had gradually gotten dark around us. Sid and Alex were still working away on the raft and they were now finishing up in complete blackness. I couldn't see them or the raft or the steel plant, but I could hear the hammer and the saw at regular intervals. Rene and I were sitting on our haunches looking at the little fire tucked between the rocks and the rail ties. Rene was pushing, nudging, and adding small amounts of carefully selected dry wood to the fire. I threw the butt of my cigarette into the fire and we both watched as it caught and burned with a blue flame.

From somewhere on the steel-plant side of the tar pond came the strain of a big engine.

"Look," Rene said. I looked over my shoulder.

Molten slag appeared suddenly out of the darkness. It sparked and flamed as it poured out of the truck and careened down the side of Slag Mountain, like lava from a volcano. The dumping made a sound like dried leaves make when you run through them. The mass of molten slag cooled quickly. We heard the sound of the truck bed lowering and a *clunk* as the bed found its rest on the back of the truck. The truck drove away in the darkness. I didn't even see a headlight. In the day, steam and smoke would follow the slag all the way down the side of the mountain. But at night the red-orange slag that came pouring down gave a great show of light and flame.

"Michael!"

"What?"

"Come and pick me up!" Sid shouted.

"Okay."

I buttoned up my denim jacket.

"Back in a minute," I said.

"Okay." Rene did not move from the fire.

I really didn't want to leave the fire, but I climbed down the rocks and into the kayak and slowly paddled away from the shore until I knew I was clear of rocks and boulders. My hands were numb from the cold air. Wearing gloves or mitts didn't help because they were ten times worse when they were wet. I paddled cautiously forward into the blackness. The sound of the paddle in the water made a *slick-slick* sound. Staring at the fire had ruined my night eyes and I couldn't see a thing ahead. The raft might have been right in front of me and I wouldn't have seen it. When I thought I was close to its position, I let my paddle slice the water behind me like a rudder and I listened for the sound of voices.

"Sid?"

"Over here."

I tilted the paddle out to the side which made the kayak turn gradually starboard, toward the sound of "over here." Sid's hand was practically touching the side of the kayak before I saw him. From the raft, he climbed into the front of the kayak. When he was seated, he took a hammer and a saw and a can of nails and put everything between his legs, part way under the canvas front of the kayak. Alex was climbing up the mast, trying to sink it deeper into its two-by-four brace.

"I'll be right back to get you, Alex," I said.

"Okay," Alex grunted. He had wrapped his legs around the mast pole and was shimmying up to the top.

I pushed off from the raft and made for the little orange flicker of fire on the shore. Sid didn't say anything and neither did I. We were both too cold. I paddled hard for three strokes on one side and three on the other. For a couple of minutes, it seemed like we weren't moving at all, but the orange dot slowly grew bigger and brighter. When I could see the boulders jutting out of the flat water near the dock, I could tell how fast we were going. Soon, we could see Rene hunched over the little flame.

I stopped at the dock and let Sid off on a big boulder. From there he passed his gear up to Rene and then climbed up and over the rail ties himself. And that's when we heard the cracking noise. It came over the water like a rifle shot.

Sid said quickly, "Alex's up the mast—"

We only had time to turn our heads toward where the raft was anchored in the blackness when there was the sound of nails ripping out of deck wood and more cracking and more nails screeching, like an old rusty door squeaking on its hinges—and then a big *splash*. We stood listening anxiously.

A moment later, Alex's voice came chattering over the cold night air of the tar pond.

"*Michael! Hurry up! I'm freezing!*"

Funny things like that happened on the tar pond all the time.

15

I WAS SITTING OUT ON THE FRONT STEP READING WHEN Rosemary Hawthorn came around the corner. I could hear her footstep on the gravel. Our front lawn was a little hill that came up to meet the foundation of our house. Grass had a hard time growing on the hill because we used it as a shortcut to get to Brook Street. Dirt and little dead sticks from the linden tree came rolling from our lawn down over the sidewalk. We should have had a retaining wall built there. Some of the dirt eventually got tracked into the house.

Rosemary was wearing a billowy white blouse and dark blue jeans. Her black hair was long, to her shoulders. Her eyebrows were black, too. Her lips were glossy pink.

"Hi, Michael. Is Heather in?" Rosemary asked.

"I'll call her for you."

"Oh, I can get her," Rosemary said. She came up the stairs, but stopped halfway.

I opened the door and shouted for Heather. Somewhere in the house Heather shouted back.

"You're wanted at the door!" I shouted.

"Who is it?"

"Rosemary!" Rosemary had put one foot in front of the other on the step and was posed there.

"She'll be down in a minute," I said. Kerby came down from the driveway and looked up at us from the bottom of the step. He wagged his tail. Rosemary sat down on the step next to me.

"Are you going to the country this summer?" she asked.

"I don't think so."

"I'm going to Inverness for a month. I love it in the country. I guess I like swimming the best. Do you like swimming?"

"Yeah, it's all right."

"I thought you really liked swimming. I heard that you were getting a lifeguard certificate?"

"That's Sid, not me. I like swimming all right, but not like him. Every time we go out to the Bras d'Or Lakes we can't get Sid out of the water. I swear he's part fish."

"What are you reading?"

"Just a book."

Heather was sure taking her good old time answering the door. When I put the book down, Rosemary saw that I had a cigarette burning.

"You're smoking! And right on your own front step! Your parents are going to kill you if they catch you."

"I'm allowed to smoke in the house, Rosemary."

"You are not!"

"Yes, I am. So is Heather."

"Oh, you terrible liar!"

"I'm not lying to you, Rosemary."

"Yes, you are! How terrible to tease me like that! What's that on your arm?"

"Just some black tar."

Rosemary leaned over and ran her fingertips lightly over the blotch of black tar that I had on my forearm. Rosemary was actually quite attractive.

Kerby was still standing at the bottom of the steps looking up at Rosemary and me as we sat talking at the top of the steps. It wasn't his suppertime or anything, and he didn't want to get in. I was looking at him and so was Rosemary. He was a very handsome dog, in my opinion. He had little black accent marks above his eyes, which were a rich brown.

"Hiya, Kerby. Do you want to get in?" I said.

Kerby wagged his tail.

"Kerby's a very, very pwetty doggie, aren't you Kerby?" Rosemary said. Kerby looked at Rosemary when he heard his name and wagged his tail weakly. And then, as we were both looking at him, Kerby started this uncontrollable *jerking*. It was as if an invisible hand was pushing his back legs under his front legs.

"What are you doing, Kerb?" I said.

The dog was looking up at us with a pathetic look as he was jerking. It was like his body was having a seizure or something. He looked up at me as if he wanted me to help him stop this crazy behaviour that he couldn't control.

"Mind your manners, Kerby," I said.

Rosemary didn't say anything at all.

"I'm sorry about him," I said.

"That's okay," Rosemary said. We were both staring at the dog.

By this time I wanted to kill Kerby. One smack with a bat and that would be that. But I didn't move from my place. He was just jerking out of control. He looked miserable, too. He didn't look like he was enjoying what he was doing. But for him to do it in front of Rosemary was unforgivable. I was happy as hell when he stopped. He just finished with a few quicker jerks and then he took a few steps on all fours to see if he could still walk. I wanted to make small talk, I wanted to say something, anything, but I was speechless. Rosemary was too. We both were completely freaked out by the dog's perverted behaviour.

"Kerby is epileptic," I lied.

"That's a sin," Rosemary said.

As we looked at the mutt, Kerby flopped down, lifted his leg, and started *licking* himself. That was too much for me. I jumped up and ran down the steps.

"Get goin'! Git! Git!"

Kerby scrambled to his feet and looked at me as if I had greatly insulted him. As if *I* had insulted *him*! He went back into the yard and fell asleep in his spot under the bushes. Heather finally shouted out the upstairs window that she couldn't come to the door because she was getting a bath and Rosemary said okay.

"You can write me a letter to my address in Inverness, if you want," Rosemary said before she left. She took a piece of paper out of her pocket with an address on it.

"Okay," I said.

"And I'll write you to tell you if the water's warm or cold and stuff."

"Okay."

"Okay, bye," Rosemary said.

"Okay," I said. "Bye."

DEPENDING UPON KERBY TO BEHAVE HAD BEEN A roulette game ever since he had barfed in the car. We'd had the station wagon loaded down with supplies for a weekend in the country. We'd had a couple of coolers filled with food, blankets for lying on the shore, a mask and snorkel, flippers, and a couple of gallons of bug dope. The car was filled to overflowing. Cosmo and I sat in the back-back of the station wagon, between the coolers. Sid and Heather sat in the back seat. Our cousin Daphne sat in front with Rory and Gloria. Kerby started out with me and Cosmo way in the back-back. He had a little place to sleep, right next to the wheel well. But he wouldn't stay put. He kept getting up and wagging his tail, looking at us. By the time we got out to Sydney River, Kerby had jumped in the back seat with Sid. We thought that he just wanted to be with Sid, since he was Sid's dog, more or less. So Kerby was in the back seat. But he wouldn't calm down. He put his paws on the back of the front seat and stuck his head between Rory and Gloria.

"Aunt Gloria, Kerby's smiling," Daphne said.

"He likes the car," Sid said. "That's why he's smiling."

When we got out to Howie Centre, Kerby barfed up a big, foamy barf behind the driver's seat.

"What the hell was that?" Rory asked.

"Kerby's barfing," Sid reported.

"He's *what?*"

"Better stop the car, dear," Gloria said.

"Let's just keep going. Clean it up, Sid."

But the stink of Kerby's barf was circulating all through the car. The smell of it started me gagging. I couldn't help puking.

"Michael's puking," Heather said.

Cosmo's chest was heaving up and down.

"Cosmo's puking, too," Heather said. She started licking her lips. The smell of one barf and two pukes in the car was nauseating. Heather put her head between her legs and began puking behind Gloria's seat. She had a good long puke.

"What the hell is going on! What the *hell*—" Rory shouted, trying to drive the car. But the car was filling up with vomit. Sid threw up next.

"Sorry, Dad," Sid said. "I couldn't help it."

"Dear, I think you should pull over."

Before Rory could find a place to pull over, Daphne had a little puke in the front seat.

"For the love of all that's good and holy," Rory swore. "What did I do to deserve this?"

"If we had a seacock in the car we could drain the puke without stopping," Sid said.

"Put a sock in it, Sid, or I'll use you to mop up."

"Yes, sir."

THE GRAVEL ROAD TO THE OLD PLACE WAS BADLY RUTted from runoff all winter and rain in the spring. In the washed-out places the bottom of the car would scrape like a boat gliding over a shoal. Boulders crunched under the tires. The tires spun for a moment against the large rocks and then caught again. Sometimes, Rory stopped the car and jettisoned the kids in order to raise the chassis up from the raised ground between the ruts. The road improved as it went into a dark wood and made a sharp left turn. A brook ran through a culvert under the road at this elbow and fell thirty feet into a ravine. Just on the other side of the woods was a pole gate. Beyond the gate was the cement lid to the well, and a rope-swing suspended from one of the arms of a hundred-year-old oak. On a little rise of lush, green lawn, surrounded by two rows of lilac hedge, was the Old Place.

There were four bedrooms downstairs, three of them off the big kitchen. The pantry where Sid once found a secret panel which hid an empty bottle of booze was also off the kitchen. The back porch door led from the kitchen to a three-hole outhouse. Our uncles and aunts say that one of us kids used the big hole by mistake once and had fallen in. I don't know if that's true. It wasn't me, I know that. A narrow stairway near the big wood-stove in the kitchen led up to two bedrooms on the second floor. The windows of these bedrooms looked out over the hedges toward the pole gate. The Old Place had been built by my father's great grandfather when he came over to Cape Breton from Scotland.

The living room had a big beach-stone chimney. A lick of black soot ran up its front and under the rough wooden mantle of the fireplace. Two huge chesterfields and three big armchairs were facing the fireplace.

I remember when I was younger the entire clan gathering in the living room of the Old Place. Our number was still small enough to do that then, to fit in one room, because only two of Grandpa's eight children had married, Rory and Bruce. Grandpa would get a fire going in the big stone fireplace as night fell. The electric light bulbs would be turned off and our faces would be suddenly made mysterious by the shadows. Cosmo and my cousin Daphne would already be asleep in the bedroom off the living room.

"Michael, do you think this fire needs a little help?" my grandfather would ask.

"Yes, Grandpa."

Grandpa would go to the kitchen and made us stay in the living room because he didn't want me or Sid or Heather to see where he got the kerosene. He'd return with a little cup of kerosene and carefully toss it on the logs. A flame would jump up from the fireplace and temporarily brighten the room.

"Oh! Did you see that, Sidney?"

"Did you like that, Heather?"

"Wasn't that fun, Michael?"

The room would darken down again, until the only light was the irregular yellow flame now flickering in the fireplace, the glow of cigarettes being smoked, or wooden matches being struck to light my grandfather's pipe. Gloria would flick the ash off the end of her cigarette and trace beautiful, red-tipped designs for us, as if she was waving a magic wand with a length of fluorescent red ribbon on the end.

Sid, Heather, and I seated ourselves between our uncles and aunts, making ourselves small at their elbows. We would listen as the unimportant shop talk turned to accounts of second sight, forerunners, and the evil eye. Aunt Marie once told a frightening story about a strange old man who appeared outside the windows of people's houses to silently stare in at the children.

"Only children can see this odd creature," Marie said. "Only children can see him as he looks at them through the glass. He presses his face right up against the pane and the breath from his nose makes a little spot of white mist on the window. His hand is a claw on the glass." Marie turned her hand into a claw. I heard a scratching sound.

"Why couldn't you run away?" Sid asked.

"Oh, you couldn't run away! If you tried to run away, he got closer and closer and closer until he was *right behind you.*"

I looked around at the shadowy faces in the room. I didn't notice that my father was absent. My uncles and aunts looked at me and smiled. I tried to smile back but it was very frightening. And that scratching sound.

"I'd run like the devil," Sid said. Heather and I didn't speak at all.

"That's the first thing that you'd think to do," Marie admitted. "But the only way to flee from this strange old man was to walk very, very slowly away from him. The slower you walked, the farther off he became until he finally disappeared. But you had nothing to worry about if you looked out a window at night *without* seeing his face looking in at you."

Another of my uncles laughed out loud. How brave he was.

"What's that about a window, Marie?" my mother asked.

Marie repeated patiently, "If you look out the nearest window and see the face of this old man looking in at you, then you know that he's *after your soul.*"

The scratching behind me had turned into a clear tapping. Nobody else in the room seemed to hear it, although I could hear it quite clearly. I turned and looked out the window.

It took my father coming in from outside to show me

the rubber mask he was wearing just to get me under control. I was screaming and terrified. My grandfather turned on the electric light bulb to take away the mystery and prove to me that I was safe and surrounded by my family. My laughing mother held me in her arms, whispering in my ear that nothing had happened and that everything was perfectly all right.

We didn't get up to the Old Place at all that last summer because my mother quit working at the union office. She said she just had to get out of the office, so, just like that, she got out. Almost immediately, she got a full-time job working for a Cape Breton MP. She bought a new Japanese car, cut her hair really short, and started wearing hoop earrings.

16

THE BUILDING OF THE RAFT'S CABIN DID NOT PRESENT a problem at all. Sid, Alex, and Rene did all the initial construction, and they did an excellent job, too. The walls went up one at a time, the back wall first. Then one side was brought up and secured to the back wall. Then the second side wall was built. Then the front of the cabin was built, only partially, because a sturdy plank door was going to be set right in the middle. The cabin took up about a third of the raft's deck space. It was about five-by-five-foot square and six-foot high, box-shaped. Rene surprised us all when he came down the tar pond with two sliding glass windows *that worked*. It took all day to cut the holes out of the walls and fit the windows. Rene got some old red-brown paint from his father's workshop and I slapped it on. We had enough for three sides, but not enough for the front. So we got some black rust paint for the front door, and we had enough leftover white primer to paint three horizontal stripes on the door and out to the edges of the front wall. Then we ran out of paint.

Some of the boards were actually groove-and-tongue and parts of the cabin looked almost professional. But the wind still came in. So I began making treks back to the hardware store to buy caulking. I could only buy one or two tubes at a time because we couldn't afford to buy them all at once.

"What do you need all this calking for?" the clerk asked.

"I'm sealing some joints," I answered professionally.

"Are they metal or wood joints?" he asked.

"They're wood joints."

"Well, you want a wood sealant."

"No, this one's cheaper."

The clerk shrugged. He didn't understand budgets at all.

Rene's father never missed his caulking gun and with it I caulked every joint. There were fourteen planks used to build each side of the cabin. That meant thirteen joints to caulk per side, plus the front, including the cabin door. I did the roof, too. I figured out later that I should have caulked and *then* painted, because the paint would hide the caulking. As it was, the black caulking ran in blobby horizontal lines along the painted boards of the cabin walls. But we'd had the paint first, so it had made sense to paint. The black caulking I selected was not only the cheapest, it also had the same smell as the tar pond.

The door was put on its hinges, and the windows

were put in, and Alex fixed up an outside battery light for above the door. The mast was rebuilt and was stronger for it, and a boom jutted out from the mast and ropes held the mast and the boom, and the planks of the deck kept our feet dry. After all that, the raft was the best thing you could ever want to have.

For its maiden voyage we poled the raft over to the barge and tied it up. There was only one problem.

"Look at that," Alex said, pointing to the back of the cabin. Black water was seeping in at the baseboard. We clambered out onto the barge and inspected the back of the raft.

"The weight of the cabin has put her under by the stern," Sid said.

"How do we get it back up?" I asked.

"Make the back waterproof," Alex said. "Seal it with fibreglass and caulking and I'm telling you nothing will get past that."

"You want the back out of the water altogether," Rene said. Rene wasn't a sailor, but he was an engineer. He thought about problems on a very practical level.

Sid agreed. "What, Rene? Nail some more wood under the raft?"

"No," Rene said slowly. He was thinking hard. "No ... tie a float to the end of the raft."

"What kind of float? What do you mean by a float?" Alex asked.

"He's right," Sid said. "I know where we can get two of them."

THE OIL COMPANY HAD HUNDREDS OF EMPTY FORTY-five-gallon drums stored near the rail line. In fact, they had a little siding all their own that went right into their property. The empty drums were stacked horizontally, one row atop another, five or six rows high, a hundred-feet long. They were stacked like bricks in a wall. Sid and I volunteered to get two forty-five-gallon drums.

We had to look them over and pick out two that were airtight. Some drums had violent dents, slashes, and rips in them from rough handling. Barrels that had paint fractures were already rusting. They were disqualified. We had to have the best that the oil company had to offer. Sid climbed up on the long row of barrels.

"Careful," I said.

"What if these all started to roll apart?" Sid said.

"Don't say things like that."

I could see the wall of steel barrels rolling apart without warning.

"Want me to jump up instead? I'm lighter."

"You're not strong enough."

"Yes I am."

Sid didn't answer. He walked gingerly on the sides of the barrels until he came to the top row. He pulled out the lead barrel by rocking it from side to side. It was very heavy, even when empty. But once it was out past the line of other barrels, Sid could put his fingers under the back rim and lever it over. It fell to the ground with a metallic bong.

"How's it look?"

"Great," I said. I kicked the barrel and inspected it as it turned.

"No holes?"

"Nope."

"Okay, here comes the next one."

The second barrel was damaged. It had a deep gash in the middle that was rusting badly. We couldn't see the damage until after Sid had pushed it to the ground and I had rolled it for inspection.

"We don't want that one," Sid said. "Just roll it off to one side."

Sid pushed down the next barrel in the row. I kicked it and watched it as it rolled.

"Looks good," I said.

"Good."

Sid jumped down from the top row of barrels and as he did the entire wall of barrels above us shuddered.

"Whoa, Nelly," Sid said, looking up at the forty-five-gallon drums. I was ready to run in case the entire line started to collapse, but they settled down almost immediately.

"Where're we putting these drums, Sid?"

"We'll hide them in the bamboo grove on the army hospital grounds until we bring the raft in to shore. Don't kick them. Here, roll them." Sid rolled his barrel across the tracks, out of the oil company's yard, and into the fence opening that led to the army hospital grounds. I kicked my barrel. But we had to push them one at a time to get them into the bushes near where we stored the kayak every night.

"No one will see them here," Sid said.

"Are we stealing these barrels?" I asked.

"Stealing them? No, we're not stealing them."

"Then why are we hiding them?"

"We're hiding them because we don't want some oil-company employee to put them back up on that top row after we just went through the trouble of picking them out, that's why."

"But if the cops came down here right now, they'd say we were stealing."

"Maybe they would, but we're not. Do you think you stole from the CN when you collected the pallet wood we used to build the cabin?"

"They weren't using the wood anyway."

"Just like these barrels," Sid said. "And do you remember the October Storm? Do you think we stole the coal we collected from the tracks and burned in our fireplace when the power was off for three days?"

"That coal warped our grate," I remembered.

"That's because the coal burned too hot and the grate was only designed to burn wood. But the coal was just sitting there along the tracks, right? The point is, I didn't see any Devco officials sweeping up the coal with a shovel, right? The coal was just sitting there along the tracks for anyone who wanted it, right?"

"Right."

"Just like these barrels," Sid said. "And if I went over to that barrel of rail spikes right there and if I took a spike or two to hold a couple of logs of the raft together, do you think that's stealing?" Situated every so often along the tracks, Canadian National had these twenty-five-gallon yellow barrels filled up with rail spikes. The spikes were always rusty because the uncovered barrels would fill with rainwater. We had already used a half-dozen rail spikes on the barge for bollards because the big bollards of the barge were too far away for our ropes.

"Why wouldn't it be stealing?"

"It wouldn't be because we aren't going anywhere with these items. The wood, the barrels, the spikes, they're all staying right here. The oil company can come down and see their barrels any time they want. Their barrels will be strapped on to the back of our raft. If we were stealing these barrels, don't you think we'd take them away somewhere instead of using them a couple of hundred feet from where we got them? And if they make a big stink about us taking the barrels, we'll unstrap them from the back of the raft and give them back, no questions asked."

"But we can use them for now?"

"Absolutely," Sid said.

A twisting feeling came in my gut.

"I think I have something we can use on the raft."

"What's that?"

"A shotgun."

Sid just looked at me. "A what?"

I took Sid further into the army hospital grounds and we went to a certain slab of cement. I reached under and pulled out the white box. The box was starting to look less new. It was dirty now, in addition to having the one crushed corner, and fingermarks were all over it. It was getting soggy from the rain. I opened the lid of the box and removed the wrapping.

"Where did you get this?" Sid asked. He didn't touch the gun, so I started putting it together to show him.

"Don't," he said. "Where did you get it?"

"There were two of them, but we put one back."

"Who's we?"

"Me and Cosmo."

I had thought Sid would be pleased to have some firepower on the raft, but by his tone of voice I knew I should never have shown him anything.

"You and Cosmo *stole* these guns?"

"No! We were just *using* them, like the barrels—"

"Where's the other one?"

"We put it back."

"Back where?"

"Back in the CN trucks down by Havelock Street. We

didn't know what else to do with it, so we just put it there."

"You mean you put it back where you got it."

"Yeah, I guess …"

Sid looked at me and looked at the gun.

"Put it away," he said. "That's stealing. You took these out of a truck?"

"Yeah …"

"That's stealing," Sid repeated.

I replaced the wrapping and put the lid on the box and then shoved it back under the slab of concrete.

"Who else knows about this?"

"Just you and me. Cosmo knows I have it, but he doesn't know where it is. I told him that I put it back in the truck."

"Stealing *and* lying," Sid said. He sure knew how to make me feel miserable. He started pacing back and forth. He always paced when he was really thinking.

"When we go back to the house tonight, you bring the gun in its box and put it in the kayak. We'll carry the kayak home and put it in the backyard. And we'll hide the gun on the third floor, under the eaves, probably, or behind the washing-machine sink, until I figure out what to do."

"Okay," I said.

And that's how the shotgun came to be in the house.

17

AT HIGH TIDE THE NEXT DAY WE POLED THE RAFT FROM its permanent dock at the barge and brought it over to the little pebbled beach between the CN and the cement company. We had hauled rocks and bricks and built a dry dock at the low-tide mark on the beach. At high tide, the raft just floated over our rock mounds. We had to wait for the tide to fall, and then the raft was left high and dry with her stern sticking out of the water. We had until the next high tide to get the two barrels secured to the end of the raft.

Rene and Alex did most of the placement of the barrels. They wrapped each barrel with a length of rope, and then brought the rope over the raft and tied it to an end piece of the cabin. When the tide came in, the empty barrels stayed underwater for a little while, but eventually they rose with the tide because the ropes couldn't keep them under water. We had to tie the raft to the shore overnight while we figured out plan B.

Early the next morning at low tide we repeated the operation, this time tying the rope around the barrels and then bringing the rope *under* the raft. The tide came in later that afternoon and we watched as the raft rose out of the water, now sitting on a sort of two-barrel sling. With the pole, Sid pushed the raft into deeper water. Alex, Sid, and Rene went in the cabin and crowded all their weight against the back wall. I watched the level of the water from the kayak. It did not rise past the floor of the cabin.

There was one more problem. The cabin had been built out to the raft's perimeter and that meant there was no way to make a complete circum-inspection of the raft by foot. Rene or Alex built foot ledges on each side of the raft. You had to hold onto the roof as you shuffled over the ledge, never putting your full weight on the boards.

You could stand on the barrels when you were at the back of the raft.

Rain came in the evening at the end of that busy week. Sid, Rene, Alex, and I looked out the glass of our sliding windows at the squall coming into the tar pond from Sydney Harbour. The whitecapped, saltwater waves of the harbour were gentled by the tar and oil in Muggah's Creek. They lost their white caps and their triangles and became rounded black, like the smooth sides of a chess piece. There was no gradual merging of the two waters. They met off the shore of the B&D Cement company, and the division was obvious: blue water up against a wall of black. Many times I had sat in the kayak with the stern in the fresh blue-green harbour water and the bow in the opaque water of the tar pond.

The driving rain blasted the side of the raft. We huddled inside the cabin and scrutinized it for leaks, thankful that we had some place of our own construction as a retreat from the storm. Some water seeped in through the places where I had missed with the caulking. I didn't care. It was good enough.

"This is the best place in the world to be," I said, looking out the cabin window.

The rain ran down the window with little upside down reflections of the tar pond in each drop.

"Look at Michael," Alex laughed. "He's dying for a cigarette!"

"No, I'm not," I said. And I wasn't—until Alex mentioned it.

"You're going to have to get wet if you want to smoke," Alex said.

"I know."

"What if we had a little outboard motor?" Sid said.

Sid had a habit of saying these things that just went right into your head. We were all immediately busy imagining the raft with an outboard motor.

"We'd have to cut a hole right here," Rene said, pointing to the back of the cabin.

"And we'd have to navigate with the cabin door open," said Alex. "Or put a window in the door."

But just the *idea* of a little outboard motor for the raft!

"How much are they?" I asked.

"Too much," Alex said.

"They're expensive," said Rene. "Even second-hand outboards would be expensive. And the motor'd probably get clogged up if we used it all the time in the tar pond."

"But what if we had one?" Sid said.

If we had an outboard motor on the back of the raft, we could set out. We could go around the world. I looked out the window at the rain and imagined we were off Cape Hatteras during a dangerous squall. With our skill and some luck we would pull through. Off Miami we would all get bad sunburns. We would have to go around the frying-pan handle and visit New Orleans because of Huckleberry Finn. We'd get as close to the Mississippi River as we could, just out of respect for the raft he floated down that river with Negro Jim. I never actually read that book because I couldn't understand a single word they were saying, especially when Jim was talking. But the pictures were good. And it looked like they had a very fine raft, much bigger than our raft. They didn't have a proper cabin or sliding windows, but they certainly had a nice raft. Powerful nice, as Mr. Finn would say. I guess I read a little bit of that book.

"Do you think the raft could cross the Atlantic?" I asked anybody.

"No way," Alex said.

"No," Rene said.

"In your dreams, maybe," Sid said. "This isn't a sailboat."

"It doesn't have a keel," Alex said. "You can't properly steer something without a keel."

"A raft like this would capsize, Michael," Rene said.

"Because it doesn't have a keel. Keels keep a boat from capsizing, too," Alex explained.

"One wave and that would be it for the raft," Sid said. "Do you know how many tons of water some of those waves in the North Atlantic can deposit on a ship?"

"A sailboat has three hulls," Alex said. "The topsides act like a hull when it's heeled over."

I looked out the window at the rain teeming on the surface of the tar pond. It looked as if a thousand trout were jumping.

The wind made a whistling sound through the window and we all smiled at each other. It was good to be indoors, an indoors that we ourselves had made. I imagined rounding the Cape of Good Hope on the raft and sailing into the Indian Ocean. If we followed the coast up and down without going anywhere near Vietnam, where the Americans were fighting, we could visit Krakatoa, east of Java, if there was anything left of it. From what I saw on television, it pretty well blew itself to smithereens. But from Java you could hit Australia with a rock. And New Zealand is down under there, too. New Zealand looks like a bigger Nova Scotia with its Cape Breton Island reversed.

"Look at Michael," Alex said. "He's shivering!"

"I'm cold," I said.

It was cold in the cabin.

Sid looked at me for a moment and then he smiled.

"WHAT DO YOU WANT WITH A STOVE FLUE?" THE HARDware-store clerk asked me.

"I want it for a stove," I answered. The clerk shrugged.

"And I also need a replacement hacksaw blade for metal."

"A hacksaw blade for metal, eh? Not a hacksaw blade for wood?"

"No, it has to be for metal."

"Okay, young feller, we have that, too."

I handed over my wad of fake, hardware-store money to the clerk, which completely took care of the cost of the flue and the replacement hacksaw blade for metal. It also took care of my wad of hardware-store money.

Sid and I went back to the oil company site and got the damaged oil barrel that we had discarded. Rene's father had a drill that could penetrate metal. Rene made an outline of a square on the side of the barrel and then we all took turns connecting the dots with the hacksaw. When we had the square cut out, Rene drilled a few more holes and got some metal hinges and some nuts and bolts, and soon we had a door to our stove. Alex hacksawed a circle in the back wall of the cabin, high up, and he fitted in the stove flue. Rene built a little fire, but it didn't catch.

"It needs more oxygen," he said.

He drilled more holes below the door which worked fine. We made a bigger fire. Sid stuffed the stove with wood. When the fire was good and roaring, the heat turned parts of the stove a translucent orange and drove us all outside where we watched red, white, and blue paint peel off the drum and curl away as noxious smoke.

18

OUR UNCLE DUNCAN, DROVE DOWN TO MEADOW STREET one day in one of the covered trucks used by the union. He had work clothes on, a shirt and pants with paint on them, dirty cloth gloves, and a baseball cap. He still wore his black-rimmed glasses.

"You'll give me a hand, fine lads that you are."

"Sure, Duncan. What are you doing?"

"What am I doing? Didn't your father tell you? We're going to take off the balcony today."

The balcony of our house was starting to separate from the frame of the house. You could see the large spikes as they became exposed. The balcony was right over the cement front steps. All of us kids had been put out on the balcony in our cribs when we were babies. We'd sleep there all day under the shade of the linden tree. You could climb up to the balcony from the front steps, too. There were places where you could hoist yourself up and over the railings. A green and white picket rail ran between the two corner posts of the balcony. The balcony had been a good place for a lookout during hide-and-seek.

"What's going in place of the balcony, Duncan?"

"A peaked roof, Sid."

"So, we won't have a door going to the balcony anymore?"

"No balcony, no door," Duncan told me. "I imagine

you'll get a small window put in where the balcony door is now."

"But why a peaked roof, Duncan?"

"Flat roofs don't shed water or snow, Michael. Peaked roofs are the way to go."

I said to Sid, "We should have put a peaked roof on the raft."

Sid shrugged at me. "Too late now."

"We built a raft, Duncan," I said.

"So Sid tells me."

"Do you want us to kick out the railings?" Cosmo asked.

That's all Cosmo wanted to do, and that's all he did. He hoisted himself up onto the balcony and had most of the railing kicked out before anyone else hardly had a chance. I got on the balcony by using the second-floor door like a normal person. Cosmo was on his back kicking the white pickets with both feet. I got to kick out four or five. They busted apart at the bottom where they were rotten, but the nails held them at the top where the wood was still sound. The busted white pickets stuck out from the green rail like buckteeth. Duncan had three crowbars. Sid, Cosmo, and I each got one. Duncan used the back of a hammer to pry the nails from the wood. Irene came out onto the front step.

"What's all the ruckus about?" she asked. She was drying her hands with a dishtowel.

"We're taking down the balcony today, Irene," Sid said.

"Are you?"

"Rory or Gloria might have told you about removing the balcony," Uncle Duncan said.

"No, no, I hadn't heard anything," Irene said.

"It might have slipped their minds. We'll try to be as quiet as we can."

Irene went back into the house and we men continued our work. Cosmo got bored and left the job site. He gave the crowbar back to Duncan, who began to use it instead of the reverse end of the hammer. Uncle Duncan and Sid and I filled the truck three times with rotting lumber and rusty nails. There was a lot of lumber in the balcony. And it took a long time to carefully take it all apart.

"Destruction is as complicated as construction, men," Duncan said. "You have to know what to take away without having the whole thing fall apart before you want it to fall apart."

"Or how to take one thing out and leave the other things standing," I said.

"Yes, sir," Duncan said.

"Like they do in the coal mines," Sid said.

"What do you mean?" I asked.

"They remove as much coal as possible and then they start removing the columns of coal that hold up the roof," Sid explained. "They take the coal from the support columns, and the roof gets weaker and weaker to the point where it's going to collapse, but they get out before it does, just at the last second. That's what I call having nerves of steel!"

"They call that 'robbing the pillars'," Uncle Duncan said. "You don't want to stay in a room after that last pillar is robbed, boys!"

"No way!" Sid made a shuddering sound.

Not only did we have to go slow taking the balcony apart, we had to be careful putting all the pieces in the truck. We couldn't throw them any which way as we could have with a bigger truck because Duncan wanted to get as much as possible in the truck for each trip. We drove each load up to the city dump off Welton Street and carefully removed the boards which were full of roofing nails and pieces of roofing splattered with tar. The nails from one board hooked onto another board, and the whole mess was worse to move than a pile of thorn bushes. We took everything from the truck and dropped it into a little trench a dozer had made.

On the way back from the third and last trip, I started asking Duncan questions about the truck. Duncan was driving and Sid was in the passenger seat. I was sitting in the middle. Duncan was explaining how a clutch works.

"Depress the clutch and then move the shift into a higher gear or a lower gear," he said. "This shift is on the wheel, but most shifts are on the floor. If they're on the floor or on the steering column, they all follow the H pattern," he said.

"What do you mean, the H pattern?" I asked.

"Well, the gears from the lowest to the highest follow a pattern that traces out the letter H."

"Even a three-speed?"

"Oh yes. The first gear could be at the top of the H, and if you bring the stick straight down you're in second gear, and then up and over and you're in third, and reverse could be straight down again. Or some variation of that pattern. Does that sound right to you, Sidney?"

"I'm not interested in driving," Sid said.

"You're not interested in driving?"

"I'll be fourteen next week," I said to Duncan. "Two more years to get my licence."

We were coming up to the traffic lights at the corner of George and Dorchester. There was a light rain falling and the street was sort of glossy. The wipers were on but there wasn't enough rain falling on the windshield to stop them from scudding. A bunch of people were waiting for a bus right in front of Central High School.

Duncan depressed the clutch and put the engine in a lower gear as he approached the red light.

"See what I'm doing, Michael? I'm putting the transmission in a lower gear which will help slow the truck without the use of brakes. This is called gearing down. *Jaysus—*"

I didn't see the girl until Duncan hit the brakes. Then I saw her. She was just out his side window and she was riding a huge balloon-tired bicycle. The bike was way too big for her, she could barely reach the pedals. I felt the truck brakes grip the wheels and felt the wheels slide on the pavement. I knew we were going to hit her. Everything at that moment started going in slow motion. Everything just slowed down and I fit a thousand thoughts into the few seconds it took for the girl on the balloon-tired bike to go from being out Duncan's driver's-side window to being directly in front of our sliding truck.

For example, I thought of mathematical problems, like how much the truck weighed and how long it would skid before striking the girl. I envisioned the investigators walking on George Street with those little measurers they use to determine when the skid began and when impact occurred in relation to the skid. That would determine speed, I realized. It was all very scientific. I hoped the rain on the pavement would be factored into their calculations. Strangely, I was very interested in the collision from a purely scientific point of view, right up until the moment of impact.

The front of the truck struck the girl. She fell onto the hood and rolled, and her hip struck the windshield on Sid's side. A big spiderweb appeared on the glass. Through Sid's passenger window I watched as the girl rolled off the windshield and into the gutter, like slush pushed there by a snowplough.

The truck slid, its brakes locked, for another ten feet or so. It took forever to come to a stop. I saw the funeral. I saw the black cars waiting outside the church with their lights on. I saw the pallbearers bring the coffin outside and put it in a black hearse. I saw the relatives weeping and the priest trying to console them. Uncle Duncan, Sid, and I were hidden in the crowd because we wanted to pay our respects. Her mother wailed and her father cursed and her brothers and sisters threw themselves on the casket and wept. It was a tragedy from start to finish.

Uncle Duncan jumped out in front of the truck and threw the big bicycle from the street to the sidewalk. The crowd, which had been waiting for the bus, was now running toward the girl, who was crumpled in the gutter. Sid was the first to reach her. Duncan came running, too. I ran to Sid and the little girl. She wasn't moving. I thought she was dead.

"Little girl?" Sid said, gently trying to turn her over.

"Careful, Sid," I said. "She could have something broken."

"Little girl?"

Sid kept trying to turn her over. She wouldn't turn over. A woman at the bus stop said, "Let me. I'm a nurse's aide." Sid got up and looked at Duncan. Our uncle was in a sort of trance. He just kept staring at the little girl in the gutter. The woman from the bus stop was speaking softly to the little girl. We heard the girl gasp for a breath.

"That's a good sign," Sid said to Duncan, who was still staring at the girl.

The girl took another few breaths. She must have had the wind knocked out of her. She took one deep breath and screamed, *"Who's the dirty bastard who hit me!"*

Sid laughed out loud. "What terrible gutter-language!" he said.

"Can't be hurt too bad," Duncan muttered to himself.

The girl kept swearing like you wouldn't believe, the nurse woman saying, "There, now, dear. There, now—" It was like trying to comfort a wolverine. All my sympathy for the girl went right out the window. A police cruiser appeared and directed traffic around the area. The ambulance appeared next, and medics put the girl, who was just blubbering now, on a stretcher and shoved her in the back. The ambulance took off with its screeching siren. Sid thought her cursing was hilarious.

"Anyone who could curse like that has nothing wrong with them," he said. "Besides, she came out of the alley like she owned the street. It's no wonder she got hit. She was lucky she didn't get killed."

"There's nothing funny about this," a uniformed man from the crowd said.

"Did anyone see the accident?" the cop asked the crowd.

"I did, officer." The uniformed man stepped forward. He looked very much like the police officer. He was wearing a cap like the police officer's cap, a dark tunic and trousers, an emblem on his chest and epaulettes on his shoulders. At first I'd thought he was a cop, but he was a security guard. He stepped forward and pointed to Duncan and said, "That man was going about sixty miles an hour!"

"I guess he *wasn't*." Sid blurted, all his humour gone.

Duncan didn't say anything. I think he was in shock.

"You lying son of a bitch," I said. The man and the cop both looked at me.

"What a punk," the security guard said.

"Who was driving?" the cop asked.

"I was driving, officer," Duncan said.

"And he was *not* doing sixty miles an hour!" Sid said.

"Do you have your licence and insurance?" the cop asked Duncan.

"Yes, I have," Duncan said. He and the cop went over to the truck and had a little talk.

The people in the crowd started to chatter amongst themselves. Sid and I were on the street between the truck and the crowd.

"I didn't think he was speeding," a woman said. She was wearing a plastic kerchief over her head and was carrying a Metropolitan shopping bag. Another woman agreed. A man smoking a cigarette and wearing a T-shirt came up to Sid and me and said we hadn't been speeding. But the security guard wouldn't give it up. He was trying to convince the crowd that he was right.

"Maybe not sixty, but they were doing well over the speed limit for city driving," he insisted, "well over the limit. I should know. I'm trained to observe such details, to observe them and remember them. I've testified in court twice and each time I have accurately recollected minute details that were crucial to recreating what actually happened. Both times my testimony resulted in convictions."

"You're a professional observer, are you?" the man in the T-shirt said sarcastically.

"You might say that, yes. And I observed that truck speeding long before anyone else even saw it. It was speeding to catch the green light at the corner."

"The light was already red," Sid said.

"We were in second gear, preparing to stop," I added. "You can't get past thirty miles an hour in second gear."

"Listen to Mr. Al Unser," the security guard said. "You're not even old enough to drive!"

"How would you like a fat lip?" I said.

"Michael," Sid said evenly, "shut up."

I couldn't give anyone a fat lip. And if I started anything, Sid knew that he would have to finish it.

"Listen to them," the security guard said, "a couple of punks! They were probably drinking in the truck when they hit that little girl! They're probably on drugs! Check the truck for alcohol, officer!"

"Why *don't* you shut up?" the man wearing the T-shirt said to the security guard.

"You're just trying to make trouble," the Met-bag woman said.

"Have it your own way," the professional observer said. He walked back to the line of parked buses and boarded one. The rest of the crowd started to disperse. Sid turned around and began walking back toward the truck. But I couldn't let it go. I ran after the security guard and boarded his bus. I saw him sitting in one of the front seats. He had an untroubled look on his face and seemed to have already forgotten about the false accusation he had just made.

"You're supposed to tell the truth," I said to him. He turned from the window and looked at me. I was standing next to the empty driver's seat.

"What are you talking about, punk? Go on. Get lost."

"You're supposed to tell the truth. That's why you get to wear that uniform. People trust you to tell the truth. That's the only thing you have to do. But you lied. You lied and you know you lied."

"What's the matter with you? I told you to get lost, now beat it."

"Why did you lie? You said you were a professional witness, and then you lied about what you witnessed! That makes you a professional liar!"

"That's it, buddy. Your goose is cooked."

The guard jumped up with an agility that surprised me. He was on his feet and in front of me before I could react. The only thing I could do was fall back into the driver's seat. But before he could put a hand on me, Sid stepped between us. He had stepped onto the bus just as the security guard had jumped up.

"Don't even think about it," Sid said.

The guard looked at Sid, who was, after all, only a boy. But he was a formidable boy and a confident boy and a boy who clearly could look out for himself—and his little brother. You could practically read these considerations as they ran across the guard's face. After thinking twice, the guard resumed his seat with the air of a man too tired to be bothered by such small fry.

"Two punks. I see your kind every day at work. Blow your brains out, what do I care."

It turned out that the girl Duncan hit with the truck was all right. She had just bruised her hip. That was the second time she had been hit by a car. She had a bad habit of driving her big bike straight out onto George Street from that blind alley. But what I couldn't understand was the security guard. You'd think, because he was a security guard, that he would tell the truth. You'd think a person who held a position like that in society would not violate the very rule that justified his profession. It was like discovering a doctor who was deliberately making people sick. I just couldn't understand the security guard falsely accusing us.

19

I THOUGHT BEING IN A CAR ACCIDENT WAS BAD, BUT MY birthday party was a disaster.

My father was home at four o'clock in the afternoon, a very unusual time to see my father. But he was home, the big sky-blue station wagon parked in the driveway. My mother's brand new car was parked on the street. It had a new-car smell and rode very smoothly for a smallish car.

"You're welcome to stay for Michael's party, Irene," Gloria said.

"I must go home," Irene said. "Happy birthday, Michael."

"Thanks, Irene."

Rory herded all of us into the kitchen and told us to pipe down.

"Listen up everybody, quiet, quiet, quiet."

"I don't want to sit down!" my cousin Mandy was screaming.

"Shut up, you little brat!" my cousin Daphne was shouting at her sister.

"Both of you shut up," Sid said.

"All of you shut up!" Rory ordered.

"Okay, shut up," Sid said. "What is it, Dad?"

"First of all, get that bloody cat off the table—"

Heather picked up Chipper and put her on the kitchen floor.

"All right," Rory said. "We all know it's Michael's birthday today—"

"Happy birthday, Kiddo," Heather said.

"Thanks, Heather," I said.

"All right, quiet! This is worse than city council!"

"Shut up everyone, *shut up!*" Cosmo shouted.

Everyone shut up.

"Are we ready now?" Rory asked. We all nodded our heads and didn't say a word. And then we burst out laughing. None of us could shut up. Rory looked at Gloria and they both smiled, which made us laugh more. Gloria went into the good room and brought out a long cardboard box that stuck out of the end of a paper shopping bag. She handed it to Rory who was sitting at the head of the table. Everyone became quiet again.

"Miss Shaw will be here for Michael's birthday—" Rory began to say. It didn't seem strange that a friend of Gloria's and Rory's from the union office would be there. I'd met her lots of times. Miss Shaw drove a white 1973 z28 Camero. It was a beauty of a car, nice throaty mufflers, and a 245 horsepower v-8 engine. I think it had a v-8 engine. It might have had a v-6. It also had a four-spoke steering wheel, which I thought was pretty cool. "Miss Shaw is going to be here for Michael's birthday," Rory repeated, "and she's bought him a gift. But there's a slight problem. *She bought him the same gift that Gloria bought him!*" I looked at my mother and she nodded her head as if to say, "It's true!"

"What did she get him?" Heather asked.

"She bought a game called Ricochet—" Rory said.

Cosmo said, "Ricochet, cool!"

"—but she didn't know that Gloria had bought the same gift!" Rory seemed honestly astonished by this coincidence.

I looked at my mother.

"I thought you'd like it," she whispered.

"I would," I whispered back to her.

In Ricochet, the playing board was in two sections, which were joined at one end by two angled elastics. You rolled a steel marble down one board, it ricocheted off the two elastic bands, and came back toward you on the other board, which had markings to count score. If the marble was rolled with too much force, it went into a gutter at the end of the board.

"He gets *two* sets of Ricochet?" Cosmo asked.

"Two sets," Rory confirmed. And he opened the Metropolitan bag and brought out the Ricochet box. The Cellophane wrapper was still on the box, but there wasn't any birthday wrapping paper. The box was almost the same dimensions as the shotgun box.

"You lucky—!" Cosmo said, and he punched my arm. I could see that we could have some pretty good tournaments with two sets. It wasn't chess, but I didn't like chess anyway. Rory put the game back in its bag. He passed it to Gloria and she put it on top of the upright piano in the television room.

"I want to play Ricochet! I want to play Ricochet!" Mandy shouted.

"Will you shut up!" Daphne said.

"Mandy, dear? Please be quiet for Aunt Gloria, okay?" Gloria said. She smiled approvingly as she rested against the range. She smoked a cigarette and sipped at a cup of instant coffee. I was starting to get a taste for instant coffee too, milk with lots of sugar.

"Birthday parties are only for family," Sid said.

"Mandy and Daphne are family, Sid," Rory answered.

"That's not who I mean."

"Miss Shaw is coming as a friend of the family, Sid," Gloria explained.

"That's right," Rory said. "She's a friend of the family.

And we don't want to disappoint Miss Shaw on her first birthday with us, right? So, this is what we'll do. Michael, when you open her present, pretend that her gift is a complete surprise. Pretend that you've never seen it before. And we'll all cheer and applaud and make all kinds of noise. All right? That's how it will go, then."

"Is it okay for me to do that?" I said. I looked at my father and then at Sid.

"Of course, it's okay," my father said. "And we'll all cheer."

"I'm not cheering," Sid said.

"Yes, you are, Sid," Heather said, hustling Sid's shoulder to encourage him to get into the spirit of the occasion. But Sid had that sour look on his face.

"I'm not cheering," he repeated so that Rory had to take notice.

"Sid's not cheering! Sid's not cheering!" Mandy shouted.

"Aunt Gloria! Will you tell her to shut up?"

"Why don't *you* shut up!" Cosmo said to Daphne. "You're screaming right in my ear!"

"Quiet, dear! Shussh!" Gloria said.

"Everyone quiet!" Rory commanded. He was starting to get pissed off. Everyone was quiet. My father turned to Sid.

"Why aren't you cheering, Sidney?"

"Because it's a lie. And she has no business sticking her nose in our family."

"It's a lie! It's a lie!" Mandy repeated.

Sid was always very upright like that. And fearless about it, too. Even if I could have thought up an objection to cheering, I could never have said it to my father. But Sid not only thought about it, he just stood there with his arms folded and said it, just the way Rory himself would have. Sid was not going along with it, and that was that.

Sid and Rory had almost done this the week before.

Everyone had been watching TV, except Sid. He was up on the third floor practising his chanter. He came downstairs when Rory got home. And Rory didn't want to hear the chanter that night.

"I don't want to hear that tonight," he said. And he sort of snapped it out as an order.

"One song," Sid said. And he started playing away. Rory grabbed the chanter right out of Sid's mouth as he was playing. The tune broke off abruptly. Sid grabbed his own lip.

"I said not tonight. Take that thing outta here." Rory pushed the chanter back onto Sid's chest.

"It's 'The Wild Colonial Boy'," Sid said, still holding his lip.

"Glad to know it. Now get out of my sight."

Rory had just about torn Sid's lower lip off when he grabbed the chanter because Sid's lip had dried to the pipe, and when the pipe was torn from his mouth, Sid's lower lip almost went with it. Sid went upstairs, and I followed after *The Waltons* was over.

"What happened?" I asked.

"Dad's got things on his mind," Sid said.

"Your lip is bleeding."

"It's not important."

I would have been pretty pissed about something like that. You only get one lip, for Chrissake. Sid had just shrugged it off. But he wasn't shrugging off this birthday thing. Trying to understand the difference was what made Sid such a big puzzle to me.

"If you think you're too virtuous to go along with a

harmless fib, Sidney, then you can leave. We don't want you here," Rory said.

Sid turned right on his heel and walked out of the house. In a way it worked out for the best because Sid sometimes had a way of making us all feel uncomfortable.

MISS SHAW SHOWED UP WITH CHINESE TAKEOUT FROM Wong-Wing's. She brought more stuff than I ever knew the Chinese ate. I liked the spare ribs the best.

Miss Shaw, Rory, and Gloria lit cigarettes after supper. Rory and Gloria had a cup of coffee. Miss Shaw wanted tea so Rory got Heather to make Miss Shaw a pot of tea. I wanted to burst out laughing when I thought of the joke we were going to play on Miss Shaw. And then it came time to open the presents. I got a pair of socks, a pen with four different colour ballpoints in it, and three more Hardy Boy books to add to my collection. There was a book on sailing from Sid. I also got a pair of brand new Dash sneakers. And then Rory handed me a long flat box wrapped in expensive birthday paper and encircled with a glittery ribbon and bow.

"This is from Miss Shaw," he said. He winked at me and I was in on the secret.

"Oh?" I said.

No one was saying a word. I didn't look once at Cosmo because I would start laughing.

"What could it be?" Cosmo said. Cosmo's a devil like that. He knew how far he could push it. Miss Shaw looked at him and smiled and he smiled back at her. I got the last of the wrapping paper off and read the box.

"*Ricochet!*" I said.

"Hey, hey!" my father cheered. And we all cheered.

"Thank you so much for this present." I said this to Miss Shaw even though I could see my mother's present lying right on top of the upright piano in the TV room.

"You're certainly welcome, Michael. I'm glad you like it so much."

"Yes, I do. It's the best present by far." Miss Shaw smiled.

And then Daphne, because she was very puzzled, said, "But he already *has* Ricochet—"

We all turned on Daphne, her own family, for this filthy thing she had said—

Shut your big mouth—stupid idiot— you dummy—so stupid that you can't even— blabbering and can't be trusted—why did you say that—ruined the nice surprise because—big mouth went and ruined it!—Twit!—

Daphne burst out crying and ran from the room.

Rory, laughing and laughing, caught in his harmless fib, did all the explaining to Miss Shaw. Gloria, laughing, went to find Daphne who was brought back to the table, her eyes all red from crying. I couldn't even look at Miss Shaw after I had so sincerely accepted her present. I felt like the biggest liar that ever lived. I wanted to be anywhere but at that table.

When the cake came, I blew out the candles, but wouldn't tell my girlfriend's name when icing stuck to the knife.

"You have to tell your girlfriend's name if icing sticks to the knife, Michael," Miss Shaw said. "It's a very old birthday tradition." I had never heard of that tradition.

"It's Rosemary Hawthorn," Heather blabbed.
"Shut up!" I said to Heather.
"Hey! That's enough of that," Rory said. "Apologize to Miss Shaw and thank her for the present."
"I'm sorry, Miss Shaw," I said. "And thank you for the present."
"You're welcome, Michael."
I ate the cake as fast as I could. I just wanted to get out of there. When Rory and Miss Shaw went to the good room to talk after dinner, I grabbed my denim jacket and was halfway down the front steps when Cosmo stuck his head out the front door.
"Can I play with Ricochet?" Cosmo said.
"Sure," I said, putting on my jacket. He disappeared back inside the house, but was replaced by my mother, who came out on the step.
"Take this to Sid," she said. She had assembled a selection of Chinese food in one of the large Styrofoam dishes. She put a piece of my birthday cake in another container. I put a can of pop in my denim jacket.
I walked down to the tar pond feeling completely miserable. Sid was out on the raft and I yelled for him to come in and pick me up. I lit a cigarette, but was too disgusted to smoke it. I lit a second one off the first one. Sid came in with the kayak and picked me up and we went back out to the raft. He had a little fire going in the stove.
"Sorry to ruin your birthday party," he said.
"No, no. You didn't ruin it. You didn't ruin it."
I just felt the worst I had ever felt.
"Thanks for the sailing book, Sid. I'll read it. I promise."

I handed Sid the container of Chinese food and the can of pop. Sid took the container, opened the lid, and dumped the contents into the tar pond. It was interesting: most of the rice sank, so did the sweet-and-sour chicken balls. The plastic fork floated. Sid then popped the tab on the can and emptied the pop into the tar pond. Miss Shaw had brought a dozen cans of pop to drink with supper, but our family had never been pop drinkers. Sid threw the empty pop can overboard. The empty Styrofoam container he put in the stove where it bubbled and turned black and went up the chimney and out the flue as inky smoke. He ate the cake, though. It was a store-bought cake from the Met on Charlotte Street and it was excellent cake.

20

A WEEK LATER, RORY CALLED US INSIDE AND MADE US sit down in front of the television to watch the live broadcast of the American president resigning. The president made a short speech and then flew away in a helicopter. A few days later, Irene quit being our housekeeper.

Every now and then Rory was liable to sit you down and make you listen to something, a poem, for example, or he'd plunk you down by a radio to make you listen to a broadcast, or make you read something from a newspaper as the rest of the family listened. He frequently announced that he was going for a drive, and press-ganged any kids in sight to come with him. Sometimes it would turn out okay, if the ride was somewhere we hadn't been before—the radar base, for instance, or the transmitter of the radio station. But most times it would be to visit one of his cronies who lived in a house in the suburbs or who owned a big building across the overpass and down a side street in Whitney Pier.

Rory would park the car and say, "I'll just be a minute." And he would be ten times longer than a minute. We'd sit in the car most times for well over an hour, sometimes longer. And the only thing we'd get out of it was to shake hands with some old geezer who was supposed to be a diehard supporter of the union. If we were lucky, we'd get a hamburger or an ice cream afterwards. I started taking a book to read just to be on the safe side.

"All right, Bodach, you and your brother get in the car."

"Where are we going?" Cosmo asked.

"We're going for a ride."

We drove to Uncle Duncan's and Rory parked the car by the curb.

"Okay, boys, in the truck," Rory ordered.

We got into the union truck and Rory started it up. Cosmo sat in the middle and I sat on the passenger side. The big spiderweb that the girl had made with her hip was still there.

"That's where the girl hit," I told Cosmo. "You should have been there. I was sitting right where you're sitting now."

"Wow," Cosmo said. He put his hand up to feel how the glass was damaged.

"Sit down," my father said. He pushed Cosmo back against the seat.

"Where we going?" I asked Rory.

"We're going to get this windshield fixed."

This was the sort of thing Rory did on his day off. No wonder we never got out to the Old Place anymore.

JOHN MATHESON OWNED A JUNKYARD IN REAR BALLS Creek, which was a little place right behind Balls Creek, off the Trans-Canada on the road to North Sydney. We took Keltic Drive to get there. On the way, I saw on the sign announcing Rear Balls Creek that someone had spray-painted "Do they?" I looked at my father to see if he had seen it, but he had his eyes on the road. He pulled the truck into a long gravel driveway and drove along a little causeway. Standing water was on either side. Rory stopped the truck by a kid who was trying to get a stump out of the ground with a long steel pole.

"Hello, Tiger," my father said. "Is your old man home?"

"He's in the house," the kid said. He looked at me and Cosmo and we looked at him.

Rory drove the truck on up to the house. It was a one-storey place with a huge cement foundation. Someone had started scraping the house for painting. The ladder was still there leaning against the shingles, but the scraping ended a few feet from the top of the ladder. There were all kinds of things scattered all around the yard—machines and parts of machines, tools, shovels, picks, and things I didn't recognize. Some parts that looked like engines just sat on the hard-packed ground and leaked oil. Grass was growing up through some of the rusting metal parts. The junked cars started just beyond the house. You could only see the first few from where Rory parked the truck. He jumped out.

"Come on, boys," he said. We jumped out, too. Rory sprung up the wooden steps and greeted a little girl at the screen door.

"Hello, Darlin'! You sure are a pretty little girl! Is your great big ugly father in?"

The little girl silently backed away from the door and Rory went in. We went in after him. The little girl looked at us and didn't say hi, so neither did we. When we were in the house the boy we had seen on the causeway came up the steps and into the house behind us. He looked at us and didn't say anything. Neither did we. Cosmo and I just stood there, and didn't say anything. We could hear somebody, a man, practically shouting on the phone.

"I don't give a lard's arse about those louse-bound bastards! They're not doin' a damn thing for the men anyway!" Rory smiled when he heard the voice of his friend.

"Listen, Tiger," Rory said to the boy, "Go get your old man. Tell him that Rory the Wrecker Chisholm is here."

The boy went around a corner. We could still hear the loud voice.

"—Jaysus Murphy, if you give 'em an inch you'll end up spilling your guts over the whole nine yards! We cave in on this one, boys, and we might as well pack up shop and work for the bastards piecework!—What do you want standing there like a retard? Speak for the love of Christ." We heard some mumbling and then the man said goodbye and hung up the phone. He came around the corner laughing.

"You ol' son of a bitch! Jaysus, let me get a picture of

you because I'm not going to see you visiting me twice! Son of a bitch!"

"How are ya, Johnny!" my father said. The two men shook hands like they were going to start arm wrestling. It would be a close call. Rory was bigger than Johnny, but Johnny had enormous arms that looked as strong as steel.

"These your boys?"

"Michael and Cosmo. Say hello to Johnny Matheson. He's going to get us a windshield."

"Hello, Mr. Matheson," Cosmo and I said. We shook his huge hand.

"Jaysus, that's about the only thing I can get these days, Rory. Them Devco sons of bitches."

We had some tea first before we did anything. And white soda crackers. We drank up the tea and I didn't ask for peanut butter for my crackers, out of politeness. They were good crackers. Salted and fresh. Rory and Johnny blabbed about some union issue regarding the men and Devco. Johnny's son served us the tea. Mr. Matheson's wife and other children were off visiting. After talking about the union and Devco and the coal mines and the steel plant, Rory and Mr. Matheson finally went outside to take a look at the smashed window.

"Da-*vid*!" Johnny shouted.

The silent boy came out of the house.

"Get the book," he said. David went back into the house and came out with a big blue book. It was more like a blue binder that held hundreds of grease-smeared pages.

"What kind of truck've we got here, David," Johnny asked.

"A Chevy, 1961," David said.

"We got any on the lot?"

"One, but it ain't got no windshield."

"What other trucks we have here, Davey?"

"We got a '70 Dodge, a Ford up on the back lot, and another Ford over the hill."

Rory had just lit a cigarette. He was admiring this display of skill.

"Anything that would fit a windshield for a '61 Chevy?"

"The '70 Dodge would fit," Davey said.

"Let him look it up," Johnny said to Davey, nodding at me. Davey brought the big binder down the steps and handed it to me. Johnny explained how to first look up the make of the truck, then to look under glass, then under windshields, then under compatibility.

"You find it, Cosmic? That's your name? Jaysus, what's his name, Rory?"

Rory laughed at Mr. Matheson's confusion. "His name is Michael."

"You find it, Michael?"

"Yes. It says that the only truck that will fit our windshield is a 1970 Dodge."

"Davey, that's pretty impressive," Rory said.

"They're as sharp as a cat-o'-nine-tails, Rory," Johnny said. "You got the keys?" Rory threw the keys to Johnny and Johnny threw them to his son who caught them with one hand.

"Boys," Rory said, "go with Davey and learn something."

Cosmo was reluctant to get in the truck first because that meant sitting next to Davey. But I pushed him up and he slid over. Davey moved the seat forward and started the truck as I slammed the door shut. I was as big as Davey and I could have driven the truck, too. But I guess he was older than me if he was allowed to drive. He knew the standard shift better than Rory despite the fact that the shift was on the wheel.

We went over the little hill at the back of the house and into the heart of the junkyard. We were in a landscape of wrecked automobiles, wrecks right to the skyline. Narrow dirt roads snaked between islands of metal and glass. The wrecks rose and fell with the contours of the earth. Some cars were tucked in behind second-growth trees that seemed to be invading the junkyard. As we reached the horizon and came over the hill, more wrecked cars stretched on to another horizon. We raced along choking dusty roads that followed a rough grid plan. The junkyard had a reassuring smell of rubber, oil, and sun-heated metal.

Davey stopped the truck and we all piled out. I felt like I was stepping out of a lunar module, the environment was so exciting. It felt like a place you wanted to explore. Cosmo got out and he had a big smile pasted on his face. I felt the same way. Davey jumped up on the hood of a dusty old truck and started peeling away the rubber stripping from the windshield using a utility knife.

"Can we walk around here?" Cosmo asked Davey.

"Yeah," Davey said. He didn't look up from his work.

"Don't disappear," I said to Cosmo. But Cosmo immediately disappeared down a narrow alley piled high with wrecks on either side. I stayed close by Davey because my place was with the truck. Davey just kept cutting the weatherstripping from the windshield of the '70 Dodge.

A crow flew by and landed on one of the small trees. The sun was almost directly overhead. There wasn't much of my shadow to be seen, it fell straight down at my feet on the dusty road. Davey got most of the upper stripping off and was working on the driver's side. I heard Cosmo opening and closing a car door somewhere over there. The distant horn of an eighteen-wheeler sounded on the highway. The sun was beating down on the metal roofs and hoods and trunks. Another car door opened, its rusty hinge chirping for a moment before it was closed. I caught the welcome scent of vinyl upholstery, coming from a car that had been sitting in the sun with rolled up windows. I moved to the wreck of an old Datsun opposite the wreck that Davey was working on, and sat down on its hood. The metal was blazing hot but I didn't move. The heat seared my butt and my calves and the backs of my thighs especially. But in a moment I was used to it.

The electrical wires of a transformer somewhere began to buzz and this buzzing went on and on and on and then died. I found out later that this sound wasn't from electrical wires at all, but from an insect named a cicada. Believe it or not, this insect lives in the ground for about fifteen years and then comes out just before it dies to sing this song that sounds like an overheated electrical transformer. This electrical sound was right at home in the junkyard. It kept starting and dying, starting and dying.

I liked everything about the junkyard. The cars, the tires, the glass and metal, the rusting wheel rims and engine blocks, the broken exhaust pipes, the trunks that wouldn't stay latched, and the car doors that wouldn't stay closed, the springs coming up through foam seats, the chrome knobs of broken radios, the bent antennas, and caved-in roofs that still held some of the last rain, the narrow paths between the junked cars, the missing rear-view mirrors, and broken side-views, and the hulking wrecks without wheels now up on blocks—all of it was good. Good, too, was the paint that peeled in every colour of the rainbow, the cool grey metal beneath the paint and the rust beneath the grey. The yard was a profusion of colour and smell and sensation. I enjoyed looking around at the great variety of geometric shapes, the circles of headlights, the triangles of back windows, the oblongs of rear signal lights. I felt relaxed in the junkyard. I felt like I belonged. I was in my place with the heat of the day upon me and the press of the sun fast upon my shoulder. Davey was flashing the utility blade with ease, sitting on his haunches, his back hunched over the windshield and his shadow falling through the glass and into the cab of the truck. I felt that something had burst in my brain and everything I looked at or thought of seemed good. It was like I had lost all judgment and all reason. Then, for a second, I thought I had a feeling of motion sickness in my stomach, but it passed.

The gleam off a chrome windshield frame struck my eye and splintered into diamonds that bore into my mind. I closed my eyes. It was just great that we were all here together and not somewhere else where we would be apart. I wanted to make time freeze so nothing would ever change.

21

I GOT A LETTER FROM ROSEMARY HAWTHORN. SHE WAS fine. How was I? She told me what the weather had been like in Inverness since she'd been there and that she had been out on a lobster boat. The ocean was kind of cold, but she still liked going for a swim, she said. She had been up to Lake Ainslie, and the water there was warmer. She signed the letter, xoxo, Rosemary. Heather called it a love letter.

"It's not a love letter," I said.

"Yes, it is," Heather said. "X's mean kisses and O's mean hugs."

"No, they don't."

Heather thought this was funny.

"She *likes* you, Michael!"

"No, she doesn't."

"Yes, she does."

"How do you know?"

"Because it's obvious."

"Not to me it isn't. She's *your* friend."

"She's not my friend," Heather laughed.

"Yes, she is. She visits you."

I thought that maybe this was what younger girls do, apprentice to older girls.

"Michael, my brother, she visits me to see *you*," Heather explained.

"No, she doesn't."

"She didn't write me a letter," Heather pointed out. "Why is she visiting me, Michael? We're not friends. I think she's a fine girl and I like her, but we're not *friends*. She's in grade eight and I'm in grade nine. There's no reason why she should visit me out of the blue. We only have one thing in common. She's visiting me because I'm your sister."

"No," I said.

This denial only made Heather laugh harder. I didn't believe Heather because her theory involved a great deal of deliberate planning on Rosemary's part. She would have to have planned the whole thing out in her head and then come over here on a false premise. It didn't make sense. I just couldn't see Rosemary Hawthorn doing anything like that. She was too honest. People who think girls can do such things don't respect girls very much. And here was the weird thing: girls were the ones who thought other girls capable of this sort of thing. I couldn't figure it out.

"Why would I tell you that if it wasn't true?" Heather asked.

"I don't know."

"Think about it."

"I don't know. Maybe you're trying to trick me."

Heather thought this was hilarious for some reason.

"I'm trying to trick you? *I'm* trying to trick you?"

"I don't know why about anything," I finally said. "I don't know and I don't care. Rosemary Hawthorn can do anything she wants, I don't give a damn."

"My little, innocent, girl-dumb brother," Heather said.

THE OFFICES OF THE MEMBER OF PARLIAMENT THAT my mother worked for were on the second floor of the Eighteen-Storey Building. This was the tallest building and the only high-rise on Cape Breton Island. It had a different proper name, but we called it the Eighteen-Storey Building. I only went up to my mother's new office once. It was on a weekend and she had to pick up some papers. I liked looking at Sydney Harbour out her office window. She had a great view. Afterwards, we drove out Kings Road and crossed the Sydney River Bridge and drove along the shore of Sydney Harbour on the Westmount side until we came to the Point Edward industrial park. Her MP boss had wanted her to be an official witness for some aspect of Devco's Scottish sheep importation to Cape Breton, planned for the end of the summer.

From Westmount, we could look across the harbour and see the skyline of Sydney. The industrial park was almost directly across the harbour from Muggah's Creek. Instead of going right down to the pier, where a large ship was docked, we made a few right turns until we drove from bright sunlight into the darkness of a warehouse. There, five or six men and one woman, all wearing overalls, were looking at about two dozen penned sheep. The pen was made of big, hollow, steel tubes and the paved floor of the warehouse was scattered with straw and hay. I had never seen a sheep before.

"Mrs. Chisholm?" one man asked my mother. He was tall, grey-haired, and had red, runny eyes. "We were afraid you weren't coming." The man spoke with an English accent. He was the chief veterinarian.

"I had to go back to the office," my mother said. "This is Michael, my son."

The shepherds drove out various sheep and re-penned them. The sheep baaahed and bleated and dumped out little deposits of black pellets every time they were touched. Although they were of two different breeds, all of the sheep were white-faced and bald-headed. None had wool on their heads or noses.

"This is a North Country Cheviot," the veterinarian said. He pointed to another. "And that's a Hexham Leicester. There won't be many of those coming over, I'm afraid. No Blackface. No Dorsets. Almost all Cheviots, actually."

I picked up some hay and offered it to the Leicester sheep that was just standing by the side of the pen. The sheep didn't want it.

"She's ill," the veterinarian said, straddling the sheep and bringing its head close to the fence. He asked Gloria to read the sheep's ear tags and confirm that they were the same numbers as the tattoos inside the sheep's ear. After she did that, he said, "Will you go for a walk and come back in ten minutes? Ten or twelve minutes? Fifteen minutes would be absolutely splendid."

Gloria and I walked down toward the harbour where the bulk carrier, the *Cape Breton Miner,* was docked. I wanted to walk right down to her but Gloria said we didn't have time, and besides she had left her jacket in the car and she was cold. Across the harbour, I could almost see where Muggah's Creek entered the tar pond. That's a good long ways across, I thought. We walked back toward the sheep warehouse, but stopped in the doorway of another warehouse to have a cigarette. Gloria opened a package of cigarettes. She offered me one and I accepted. Her cigarettes were such light cigarettes that you nearly went cross-eyed trying to draw on the stupid things. The wind was cold. We smoked hidden in the doorway of the warehouse. I noticed that I was now taller than my mother.

"So, those sheep are from Scotland?"

"Yes, isn't it exciting? Devco flew them in last week. And in September they'll fly in over three thousand!"

I couldn't get used to my mother's short hair.

"So Heather went up in an airplane with Miss Shaw."

"A single-prop plane," Gloria said. "Heather says it was the greatest fun."

"Why didn't Miss Shaw take the boys up in an airplane?"

"Well, maybe she will yet."

"Is Miss Shaw Rory's girlfriend?"

"Would it be so bad if she was?"

"Are you saying she is?"

"What do you think I'm saying?"

"I don't know. I'm just asking a question."

"All three of us have consented to this arrangement, Michael. Nobody is dumping anyone. Miss Shaw is a wonderful woman. I like her."

"Sid says she's interfering in our family and you're not doing anything to stop it."

"Don't listen to Sid. He has a lot of anger to work out. You have to clear your mind of jealousy and traditional notions about relationships. We have to get used to the idea of an alternate family structure based upon *positive* feelings toward individuals, not negative feelings. We always think we *own* someone or that somebody *belongs* to us. But we must open our minds and not be restricted by outdated conventions or what other people think. You mustn't have a closed mind, Michael."

"Sid says Miss Shaw uses you like a welcome mat, that she wipes her feet all over you."

"That's nonsense, utter nonsense. I *like* Miss Shaw, I really, really do. She's a sweet, sweet girl. Besides, in an open relationship, can one wipe their feet on another if all are consenting parties?"

I didn't have any idea of what my mother was talking about.

"I don't know," I said.

"They can't," she said firmly. "Remember, Michael, nobody can make you feel second-rate without your permission."

"Oh," I said.

We finished our cigarettes and returned to the warehouse, where Gloria had to confirm that the autopsied sheep was the same one she had seen alive. Its pink and blue guts were all over the floor of the warehouse. The smell of its intestines made me want to puke.

AT FIRST, RORY HAD SUPPORTED GLORIA'S NEW JOB. But he didn't like her promoting this sheep-importation business. They discussed it at the kitchen table after we returned from Point Edward. Their discussions were becoming less and less like discussions and more and more like arguments.

"Rory, it's my *job* to promote the sheep importation. I also happen to think it's a great idea."

"How great is it, Gloria? In what way is it great? Tell me."

"It's a great publicity event for Cape Breton, Rory. No one has ever flown thousands of sheep across the Atlantic Ocean. This is an historic event. It's a first and it's happening here. You might point that out to your union cronies."

"I don't care if these bloody sheep are *swimming* across the ocean. Do you know the circumstances of how Scottish Highlanders came to be Cape Bretoners, Gloria?"

"Yes, I know the circumstances of how we got here! Everyone on this island is not as ignorant as you think they are, Rory."

"I don't think everyone is ignorant. But you tell me you know about the Highland Clearances."

"Yes, I know about the Clearances! Yes, yes, I know about all that!"

"And you know that we were cleared from the Highlands in order to make way for sheep?"

"Yes, yes! So what? So what? *So what!* Who doesn't know about all that? You talk about it as if it happened yesterday."

"It did happen yesterday, Gloria. And that makes it historic. I know you value history."

"I value history when it doesn't make fools out of people because they can't forget."

"People will only become fools if they don't remember."

"Rory, the government is *trying* to do something for Cape Breton. In this case, to improve these bloodlines—"

"Have you ever heard of artificial insemination, Gloria?"

"—and all you can do is cut the whole project off at the ankles—"

"Why doesn't Devco just have the semen shipped over instead of the whole animal?"

"Why? Why? I don't know why! I'm not a farmer, for heaven's sake!"

"I know you're not a farmer, Gloria. But you might ask a farmer what's reasonable and what's practical while you're taking part in this publicity stunt with those Limey bureaucrats—"

"This is about your prejudice against the English!—"

"—who have nothing better to do than dream up idle schemes to waste tax dollars—"

"—I might have known!—"

"—on fantasies of British sheep imports to Cape Breton. Not only is it a waste of money, it's an insult to every Highlander on Cape Breton, or in the Maritimes, or on the entire continent, for that matter."

"I'm not insulted," Gloria said firmly. "I am in no way insulted."

"How dumb can the Scottish Highlander be? We'll show you how dumb! Clear them from their lands and replace them with sheep. Wait a hundred years and then fly the sheep to Cape Breton where the dumb bastards will receive them like visiting dignitaries! Where the wife of a Highlander will praise the Englishmen at Devco for their concern for animal welfare during transportation! Gloria, they're treating those precious sheep far better than they treated our own grandfathers who came over here on death ships!—"

"—You are so in*sulting*—"

"—but you with your tomming to the Limeys wouldn't understand that, because history is only 'all that' to you."

"You're just jealous because I have a newer car than Miss Shaw!"

22

SID WENT TO CAMP DURING THE LAST TWO WEEKS IN August. On the day he was leaving, I saw his packed duffle bag resting next to the radiator in the hall. He and Alex would be leaving with the rest of the corps for Cornwallis base in the Annapolis Valley, on a chartered bus, right after lunch. Heather was cleaning the kitchen when I came in.

"Where's Sid?"

"Do you know where the clothesline poles are? We had two clothesline poles in the backyard and now I can't even find one. This place is starting to drive me crazy!" Heather said.

"Where's Sid?" I asked again.

"Next door," Heather snapped. The kitchen smelled like bleach.

"What are you doing?"

"The people who live in this house are slobs! That's what I'm doing!"

I didn't blame Heather for being so angry. After Irene quit, my mother was away from the house as much as my father had been. The house looked spic and span for a while. But then you started noticing that the kitchen was always dirty. There was green algae growing around the kitchen sink. The kitchen table was never clear of dirty plates or bowls. Congealed milk rings marked the table. On the counter, blobs of mayonnaise hardened over where someone had made a sandwich. If you pushed a cigarette into the mayonnaise blob, you could tell that it was still wet under the crust because the tip of the cigarette sizzled. Uneaten macaroni hardened into the corners of pots that were forgotten on the back burners of the stove. We spooned the cats' canned food directly onto the enamelled top of the used dishwasher that Gloria's mother had given us. The dishwasher top was now covered with a hard paste from the buildup of uneaten food, and the whole mess stunk like rotting fish. And you didn't want to open up the dishwasher at all because it reeked of sour milk. You didn't want to open the back porch door because the kitty litter absolutely stank. Mopping the floor was impossible because it had to be swept first and it was useless to sweep it because it would just get dirty again. I was glad Heather was cleaning the house but I didn't want to be anywhere near her when she was doing it. She was very angry about the entire arrangement. I only knew that I wasn't cleaning it.

I hopped the little fence that led to the Carsons' driveway and I went into the back porch of their house. There was a lawn mower in the back porch and it made everything smell of fresh-cut grass. All sorts of rakes and shovels were hanging up on the back porch wall. Empty bottles were all neatly arranged on shelves. I knocked on the inside porch door and heard Tim hollering for me to come in. I walked in. Sid and Tim were sitting at the kitchen table.

"Hallo, Michael, and welcome," Tim said.

"Hi, Tim."

"Big Sid is going on his trip today, Michael," Tim said. "Right off the island."

"I know," I said.

"Tim is going to give me a drive to the bus stop," Sid said.

"Come on in, Michael. Take a load off, son, take a load off. You make me nervous standing there like you have a summons to deliver." Tim indicated an empty chair at the table.

The kitchen walls and the cabinets were painted a nice

light yellow and the floor had butterflies in the centre of each tile. There were little special shelves that fit right into the corners of the walls. Tiny porcelain dolls were on one shelf and some letters and papers on another. A fancy battery clock with big gothic numbers on its face was on a shelf by itself. There was a little framed saying over the kitchen sink that said "God Bless This House." Over the door there was a crucifix. But you didn't see the crucifix until you sat down facing the door or until you were leaving the house. Irene kept everything in the house spotless.

"Did you go for your test, Tim?"

"The bastards really got me this time, Michael," Tim said.

"What bastards?"

"Doctors," Sid told me.

"What did the doctors tell you, Tim?"

"Sons of bitches," Tim said bitterly. "They told me my guts were in shreds, that I got holes and pieces missing and I don't know what else."

"That's from that test you had to drink?"

"Barium test," Sid said.

"They will be burying me, too, boys. They might as well bury me, Jesus H. Christ." Tim crossed himself after he said the Lord's name.

"Do you have to have an operation or something?"

"I'd take an operation if they told me I had to have one. But they say there's nothing they can do with an operation, Michael. They say that there's only one thing that can be done and that's to change my diet."

"Your diet? What do you mean?"

"Look at this," Tim said. He pushed a tall glass of what looked like milk toward me. It had a little place on one side where someone had drunk from it, and some lumps were streaming down from the spot. "Have a drink of that."

"What is it?"

"I just took a drink," Sid said. He was about as gloomy as Tim.

The milk in the glass smelled funny. I took a little drink and nearly gagged. This brought Tim's spirits up a little.

"What *is* that?" I sputtered.

"Buttermilk," Sid reported.

"Buttermilk? You have to drink buttermilk because of your guts?"

"I'm afraid so, boys. They want me to eat salads and fruits and I don't know what goddamn else. Flowers, I expect. All pussy food, boys. No more spaghetti and meatballs or hamburgers on my plate. No more meat and potatoes for poor old Tim. No more beernuts or chips or breaded smelts. They don't even want me eating white bread, boys. Fruits and salads. You heard right! Fruits and salads! Lord love a duck, boys!"

I was stunned. It was like Tim got hit with lightning or something.

I didn't know what I'd do if I couldn't eat peanut butter. When I was hungry, I especially liked eating salted soda cracker sandwiches, pasting one cracker with crunchy peanut butter and the other cracker with butter. I could go through an entire row of soda crackers for supper. It was a lot easier than trying to cook something. I'd wash the crackers down with my favourite milk drink that I was starting to drink all the time. It was a tall glass of milk with brown sugar mixed in. I'd just take two heaping tablespoons of brown sugar and mix it in with the milk. This turned the milk a rich brown. Most of the sugar came to rest at the bottom of the glass no matter how many times you stirred it. After I drank the milk, I'd scoop the brown sugar out of the glass with a spoon. Sometimes, I'd stir the milk and drink the whole thing down the hatch with the sugar still turning in the glass.

"What are you going to do, Tim?" Sid asked.

"Can't do anything, boys. Can't do a goddamn thing but eat what they put in me lunch pail. Sons of bitches."

"You're going to starve to death!" I said.

I thought he would, too. If you couldn't eat potatoes and pork chops or gravy and white bread or crackers, what would you eat to stay alive? Tim couldn't even eat Irish stew.

"Irene's the one who's going crazy, boys. She doesn't know what in hell to make for supper. And I don't know, either. I can't even eat fried chicken, for the love of Mike!"

"No!"

"It's true, boys. They call it a diet but I think it's some kind of goddamn torture."

We all sat looking down at the checkered tablecloth under its transparent plastic cover. Tim drew a cigarette out of its package.

"You want a cigarette, Michael?"

"I got one," I said.

"If you're old enough to smoke I guess you can do anything. You're allowed to smoke in the house, too? I guess I brought up all me brats wrong in that case, eh, Sid?"

Sid and Tim exchanged looks.

"Doctors still let you smoke?" I asked. I took my own cigarettes out of my denim jacket and lit one. I didn't want to offend Sid, who leaned back from the table, but I wanted to smoke with Tim.

"Oh, they want me to stop smoking, too. I forgot to tell you that, Sid. Yeah, they want me to stop smoking. 'Give them up if you can, Mr. Carson,' the doctor said. 'Make an effort for your own good and the good of others,' he said. I told him, 'Doctor, I don't see that happening any time soon.' Son of a bitch. What's it to him? He's not the one who has to give up eating for Jaysus sakes!"

"What about having a beer, Tim? Are you still allowed to have a beer?"

"Now that's one bright spot, Sid. Here they are telling me I can't have this and I can't have that but they turn around and tell me that I can have a beer every now and then and that I can still smoke if I can't do without them. It's better to give up everything, according to those pill-rollers. But they left me with my beer and I'm grateful for that, boys."

"They can't expect you to give up everything, Tim."

"Didn't ol' Tim go and ask the doctor whether he wanted me to give up the pussy on the weekends, too."

"You didn't," Sid said.

"Oh, I did, boys, I did."

"What did the doctor say to that?"

"Looked like he had a rod up his arse. I must've offended his delicate sensibilities. To look at him, you'd think that *he* was the one whose guts were shredded. But maybe he doesn't like pussy, boys. I wonder what *he* does on bean-and-tail night."

We started to laugh but Tim winked and shushed us up because Irene had come into the kitchen.

"Hi, Irene."

"Hi Sid and Michael. How are you both?"

Irene looked at my cigarette in the ashtray. I nubbed it out and put the butt back into my package.

"Tim was just telling us about his barium test," Sid told Irene.

"Isn't it terrible? But I guess it could have been worse. It wasn't the c-word, anyway."

"Yes, boys, it wasn't the c-word," Tim said. "Irene, what is the c-word? Is that a four letter word? The c-word?"

Irene gave Tim a quick smack on the shoulder.

Tim winked at us. He liked teasing Irene. She was very religious and very proper about observing religious things. She was always like that. I found out much later that she had quit being out housekeeper because she found out what Rory and Miss Shaw were doing. She was still friendly as anything, though. She always asked about us. And she always gave Heather advice about cooking and housekeeping. But she never went back in the house. Not one foot did she put back in our house. And she had practically raised us from scratch.

"How are you, Michael?"

"Fine, Irene."

"Are you eating enough?"

"Yes, I think so."

"Do you want a sandwich?"

"No, thank you."

"Sid?"

"No, Irene, thanks," Sid said.

"Did Tim offer you a cup of tea?"

"Oh course I offered them a cup of tea! Boys, do you want a cup of tea? It's right on the stove if you want it. Help yourselves. You know where the cups are and where the milk is in the fridge. Don't be shy, your mother wasn't."

Irene clucked disapprovingly at Tim's comparison as she left the kitchen.

I got up, found a cup, and tried to pour tea from the glass teapot on the stove. I couldn't see any tea in the pot itself because it seemed to be filled with tea bags.

"Tim, do you mind if I take out some of these tea bags?"

"I've been throwing them bags into that pot since this morning," Tim said. "It should be good and strong. Here," he said, holding a saucer, "fish them out with a spoon and put them on this."

I scooped out a few tea bags, enough to allow the tea to pour properly, and plopped them on Tim's saucer. He returned the saucer to the table in front of Sid. I filled my cup. The tea smelled very strong.

"You want a cup, Sid?"

"No, thanks," Sid said.

"Tim?"

"No," Tim said.

I put the cup of tea at my place at the table and went to the fridge, which was in the pantry, to get the milk. I brought the milk into the kitchen, splashed a bit of milk in my cup, and returned the milk to the pantry. I was about to sit down and enjoy my cup of tea when I happened to look at Sid and noticed an almost imperceptible smirk on his face—and a salt shaker in his hand. I looked at my tea. Without tasting a drop, I took the cup over to the sink and emptied the cup in the sink.

"What are you doing?" Sid asked.

"You know what," I answered.

"Don't waste a cup of tea," he said.

I repeated the steps of getting a fresh cup of tea, but this time I took my cup of tea with me to the refrigerator in the pantry, instead of leaving it on the table. I came back and Sid had a huge smile on his face. Tim, too, was smiling.

"You got to watch out for this guy," I said to Tim.

"I know, Michael, he's full of tricks," Tim said.

"He can salt your cup in a split second," I told Tim.

"He's a devil, all right," Tim said. "But you figured him out in time."

"I didn't put salt in your tea," Sid said. "I swear to God."

"Sure, you didn't," I said. I put the new cup of tea back before my place at the table and took my seat.

Sid leaned forward, studying my face.

Tim cocked an eye in my direction.

I felt a warm, wet sensation as the wet tea bags soaked through the seat of my jeans. I looked at Sid, who was now grinning, waiting for me to acknowledge his supremacy.

"Good one," I said, as I stood and removed the wet tea bags from the seat of my pants.

Sid almost laughed his head off. Tim was laughing. I was laughing, too. It was a good one. Tim slid the glass of buttermilk across the table.

"Here, Mikey," he said. "You'll be wanting some milk with your tea."

This caused Sid and Tim to laugh more. I had to laugh with them. It was a good one.

"Sid's one tricky son of a gun," Tim said, enjoying the trick.

Irene came back into the kitchen. She didn't think Sid's trick was very funny at all. She made that clucking sound again and gave me a dry cloth to sit on to absorb some of the moisture. "I'm going to Dottie's," Irene said. "Your dish is in the fridge, Tim. Eat it all with your cottage

cheese. Dottie said she had some recipes for me. Her husband had a heart attack, you know."
"Did he?" Tim said full of sarcasm. "Poor man, poor, poor man."
With Tim you just wanted to burst out laughing all the time.
Irene put her jacket on and tied a kerchief on her head. She gave Tim a little peck on the cheek and he brought his hand up under her jacket and goosed her.
"Tim! For heaven's sake!"
"That's all right, Irene! It's nothing the boys themselves won't be doing soon enough! Probably doing it already, I'd bet. But a woman like Irene's a handful, boys. Best get yourself less of a woman, if you want my advice."
Irene turned completely red from the neck up.
"*Tim!*" she said.
Sid and I laughed even more at Irene's embarrassment. I think I laughed so much at Irene's embarrassment because I was still laughing at my own embarrassment from sitting on wet tea bags.
"She's still got that stuff and that's all that matters, eh, boys? Isn't that what they call it? Stuff? You're all the stuff I need Irene, dear. You're my soul's desire."
"You're supposed to drink ten full ounces of buttermilk with your fruit, Tim. Don't forget. Make sure he does it, boys."
"We will, Irene," Sid promised. Irene left the house and Tim watched her go. I relit my cigarette. Tim turned to us and raised his glass in a heartfelt toast and then downed the buttermilk in a gulp. "Boys," he said, "pussy's the most powerful thing in the world."

23

A COUPLE OF VERY SIGNIFICANT THINGS HAPPENED while Sid was away at Sea Cadet camp. For one, the south tar pond caught fire one day. The fire chief thought that someone, a steelworker, had thrown a lit cigarette out the car window and this had started the blaze. It had been low tide and a lot of the bottom of the south pond had been exposed. Three pumpers poured water on the fire, but they couldn't put it out. Some kind of special foam was then sprayed on the flames, but there wasn't nearly enough of it, and the foam couldn't reach the fire that was farther out in the pond. Vehicles couldn't be driven too near the tar pond shore because they would sink in the tar. Big billows of black smoke curled up from the tar pond and drifted over the city. The fire chief was alarmed that both ponds, north and south, would ignite and all hell would break loose. High tide finally put the fire out. Everyone went away and forgot about the tar ponds, except the alderman of our ward.

Mr. MacDonald was down our house the next Saturday. I saw the big Lincoln pulled up in front of our house like an ocean liner at a pier in New York. He and Rory were talking in the kitchen. There was a bottle of Scotch alcohol on the table and the room was blue with smoke. I stayed around the kitchen while they were talking. I wanted to ask Mr. MacDonald if I could sit in his car.

"You know yourself, Rory, that that son-of-a-bitch mayor isn't going to do a goddamn thing about cleaning up that mess."

My father raised his eyes at Mr. MacDonald and looked at me.

Mr. MacDonald looked at me and said, "You know what a son of a bitch is, don't you Sonny?"

"I sure do!" I said.

"What can the mayor do, Neil?"

"What can he do? Jaysus, Rory, he can bury the dirty soil, or he can truck the damn stuff away and dump it down a mine shaft, or he can dam up the jaysus ponds where they empty into the harbour and cap the entire thing with slag. God knows we've got enough of *that* crap. There's lots of things he can do, Rory, lots of things. Every time I bring the matter up in council that son-of-a-bitch mayor laughs it off. He lives in Boulderwood, for Chrissake! I live in the north end and I see the goddamn tar ponds every time I step outside my front door!"

"Move to Boulderwood, Neil. You can afford it."

"You sound like the mayor now, Rory. He says if the delinquents in Ward One don't want to go to bed hungry they'll have to bite the nail and steal more food. That son of a bitch."

"Neil, what are you saying? That we should stop steelmaking because of a little pollution?"

"Bollocks, Rory, you know I'm not saying that! I've been at that goddamn plant for thirty years and I know what it takes to make steel. But I'm not saying I like staring at the arsehole of industrial Nova Scotia every time I look out my window, either!"

"No smoke, no baloney, Neil."

"Don't give me that we-have-to-put-up-with-it-if-we-want-to-eat argument, Rory! I heard all that bullshit before. It used to be that anyone who wasn't in the war wasn't a man. And anyone who didn't get his brow dirty wasn't a man. Now it's starting to be that anyone who's not on unemployment insurance isn't a man, because, God help them, Rory, that's where all the men are these days. On top of that, now you're telling me we have to eat crap to be men? I don't think so, Bye. I don't think so."

Mr. MacDonald himself had been in the Second World War. I remember he and my father had a conversation about that. My father said he felt guilty for being too young to fight. Mr. MacDonald said that he felt guilty for surviving the war when so many of his friends had died. "We all have to swallow things we don't like, Neil."

"But we don't have to say it tastes good, Rory."

"Look at it this way, Neil, a pick-and-shovel job, by description, is going to be a dirty job. There's no way around it."

"You're telling me? I'm the bastard who works the pick-and-shovel job, Rory. You're not bloody-well qualified to talk about a pick-and-shovel job. Jaysus, *you're* the one who should be living in Boulderwood if anyone should! You're not working class!"

"The *hell* you say—"

"—and we don't need any highfalutin advice saying how lucky we are to live with crap shoved down our throats."

"I've always defended the working man, Neil—"

"Who can't understand a bloody word you're saying—"

"—I esteem him, I admire him. I admire the strength it takes to survive in a world where nothing is given him. Nobody's handed him any privileges. Nobody's had a trust fund waiting for him on his twenty-first birthday. By his own wits he's had to figure it out and by his own mettle he's stood the gaff. Now, what the hell's the matter with recognizing that sort of courage and fortitude?"

"Just the same way you organized the union."

"You're damn right it is."

"By the Jeeze, Rory, if I could give my kids a trust, I would in a second. If I could give them a nice home away from this stink hole, I would. Any man in my district would, if he could."

"I don't know if I would, Neil."

"You're full of it, Bye. You're telling me that if you won the lottery tomorrow, you'd stay right here, living by the steel plant, breathing that orange smoke? You'd be packed up like Judd Clampett, Rory. You'd be the first one outta here, don't shit me. You're full of it, Bye. Isn't your father full of it, Sonny?"

Mr. MacDonald looked at me and grinned and I grinned back. But my father was very serious.

"I don't know if I would."

"Ah, you're full of it! The north end is no privileged place, Rory. It's all right by itself. I've lived here all my life and I like it well enough. But I can think of better places to live. The north end isn't any better a place because it's next to the steel plant or the tar pond. The only special thing about the north end is the people. And that's the goddamn truth. The best people in the world live here. But they'd be just as nice if they were living anywhere else."

"Neil, for cryin' out loud, that's the entire point of the north end! That's the whole point of Sydney, of Cape Breton. If we were anywhere else, we wouldn't *be* north-enders or Cape Bretoners. Our neighbourhood makes us who we are, it gives us our character. The people in your district are the best people in the world *because* they live here! If we lived anywhere else, we'd be just like the rest of them—ordinary mainlanders."

"What's wrong with you, boy? You talk about Cape Bretoners being a big family, and how family has to look out for each other, and you get all upset over some English sheep coming here on a jaysus airplane instead of being upset that our children grow up playing in filth left behind by the likes of Dosco and Hawker-Siddeley—imperial Brits, the last time I looked, Rory."

"You're going to beat that pollution drum until it breaks, Neil."

"That's why I'm on city council, Bye! I'm a professional drum-beater!"

Mr. MacDonald laughed and took another drink from his glass. Rory took another drink and lit another cigarette.

"Seriously, Rory, I was talking with a few other councillors and one of them says to me, 'Neil, bye, can you imagine saying what Rory's been saying lately?' And, jaysus Rory, I have to be level with you, I can't imagine it."

"You can't imagine saying it? Neil, can you imaging *doing* it? All I said was that federal civil servants should not be given hardship pay when they transfer to Sydney. Hardship pay! As if they were being sent to the Arctic, for cryin' out loud!"

"We're the poorest city in the country, Rory. Don't you think we all deserve hardship pay if we could get it? I don't begrudge them a penny of that hardship pay, not a penny."

"Now who's full of it, Neil?"

"You know what your problem is, Rory? You know what your problem is? You're too smart for the mines and you're too proud for college. And so you've found a place halfway in between. You use your brain to praise the work of the back. You're just like all those journalists who want it both ways. You want to be smart and respected without being beholden to any teacher, and you want to be a regular joe without getting your hands dirty."

"Walk with kings and keep the common touch," my father quoted.

"That's it, walk with kings. You can bet a worker didn't say that. No, sir. You can bet your life no worker ever said something like that. A jerk-off journalist said it."

Mr. MacDonald was right. Rudyard Kipling said that and he was a journalist.

"Give the man a Kewpie doll," Rory said.

"You goddamn idiots are all the same. You think you're untouchable because you sit in judgment without ever being judged yourselves. But, jaysus, Rory, you can be as dumb as a post sometimes, too stupid to know that you're just as vulnerable as all of us."

"In your own colloquial idiom, Neil, what is it you're trying to say?"

"I'm saying this, Rory. I'm saying this as a friend. The District Council is talking about imposing what they call a social reprimand against the little domestic arrangement you've got going here."

"Social reprimand? What the hell does that mean?"

"Jaysus, you're thick. It means, Rory, that as far as the membership goes—the membership, Rory, do you hear that? I'm bringing you a message from the *membership*—if you don't start practising the family virtue that you're preaching, you won't have a paycheque left to wipe your arse with."

"Michael, go outside and play in the traffic."

I never got to sit in his car and that was the last time our alderman visited the house.

24

SID MAILED A POSTCARD FROM CORNWALLIS BASE. THE picture showed a jet plane positioned on top of a pedestal. The caption said, "Cornwallis Military Base, Nova Scotia." He addressed the note to the Chisholm Clan at Meadow Street.

> *Hello Mum, Dad, Heather, Michael, Cosmo. I hope you are all well. I am fine. This is my first full day here. Alex is at another barracks. He joined the precision drill team. I'm learning gunnery, music, & sail. And I'm studying to be a boatswain. Before I leave I will have my swimming certification. If I go to camp next year they'll give me $75.00 dollars in training bonus. I have to go to parade. Your son and brother, Sid (petty officer, 2nd class) Chisholm.*

I don't know why I didn't send Sid a letter while he was away at camp. I wish I'd sent him at least one. I know he would have appreciated it. I could have taken a photograph of Rene and me on the raft so he could show the raft to his friends. I should have done that. But I didn't do it. I didn't send Rosemary Hawthorn a letter, either. But Sid was my brother. I wish like hell that he could have come home earlier. My days were all mixed up and even my dreams were bad, dreams all involving disaster.

Sid and I were on a small sailboat in the middle of a violent storm. Tons of water splashed over the deck as Sid tried to keep the keel even. He gave me an order to trim the sail and I was starting to do just that when I saw a reef dead ahead. It was only exposed for a moment before it was covered again by the sea. But I had seen it. I tried shouting to Sid at the wheel but he couldn't hear me above the storm. The boat suddenly lurched sideways as it struck the reef and both Sid and I were thrown into the dark churning water.

At that moment, I felt a hand on my shoulder. I woke up immediately. Heather whispered directly in my ear, "Come downstairs." And she silently withdrew from the room. I dropped from the top bunk and in the dark I put on my pants and a shirt and a pair of Cosmo's socks and made my way down the narrow third-floor staircase, feeling my way as I went. The bathroom light on the second floor blinded me, but I went in there first. And then I came down to the first floor where I could hear voices from the good room. I didn't know what time it was. It was late.

I opened the good-room door and the room was clouded with smoke. My father was sitting in the big yellow chair next to the bookcase, the same chair he had sat in when we had our family picture taken. He had a glass in his hand and a bottle was on the coffee table. Gloria was wrapped in her nightgown and was sipping a cup of coffee and smoking a cigarette. She looked tired. Heather was smoking a cigarette and drinking a coffee. She offered me a cigarette, but I didn't want one. I was still too shy to smoke in front of my father even though he had said it was all right. I sat in the big chair opposite Rory. Gloria and Heather sat on the chesterfield.

"And now we have a quorum, do we?" Rory said when I came in the room. "Michael, do you know what quorum means?"

"No," I said.

"You don't? Too bad, too bad. You should know what it means, little boy. I knew what it meant when I was your age."

"What does it mean?"

"Look it up, little boy! Don't depend on me to tell you! Look it up for yourself, like I did!"

Rory plucked a book out of the bookcase and flung it at me. I caught it with a lucky catch and pretended like it had been a polite toss. I looked at the book. It wasn't even a dictionary but a book on labour relations. I looked at Rory and he looked like he wanted to pound me.

"Keep your voice down, please," my mother said.

"What's going on?" I asked Heather. My father answered. His words were slurred.

"What's going on? The little boy would like to know what's going on. I'll tell you what's going on, little boy. We're having a little secret meeting to split up the family, that's what's going on. Your mummy and daddy are going to get a divorce, that's what's going on. Because your mummy has decided that we can't live as a family anymore, that's what's going on. Now you know what's going on."

I looked at Gloria and she was just staring at the blue glass ashtray. Heather looked at me with an unmoving face.

"I don't see why this can't be handled in a mature, responsible way," my mother said.

"Gloria, we tried your mature and responsible way before, remember? No jealousy can exist between mature, responsible people who want to love freely, remember?"

"That's perfectly true, Rory! Jealousy is a learned response. The Eskimos at the North Pole and the Siriono in South America have relationships unmarred by such a stunted, life-denying emotion as jealousy. I hate jealousy, I just *hate* it!"

"For such a loving person, Gloria, you're chock full with hate."

"You haven't been the loyal husband, Rory. Let's not pretend that you were."

"If you're not jealous, why do you want a divorce?"

"Because it's clear that Miss Shaw wants the divorce, Rory! Miss Shaw would like to have you all to herself, that's obvious. And it's just as obvious that you would like to be with her. She's a younger woman and maybe a man at your stage in life—"

"—Gloria that's bullshit!—"

"—needs to feel like he's still young—"

"—cockeyed psychobabble—"

"—and perhaps the urge was uncontrollable and I can understand that."

"You can understand that, can you, Gloria? That's news to me."

"You need to be with her, that's clear. You certainly haven't been here with me or your family."

"I've been working, Gloria. I've been at the union office day and night for fifteen years. It's been the union that has kept us fed all this time, in case you've forgotten."

"I'm not being judgmental at all. I'm only making an observation."

"That's all you're doing. Oh." Rory smiled so that his mouth looked disconnected from his sad eyes. "So, you're not jealous of her?"

"No, I'm not jealous, Rory. Miss Shaw is jealous of you spending time with me and your children."

"So, you're giving me to her? You're not going to make any sort of objection?"

"You're a mature adult. You can make your own decisions."

"Gloria my dear, my wife, my lawfully wedded wife, why don't you tell me you don't want this to happen? You've never once said it. Not once. Tell me right now, right now, tell me that you don't want this to happen and it won't happen. Tell me."

"I don't bark every time you snap your fingers."

"So you *do* want it to happen. I suspect you, Gloria. I suspect you. You're always trying to be the chief victim. When our kids flunk out of school, it helps you in your victimhood. When your husband is forced to go elsewhere than to his wife, you get sympathy. Pity me: delinquent kids, unfaithful husband, failed family. But you love it, don't you Gloria, you love it because you're a goddamn sob sister who's not happy unless she's whining about being victimized. I suspect you, Gloria. You've encouraged this thing all along."

"I don't know what you mean. You're drunk. And I resent your insinuations."

"You know what I mean, Gloria. Tell us, tell your children, do you want to continue as a family?"

"I am my own person."

"I know you are your own person, Gloria. God forbid that I should intrude upon your sacred personhood or upset your precious self-esteem, but you also have responsibilities as a wife and a mother. And I'm asking you, in your capacity as wife and mother, whether you want this thing to happen. Because if you don't want it to happen, it won't happen. I'm telling you it won't. Yes or no, Gloria, my dearly devoted wife."

"I am my own person."

"That's not an answer," my father said. He waited for another answer and looked unsteadily at my mother who had pulled her feet up underneath her as she stared at the blue ashtray.

"That's not an answer," my father repeated.

But that's the only answer my mother had.

I still hadn't figured out why Heather and I had been called to this discussion. I suppose it was our parents' way to practise democracy and be inclusive in the modern way.

"Who would you go with, Michael?"

"What?"

"That's an unfair question," my mother snapped.

"Do you mind? I'm asking my son a question. Who would you go with, Michael? Your mummy or your daddy?"

"I don't know. I haven't thought about it."

"I know who you'd go with, little boy. I know who you'd go with. You're full of shit just like her. Get out of my sight before I take notice of you."

Gloria said that kind of language was uncalled for. Rory said Gloria had absolutely no idea of what was called for. Gloria called Rory a bully. Rory called Gloria a flake. Gloria said Rory had always been too uptight for her and she was tired of being penned in by his conservatism. Rory said he was sick of correcting Gloria's fuzzy thinking and tolerating her moral degeneracy. Gloria called Rory abusive. Rory called Gloria perverted. The two of them were swinging away at each other, almost like each was daring the other to say the one unforgivable thing that would make the situation irreversible. I wanted to get out of the room before the roof collapsed.

I looked over at Heather. She was awake, but she had her head down and her eyes closed. She was curled up in one corner of the chesterfield with her feet under her, a cigarette still burning in her fingers.

After a silence, Rory said, "I'm sorry if I hurt you."

"You didn't hurt me," Gloria said.

"Gloria," my father said, "I'm sorry for hurting you."

"You didn't hurt me," my mother insisted.

Without another word, my father left the house. Gloria followed him out to the front step and offered to call him a taxi. He laughed at her concern and called her a hypocrite. My mother stood on the step for a moment before coming in. She locked the front door and turned the outside light off.

And that was the one and only discussion we had concerning the end of the family. As my father had noticed, there had been no protest, no outcry. His had been the only raised voice. Afterwards, he had staggered off into the night. Heather drifted back to her bed. Gloria shuffled to her room and closed the door. And I put one foot in front of the other and stumbled up the third-floor staircase to my top bunk. It was hardly what you'd call a Parade of Concern.

I THINK OUR MOTHER WENT OFF THE DEEP END AFTER Rory moved out. When I asked her what was for supper, she had a first-rate blow out.

"I don't know what's for supper! Make your own supper for a change! You can cook just as well as I can!"

"I don't know how to cook," I said. I wasn't complaining or anything. I was just stating a fact. But Gloria flipped her wig.

"You *can* cook! *Yes,* you know how! I can't do it, so you

do it! For heaven's sake! Take some responsibility for yourself! *And stop asking me about supper.*"

Gloria would come back from the health food store every third day and plunk a big loaf of multi-grain bread on the table. We attacked the loaf like a pack of rats. Breakfast was always oatmeal and if you could get a multi-grain sandwich at lunch and a plate of five-minute macaroni at supper, that was just fine. We could all make macaroni. We were experts at it. We started living on it. All you did was boil up a box of noodles and dump in a can of tuna and you had a tuna casserole. Simple. The problem was that nobody made enough for anybody else. When Heather cooked, she made enough for everybody, but she didn't cook every single day. And when she did cook, she said if anybody wanted to eat, they had to be in the house at five. She was as grumpy as hell about cooking and she put onions in everything.

I was never in the house at five, so I started making my own suppers. But the *mess* you had to clean up just to get a clean pot to cook in was starting to get to me. If it was bad after Irene left, it got twice as bad when Rory officially moved out. I smoked a lot of cigarettes and drank coffee. That way, I didn't have to eat as much or as often, which saved me a lot of grief with the dishes. If I didn't dirty them, I didn't have to clean them up. My solution was to bring a row of crackers and a jar of peanut butter down to the tar pond and eat lunch on the raft. I had to drink pop with the crackers because I couldn't think of a way to keep milk cold.

"Are you going to start sleeping here, too?" Rene asked.

"That's not a bad idea," I said.

25

THE BEST PLACE TO BE IN THE WORLD WAS ON THE RAFT. We had shelter if we needed it, we had a stove if we were cold, we could be mobile by simply casting off and poling to a new berth. And when you were alone on the raft, when you paddled out from the shore and looked back at the north end, you got a sense of safety knowing you were where no one could reach you without drowning.

With Sid and Alex at camp, and Rene at home working on his new idea of a flat-bottomed boat, there wasn't a whole lot going on at the tar pond. I spent most of my days there, anyway. I paddled out with a book and a package of cigarettes and read. It was great. Those late August days were the hottest days on the tar pond. The sun really brought up the smell of creosote. Railroad ties were all soaked in creosote. The abandoned dock built for the army hospital was made with creosote rail ties. But there were other smells, too.

Sometimes you could smell the good smell of gasoline, like the smell that fills the inside of a car at a service station on a hot summer day. And the smell of oil was a good, strong smell on the tar pond. After a heavy rain there was always a refreshing aroma in the air, a pleasant chemical odour like a bathroom spray or scented chlorine. On hot days, when the city was paving a street, the new asphalt, steamed and rolled, smelled a lot like the tar pond. Roofer's tar smelled like tar, all right. But the smell of roofing tar was very concentrated compared to the smell of the tar pond, which was a steady and not too overpowering sweet smell. Occasionally, the pond smelled as pungent as plastic wires overheating. But even that smell was nothing like the stink of garbage. The tar pond didn't smell anything like the city dump, which was a kind of putrid reek. And it was nothing like the stench of sewage. Occasionally, you'd catch the smell of diesel exhaust that drifted on the breeze like the scent of some heavy metal flower. I don't think there's anyone who doesn't like the smell of diesel exhaust.

And here was a weird thing. Thirty sewer outfalls emptied into the tar pond, but even when you stood right on top of the pipe at the corner of the Ferry Street causeway, even when you sat down on the pipe and let your legs dangle above the gushing water, the sewer smell didn't reach you. If anything, the water smelled sort of fresh. In fact, the only way you would know the pipe carried sewage was by the reams of toilet paper streaming out of it. The paper got stuck on wires and rebar and fluttered like tinsel on a Christmas tree. And this sewer water, so much of it gushing out of this pipe, completely disappeared into the tar pond. Nothing floated, no paper, no turds, no nothing. Truthfully, I never saw any turds at all. They must have been completely destroyed on the way down the pipe. When you think of it, although they're called solids, in truth they aren't very solid at all. And even if one survived being flushed, it still wouldn't float in the tar pond. It just vanished. If you wanted to see the sewer at the outfall, you had to go right to the pipe, otherwise you wouldn't have known there was any sewage in the tar pond to speak of.

I started going to the sewer outfall every day during that last week. I smoked cigarettes and listened to the pleasant music the water made as it spilled out of the pipe and into the black pond. It was the same sound as the cold-water brook running over mossy stones at the Old Place—very peaceful when you closed your eyes. It could even be peaceful with your eyes open. Listening to the sound of water spilling out of a pipe, and watching it course by rusty old wires and empty buckets and half-submerged rubber tires was very relaxing and restorative. The entire estuary was placid and quiet and still. The tar pond was like one of those Japanese rock gardens where people go to meditate if they are tired. I don't know why more steel-plant workers coming off shift didn't pull their cars over on the Ferry Street causeway and take a few minutes to contemplate the tar ponds. Like them, the ponds expressed deep physical exhaustion after many years' work.

Most days I stayed on the raft reading my Hardy Boys books. Rene usually made all the fires in the raft's stove because he was good at building them. He was careful and picky about what sticks of wood he'd put in. On one particular day, Rene was not on the pond, and I had collected a considerable pile of firewood from the steel plant shoreline along the foot of Slag Mountain. The shoreline was not gradual like a beach. It plunged straight down into the water. So I collected driftwood without ever leaving the kayak. I just came parallel to the shore and picked up the driftwood that was hanging on the rocks, left there by high tide. Some of the wood was punky, and some was wet and hard to burn. But we had a container of kerosene. Kerosene was cheaper than gas and started fires just as well. I had brought a cooking pot from home, a can of pea soup, a can opener and a spoon.

I filled our forty-five gallon oil-drum stove with driftwood and a wedge of shattered plywood that had red paint on one side. I turned the big kerosene jug into the stove and heard the kerosene gurgle out over the wood. I stopped when I figured the wood was good and soaked. I had only one match, which was very unusual for me because I accumulated books of matches left, right, and centre. (Louie V sold "Success Without College" matches. The booklet had a long list of careers a person could succeed in by contacting the Success Without College Institute.) I lit my one match and then I lit a cigarette, and then I lit the empty matchbook, making sure it caught. Crouching down in front of the open door of the stove, I threw in the burning match.

Nothing happened.

I figured the kerosene had probably put the match out. But I had the burning matchbook as a fail-safe. I let the fire catch by holding the booklet upside down. When it started to burn my fingers, I tossed the booklet into the stove.

An orange flame came roaring out of the hole that we had cut in the forty-five gallon drum. My legs sprung me backwards as my head was encircled by fire. The blast blew me straight out the door of the raft and onto the deck. I lay flat on my back next to the mast. My arms and legs trembled as if I was having a fit. My eyes were locked shut. I had gone deaf. The smell of burnt hair made me feel sick. That was enough of that.

"WHAT ARE YOU BUYING THIS TIME, SONNY? A LEISURE Log?"

"Yes, sir."

"I suppose you're going to put that in your stove?"

"Uh-huh."

"I figured. Here's your change. You'll be wanting your hardware-store money."

"Yes, sir. Thank you."

"Oh, no, son. Thank *you*."

"You're welcome."

RENE AND I LAUNCHED THE FLAT-BOTTOMED BOAT THE day before Sid and Alex got back from Sea Cadet camp. Rene had built the boat in his father's garage. It was simply a small box, like a small square barge, but it floated. The problem was that it would spin almost completely around when you paddled it—the problem of no keel again. We splashed the boat into the tar pond from the CN shore. I followed Rene in the kayak and laughed every time he tried to paddle the boat in a straight line. Rene finally had to throw me the yellow nylon tow rope and I tied it to the back strut of the kayak. Rene paddled on the port side, I paddled on the starboard. By this method we finally got out to the raft. The boat had to be hauled up on the barge and emptied of the black water that had sloshed around Rene's ankles.

"It needs more caulking," I said.

"No, I'm going to put fibreglass over it," Rene said.

"Caulking would work just as well," I said. Since I had done the caulking on the raft's cabin, I had some right to give my opinion.

"Fibreglass would be better," Rene quietly insisted.

"What's that sound?" I asked. Rene paused and listened.

"Boat," he said.

Slag Mountain caught the sound of the boat and funnelled it into the north pond where it resounded. Soon we could see the boat rounding Battery Point. It was a Zodiac, the kind of pontoon boat that Jacques Cousteau used. I had never seen any sort of boat in the tar pond other than the raft and our kayak. One day, two guys in a canoe paddled in, but they paddled out pretty quickly when they saw their precious Chestnut canoe getting stained.

Rene and I stood out on the raft and watched the Zodiac come slowly into the pond. Two people were in the boat. One of them spotted us and raised his arm, pointing to us. The man who sat in back with the outboard motor turned the boat toward us and gave it a little gas. You could tell they didn't know the pond very well because they advanced very cautiously, as if they were afraid of hanging up on a rock. The Zodiac came right alongside the raft and brought a big wake with it. But the wake washed below our feet as Rene and I stood on the raised deck of the raft.

The two men looked very official in identical light grey windbreakers. They were not police. They were smiling, both of them, and police wouldn't have smiled. And they greeted us before we greeted them. They were not police. The large man in the back controlling the outboard motor had a black beard and wore a baseball cap with the initials DFO written on the peak. The man in front had red hair and was much thinner than his companion. He didn't have a cap. They behaved like explorers who were just making contact with members of a lost race. They were scientists.

"Hello," the man at the outboard shouted.

Rene didn't say anything.

"Ship ahoy!" I shouted back.

The man in front smiled and looked at the man in the back. What a fine boat it was. It was as long as the raft and almost like a catamaran, two-hulled with seats slung between the pontoons. The outboard motor was a big

Evinrude 500. It made a wet, spitting sound as it idled. We'd have to have four barrels on the raft if we had a heavy motor like that on the back.

"You boys look as if you know these waters," the man in the front of the Zodiac said.

"We sure do," I said. "We know everything about these waters."

"Are there any shallow areas here? Anywhere we're likely to run aground?"

"No, nothing," Rene said. "All the wrecks are above water. There are a few boulders near the CN dock that you have to look out for, but only at high tide when they get hidden."

I went scrambling into the cabin and emerged two seconds later with Alex's rolled up charts. The men just looked at the raft and didn't know what to make of it.

"Don't go too far up toward the Ferry Street bridge," I said. I rolled out the chart for the two scientists. "See here? Right at the narrows? I wouldn't take your boat past that point."

"That's very helpful," the man in the front said, looking over Alex's chart.

"You work for the government," Rene noted.

"Department of Fisheries and Oceans," the man said.

"Fisheries? You're not going to catch any fish in the tar pond!" I joked.

The two men from the government laughed. They were good sports. And they were friendly. They were the only visitors we ever had in the tar pond. Too bad Sid and Alex weren't there to meet them.

"No, I don't expect there would be much fishing in this place."

"Why are you coming in here, then?" Rene asked.

"Oh, just to look around," the red-headed man said. He took a plastic sample jar out of a box, put on rubber gloves, carefully leaned over the pontoon and filled the jar with black water. When it was full, he resealed the lid and wrote something on the label.

"Why are you taking samples?" Rene asked.

"Oh, curiosity."

That sort of an answer wouldn't satisfy Rene. "What are you curious about?"

"No harm telling them," the bearded man said to his passenger.

"I guess not," the red-headed man said. "The lobster fishery is being closed in the harbour because of high toxin levels. We think Muggah's Creek is the likely source of contamination."

"Sure, it is," I said.

"You bet it is," Rene agreed. "What are you going to do now?"

"We aren't going to do anything," the passenger said. "We're going to turn it over to Environment and they'll take a few drill samples. We just came in to have a look-see for ourselves. That's a fine-looking raft you have there, boys."

"Thanks," I said. "That's a fine-looking boat." How lucky they were to have it.

THE NEXT DAY SOMETHING INCREDIBLE HAPPENED. I was at home getting ready to go down to the tar pond when somebody banged on the front door. It was the postman and he had a package. It wasn't a huge package, but it was big enough that he couldn't stuff it into our mailbox, which was nailed to the outside wall. He had to knock on the door and leave it inside.

"Come in," I said. I was the only one around and I was having a smoke and a cup of coffee in the kitchen. Actually, I had my feet up on the kitchen table and I was reading my Hardy Boys book.

"Is the dog in there?" the postman said, keeping his hand on the door to prevent Kerby from bursting out and getting him. He was a new postman. I hadn't seen him before. But he knew enough to know that we had a dog.

"Don't worry," I said. "He's outside."

"He's outside?" the postman said, looking over his shoulder. "Is he tied up?"

"No," I said. "But he doesn't bite." And that was true.

But now the postman was looking up and down the street nervously. I came to the door and took the package from him.

"He won't bite you," I promised.

"Okay," the new postman said. He handed me the package and walked quickly up the street. I looked at the package and was surprised to see that it was addressed to me. I opened it right there on the front step. I couldn't believe what it was. It was an entire carton of cigarettes. A little note was attached to the carton that said, "With Our Compliments." A whole carton! I couldn't believe it! This was about the only good thing that had happened all summer.

26

SID CAME HOME LATE SATURDAY AFTERNOON ON Labour Day weekend. His hair was cut even shorter than it had been when he left. His face was tanned and he looked really fit and healthy. My hair was longer than ever and it overgrew my face. You'd never have suspected I had a forehead, just long bangs and a nose. I saw Sid from the third-floor window getting out of the taxi, a sailor home from the sea. If I'd had my driver's licence, I could have picked him up at the bus station. And if I'd had my own car, say a 327 Chevy Nova ss three-speed, with jacked up mag wheels, shag carpet, and a Pioneer sound system, then picking Sid up at the bus station would have been something else. I'd blast the horn and Sid would see the car and hear the low idle and smile and throw his gear in the back and jump in. And man, coming out of that dirty old bus station, I'd lay a strip of rubber a mile long. Sid didn't think much of muscle cars. He said once that a fuel-injected engine was superior to a carburetor engine. And as far as cars went, he only liked the Mercedes Benz. He thought the Mercedes Benz was the Rolls-Royce of automobiles.

Sid came up the third-floor stairs two at a time.

"Guten Tag, mein Bruder! Wie geht es Ihnen?" He swung his duffle bag around like it was a small anchor and flung it straight up onto the top bunk, where it landed on top of me.

"Dump your stinky old clothes in the washer, Sid!" I complained.

"Good idea," he said. I jumped down from the bunk. Sid put his hand out and I shook it. He exerted pressure, and I resisted. He exerted more pressure and looked at me, smiling. I resisted, and winced. I was making my hand as small as I could make it. I was folding my hand in two by bunching all my fingers together. Sid was starting to crush the palm of my hand, which I couldn't collapse.

"Okaaaay! I give, I give," I yelled.

"Ha-ha!" He was happy to be home. He let go.

"You didn't have to crush my hand, Sid!"

"That's my bad hand, too," Sid said. He opened and closed his fist. "I got in a couple of fights at camp." He dumped his clothes from the duffle bag into the washer and stripped down to his underwear, throwing the clothes he was wearing directly into the washing drum as it was filling with water.

"Did you win?"

"Cleaned their clocks, Michael. I didn't want to fight. But there was this jerk who thought he could terrorize the entire barracks. He was there a week earlier than me and Alex."

"Did you and Alex stay together?"

"No, we got separated. So this jerk thought he owned the place because this was the third summer camp he'd signed up for. And he's older too, seventeen. Petty Officer First Class. So it was his big thrill to snap a wet towel at everybody when they were in the shower. He'd stand there at the shower doorway with this grin on his face, waiting to snap the towel at you. I said to him, 'You better not snap that towel at me, Buddy'. I didn't know his name or anything about him. But he snapped the towel at me anyway and I just turned around and clocked him one. He was on his ass with a split lip wondering what hit him. Believe me, he never snapped that towel at me or anyone else after that. That was on the first day, too. Clocked him one. Knocked him right out."

"Knocked him out?"

"Well, almost."

"What about the other fights?"

"They were nothing. He said he had friends that would

beat the shit out of me and he brought these two idiots around to the mess one day. You should have seen them. One was as skinny as a pole with pimples all over his face and the other was a fat pig. I don't know how they got uniforms for them. They came over to me in the mess and said they were friends of the jerk. And before he could even finish threatening me I grabbed the fat one and pushed him up against the wall and put my fist right up to his face and said, 'You want some of this, too?' And he said, 'No, sir'. Ha-ha. No, sir. Real tough guys. The skinny guy stood there stamping his feet. Didn't help his friend at all. Just stood and stamped his feet like he was trying to fit better into his boots. So, I guess that didn't really qualify as a fight. More like a joke. You would have laughed, if you'd have seen it. Where is everybody?"

"Louisburg," I said.

"Louisburg? What are they doing out there?"

"Cosmo went with Rory and Miss Shaw. I didn't want to go. Heather's downstairs cleaning."

"I didn't see Heather downstairs."

"I don't know where she is. She was there a few minutes ago."

"Where's Mum?"

"At work, I guess."

Sid found a clean change of clothes and then went downstairs to shower. I climbed out of the third-floor window to sit on the second-floor roof. I lit a match, cupped it with my hands, and lit a cigarette. I flung the expended match over the edge of the roof and hoped it wouldn't land on Tim's Chevrolet, parked in the driveway below. I looked around the neighbourhood and saw the back of the Carmichael house. I could still see where the pellet gun had put dents in their aluminum siding.

Sid had a pellet rifle last year and he thought it would be a good idea to shoot a few pellets just below Mary Carmichael's bedroom window to get her attention. Instead, Mrs. Carmichael, Mary's mother, phoned our house and asked Gloria to ask Sid to stop shooting bullets at their house. It was sort of funny, now that I think of it. The Carmichaels moved away some time after that, but the dents were still there on the aluminum siding.

Heather came up the third-floor staircase and opened the lid on the washing machine.

"This Sid's wash?"

"Yeah," I said from the roof.

Heather came over to the window and leaned out. She still had a dishtowel with her. It was a checkered red and white dishtowel and she had just carried it all the way up to the third floor unconsciously. She looked like a teenage housewife.

"Got a cigarette?"

I handed her the package and she lit a cigarette.

Sid came bounding up the stairs and disappeared into our room.

"Hiya, Sid," Heather shouted.

"Guten Tag, meine Schwester," Sid shouted back through the closed door.

"Sid said there was nobody downstairs when he got home."

"I was next door talking to Irene," Heather said.

Sid came out of the bedroom wearing a clean pair of jeans and a clean T-shirt. The shirt was an undershirt from his cadet uniform. It had a length of coiled rope embroidered on the left side of the chest.

"How was Sea Cadet camp?" Heather asked.

"Okay. I liked it."

"You must have learned some German at camp," I asked.

"Jawohl," Sid replied.

Sid gave Heather a big hug despite the fact that she had a cigarette in one hand. Sid was becoming accustomed to our smoking. He still didn't like us smoking and didn't like the stink of cigarette smoke, but he was becoming accustomed to it all the same.

"Whew! You smell like Old Spice," Heather said.

"Yup!"

"It's, well, nice," she said.

"Yup!"

"Did Michael tell you about Mum and Dad?"

"I didn't have a chance," I said from the roof.

"What about them?"

Sid stood before Heather with his head back and his arms crossed. He appeared to have grown bigger in two weeks, if that was possible. He was a petty officer now and he was getting used to command and leadership. You could tell that right off. He had more control. He was a very controlled guy anyway, a natural leader. We'd always lined up behind Sid. But you could tell that camp had done something good to him. At least it seemed obvious to me. He was standing in a certain way now, a mature or adult way, which was quite formidable.

"I thought Mum was supposed to call you at Cornwallis," Heather said. "She said she was going to call you. I guess she forgot."

"What's the matter?"

"They're getting a divorce," I said, leaning in from the roof.

"Who are?"

"Mum and Dad," Heather said, drawing on her cigarette and not taking her eyes off Sid. She blew the smoke back out the window through the side of her mouth.

"Since when?"

"Since Dad and Miss Shaw have started living together."

Sid didn't say anything. Heather was staring right at him, looking for a reaction. He looked at Heather and then he looked at me.

"Is that true?"

"Yes," I said.

"What's been done to stop it?"

That was Sid, a commanding officer weighing the report of a subordinate.

"What's been done? What's there to do?" Heather asked.

"There's always something that can be done," Sid said.

"It's not as if they're asking for our permission, Sid," Heather said. "They're getting a divorce and that's that. I don't see how there's anything we can do. What can we do? Dad's living with Miss Shaw and not coming here at all. He hasn't spent a night here since long before you left for camp. We just didn't notice he wasn't coming home. I haven't seen him at all for almost two weeks. Have you seen him, Michael?"

"No."

"I haven't seen him either," Heather said.

"Let's go visit him at her apartment," Sid said.

"And do what, Sid? *What are we supposed to do?* Gloria thinks the divorce is absolutely fine. She's acting like Dad's dumping her was her idea in the first place. And maybe it was. She told me that although it may not seem like it now, someday we'll see that everything that's happening is for the best."

"What does Dad say?" Sid asked.

"You can't get a straight answer out of him. I asked him whether or not he was going to let Mum move out of the house, because if she does that—"

"It's final," I said for Heather.

"Right. Once she's out, she's never coming back."

"And what did he say?"

"He said that you've got to play the cards you've been given and that life is a river," I told Sid.

"Right," Heather remembered. "Mum said that life was a river, too."

"So did Rory."

"A river," Sid repeated. He walked back and forth in the space between the washer and the dryer. Heather and I looked at each other. The wash was into its second rinse spin and by the time this ended, Sid had made his decision. I finished my cigarette and climbed back through the window. Heather and I stood there, not knowing what to do. Sid knew, though. And we were waiting for him to tell us.

"I wonder what they'd say if they were looking down the barrel of a twelve-gauge shotgun," Sid said.

These words went through me like a shock. I could not believe what I had heard. And the way Sid had spoken them, so offhandedly, so matter-of-factly, made it seem as if Heather and I were somehow negligent for not considering this obvious plan of action much earlier.

"Good idea, Sid," Heather said, "but not very practical." She had completely misunderstood Sid. As far as she was concerned, he might as well have suggested dropping an atom bomb as using a shotgun, since both were equally unattainable. "We have to think of something positive," she said. She had completely missed the danger in what Sid had said because she didn't know about the shotgun. "We have to think of a way that will make everybody happy."

"Making everybody happy is just going along with it," Sid objected.

"Sid, we have no choice."

Heather assumed that the entire weight of our parents' impending divorce had fallen on her shoulders, since the best Sid could offer was only some expression of anger. It was that, all right, but it was much more. Sid had put an image in my head and I didn't want anything to do with it.

"No way," I said to Sid. He looked at Heather and me with disappointment before he turned and descended the third-floor staircase. Heather looked at me and rolled her eyes at Sid's supposed inability to grasp the situation as it was. She followed Sid downstairs.

As soon as Heather had gone, I searched under the washing-machine sink and in all of the crawl spaces on that side of the house. I searched on the other side of the house and checked there too by feeling around in the dark. I had to crawl on my hands and knees all the way down to the end of the eaves without lifting my head, because the roofing nails would get me if I stood up. I didn't find the shotgun. I searched in the closet and up in the attic. I didn't find it.

I WAITED ALL DAY AND ALL SATURDAY NIGHT FOR SID to return. But he didn't come home. I finally fell asleep on the top bunk with my clothes on. I was awakened Sunday morning by some noises in the room.

"What are you doing, Sid?"

"Sussh. Don't wake Cosmo. I'm getting ready for church," he said.

"But it's still night."

"I know. I'm going to Alex's first. Coming with me today?" he asked.

"No."

"Come on."

"No."

"Why not?"

"You'll never get me going to church, so stop trying."

This would prove to be untrue. Four days later, Sid had me in church. I've been going ever since.

We used to go to church as a family on Sunday mornings all the time. Sacred Heart Church is a big church, painted white, and has five big doors and two steeples. One steeple is much shorter than the other because it has been hit by lightning and was never rebuilt. Inside at the entrance there are marble bowls filled with holy water. The backs of the pews run in an unbroken line up to the altar.

The columns near the altar start out as columns but somehow they turn into the ceiling. They just begin flaring halfway up and expand into vaulted arches. The ceiling is nice to look up at. The windows are all made from stained glass and show different scenes from the Bible. There is a choir loft, too. You have to climb a narrow stairwell, and then you can look down over the congregation. The sound of voices singing and the music blasting out from the speakers gives you a good feeling all right. I used to sing in the choir during Christmas concerts, and one time we even sang on television during a live broadcast at suppertime.

Over the altar is a huge portrait of Our Lord holding his Sacred Heart in one hand with a look of great compassion on His face. The painting is mostly dark, mostly browns and blues. There are storm clouds in the background that look as if they had just parted to allow this terrific beam of white light to strike Christ on the back of the shoulders. This beam of light produces a blaze of white around His head. There are all sorts of smaller angels flying in and out of the thunder clouds. One of them looks at the viewer and points at the Saviour.

The altar used to be surrounded by a railing with little gates placed here and there. I remember that very clearly from my first communion. The railing was painted brown. And I remember when they got rid of the railing and made the altar come down to meet the pews without any obstruction. And I remember my father complaining about there being no more Latin in church. I think that's why he stopped going to listen to the Mass, because it wasn't in Latin.

Sid had turned on his little bedside lamp, which threw his big shadow across the room. Cosmo was sleeping in the lower bunk. I turned on my stomach on the top bunk and watched Sid get ready. After his pants came his shirt, tie, and shoes, and then he brushed his hair. He prepared for church with the same meticulous single-mindedness he displayed when he was getting ready for Cadets.

"You should come to church. The whole clan will be there."

"I don't want to see them."

"They want to see you. They always ask how you are."

"Who does?"

"Uncle Duncan does. Bruce and Marie and Paul always ask."

"So what."

"It's good to be a part of a large family, that's so what," Sid said, knotting his tie. Sid knew every knot possible. Cadets had taught him most of them. Rory had taught him about necktie knots.

"Why don't you get Heather to go with you?"

"She doesn't want to go anymore," Sid said.

"I know," I said. "But I don't want to go, either."

Sid walked over to the hallway window as he knotted his tie. By this time I was fully awake and had remembered what I wanted to ask him. I jumped down from my bunk and went out into the hallway. Sid was looking out at the harbour.

"Sid?"

"Yes?"

"Where'd you go last night?"

"I stayed at Alex's," Sid said. "We played chess all night."

"Oh."

It was getting light over by the steel plant. I could see the lights of North Sydney across the harbour. I knew that somewhere in the darkness the blue-hulled Newfoundland ferry was tied up at its North Sydney dock.

"Sid?"

"Yes?"

"Where's the shotgun?"

Sid didn't appear to hear me at first, but then he turned and looked at me.

"At Alex's. Are you coming to church or not?"

"No."

"Suit yourself."

27

FOUR DAYS LATER, AT SID'S FUNERAL, THE PRIEST SAID that there would be a time when the reality of having lost Sid would strike us powerfully and that it would be okay to cry when that time came. It might be during the funeral ceremony, or afterwards at the gravesite, or maybe a week later, or a year, or many years later when looking at family pictures. But it was okay to cry when the time came and quite natural to cry, he said. Heather and Daphne took him up on the offer right away and had big puffy faces and watery eyes. They kept blowing into handkerchiefs and blubbering. An aunt would come to console them, only to start crying herself. And when they all cried, they got Mandy upset so she would start crying, too.

Because Sid's body was never found, we were told that we could put something of value in the casket, an item that meant something to us. Heather put in a book of poems about the sea. Cosmo put in a sealed envelope. Gloria put in flowers. Rory put in Sid's chanter. I put in the red life jacket. And that's what we buried instead of Sid.

They had bagpipes at the church. After the Mass, the piper played "Flowers of the Forest" as everyone slowly came out of the church, one step at a time. Alex and five other Sea Cadets were the pallbearers. Rory had asked me if I wanted to be a pallbearer and I had said no. I didn't want to carry an empty casket. Sid's Sea Cadet lieutenant had offered the members of Sid's corps. I thought that was a pretty smart idea. Sid would have liked seeing his casket being handled by the Sea Cadets. They were all spit and polish. The hearse was parked with its lights on in front of the two main doors of the church. The casket filled with flotsam and jetsam was brought down the steps by the Sea Cadets and put in the back of the hearse.

I listened to the drivers of the funeral procession discussing how they would just head out Route Four, and how the ceremony would wait until everybody got to the graveyard. A second big black car at the curb was reserved for our family. Alex and Rene couldn't come with us. They followed in Rene's father's station wagon. I kept looking around at the small crowd in front of the church, half expecting to see Sid hiding among our uncles and aunts, waiting for me to acknowledge his masterpiece. Good one, Sid. The best one yet. I began to follow a small procession from the church that was walking slowly up toward College Street. Cosmo was sent to get me and bring me back to the family.

The inside of the black funeral car had two long seats facing each other. I had never been in a car like that. Rory and Gloria sat on one seat. Heather, Cosmo, and I sat facing them in the other seat. It was weird not having Sid there. But maybe it was just as well because there wasn't any room for him.

Sid's empty casket was buried in a little graveyard that overlooked the Bras d'Or Lakes. The air was always cooler over the lakes than it was in town. Wispy clouds were over the purple shore of Iona, a long way from us across the blue water of the lake. This church was tiny compared to Sacred Heart. It was painted white and had one set of steps leading up to one little door. We didn't even go in. Two gravediggers were having a cigarette up near the back of the church, a respectful distance away from the funeral party. They looked like two regular joes. Uncle Angus approached them and they had a conversation in Gaelic.

"What did they say?" my father asked.

"They were just trying to see how much Gaelic I knew," Angus said.

The graveside ceremony was very brief. The priest said a few words and the flower-strewn casket was lowered into the earth. Alex played "Last Call" on the trumpet. He made a few mistakes because he'd only had a few days to learn it. But he hit a couple of pure notes that felt like a sword was stuck right through your heart. Just in case you came through that without bawling your eyes out, the bagpiper played "Mist Covered Mountains," a horrible Scottish lament designed to make you cry like a baby. Sid used to play it on his chanter.

We were standing in front of the black car, ready to make the drive back to Sydney. My aunts hugged all of us. My uncles shook my hand and Cosmo's hand. Duncan said to me, "Be strong." My sister was crying all over the place. Everyone was hugging us and shaking our hands. Aunt Marie hugged me and squared me up with her arms and gave me a good, steady look. I was taller than she was.

"Gloria," she said, calling my mother.

"What is it, Marie?"

"Look," Marie said, pointing at me. My mother looked at me.

"What?" she said. "Is there something wrong? What? What?"

"Gloria, your son doesn't have any *eye*brows."

MY MOTHER MOVED OUT OF THE MEADOW STREET HOUSE in September and my father and Miss Shaw moved in. Cosmo went with my mother to a small apartment in the south end. Heather and I stayed in the north end with my father and Miss Shaw for as long as we could. But then we followed my mother, too, because Miss Shaw and my father left for Toronto shortly after he lost his job. Heather, Cosmo, and I dropped out of school as soon as my father was far enough away that he couldn't do anything about it. When Rory phoned to complain, Gloria told him that she could only do so much under the burden she was carrying. But it wasn't all bad news. Gloria told us that society had placed far too much emphasis on credentials, anyway, and that she had read that de-schooling society was the wave of the future.

Rory also was infuriated that Gloria had Heather and me testify at the divorce trial. There wasn't anything called "no fault" divorce, so someone had to accept responsibility. Gloria's lawyer, one of the first female lawyers in Sydney, was very sympathetic. She patted Gloria's shoulder as we were going into the courthouse and told her to hang in there. That was my first time in a courtroom. But it was okay because we knew the judge, Judge Sinclair. He had been down to our house every Christmas. He was very considerate to us and sympathetic to Gloria, whom he viewed as a single parent doing the best she could under extremely difficult circumstances.

"Just have a seat, Michael. I want to ask you a few questions."

"Okay."

I had a seat in the witness chair and Judge Sinclair

asked me a few questions from the bench. It's not really a bench. It's a table on a platform that's been elevated from the floor.

"You understand that a divorce cannot be granted unless certain conditions are met. In this case, in the case of your parents, the petition for divorce is based upon the assertion that the respondent, your father, has committed adultery since the celebration of his marriage with your mother. Do you understand what adultery means, Michael?"

"Yes, sir."

"Can you tell me what it means?"

"It means when a married couple sleeps with someone else."

"Well, that's right. In this case, we must know whether you can testify if the respondent, your father, and Miss Shaw have ever had sexual intercourse."

"Yes, sir."

"They have?"

"I didn't see them, sir."

"No, but you believe that they have had sexual intercourse? You have a reasonable suspicion that they had sexual intercourse?"

"Yes, sir."

"When was this, Michael?"

"When they went to the bedroom, Your Honour."

"The bedroom in your home at Meadow Street?"

"Yes, sir."

"And you will testify that you believe they had sexual intercourse in that room?"

"They went in the room at night and came out the next morning."

"I see. I think that's all, Michael. You may step down."
"All right."

28

ON THE DAY THAT SID DROWNED, SUNRISE OVER THE city of Sydney had been artificially enhanced by the orange smoke from the steel plant's six giant smokestacks. The morning light caught the smoke as it poured out of the stacks and made it look first like orange billowy ribbons on the ends of magic wands, then like cotton candy. A steelworker's name for the ribbon of smoke that issued from the stacks was "plume," like a billowy feather. From the north end, we could only see the beginnings of plumes before they stretched into six long fingers that reached across the horizon and dissipated over the Atlantic. Sometimes the smoke that came out of a stack was black to start, but it soon turned orange, making the lengthening plume look like a fox's tail tipped with soot.

After Sid left for church, I watched the sunrise from the third-floor window. The tar pond, in the shadow of Slag Mountain, was complete blackness. I went downstairs to the second floor and used the bathroom, then continued downstairs to the kitchen, passing my parents' bedroom where now only my mother slept. The kitchen was a mess again. Chipper, our striped cat, was sleeping on top of the fridge. Our black cat, Cinder, was playing with a steel marble on the television room floor. Kerby was having one of his dog dreams on the chesterfield. I took two of my mother's cigarettes, smoked one of them, and drank a cup of coffee. There was nothing to eat so I went out the front door and let it lock behind me.

The entire neighbourhood was quiet and filled with slanting shadows. I was glad I had taken my denim jacket because it was chilly. I was still wearing the same T-shirt and the same old jeans that I had worn all week. I walked down Brook Street and turned down the dead end of Louisa. I followed the path through the reeds and the bulrushes, and climbed the little rise to the CN tracks. The kayak was tucked neatly away in the bamboo grove and I hauled it out and put it on my shoulders, placing my head in the space for the seats. I was wearing it like a huge hat. The tar pond was jet black and as flat as a piece of black marble. Slag Mountain was a huge, black, horizontal bar. The dawning sky behind it was becoming overcast. I eased the kayak off my shoulders and put it nose first in the water. Then I jumped down to one of the boulders near the dock and got in. I pushed off from the boulder and started paddling for the raft. Out on the water there was a slight breeze. It was full tide.

My plan was to light the fire log in the raft's stove and get warm. I paddled across the black liquid and lit my second cigarette when I was halfway across. The only sound on the tar pond was the little squelching sound the match made when I threw it into the water. I came gliding around the barge using my paddle as a rudder and came up against the raft in a perfect side-swipe docking. I put my hand out and held onto the raft and climbed aboard. That's when I heard Sid yelling.

"Michael! Come pick me up!"

I looked back over at the CN shore but couldn't see anybody. The shore was still in the night shadow of Slag Mountain.

"Okay! I'll be right there!"

I got back in the kayak and pushed off from the raft. It only took a few minutes to make the crossing, but Sid shouted "Hurry!" twice in that time. My stomach started to get that twisty feeling. I glided in against the boulder Sid was standing on, and he clambered into the front of the kayak.

"Thanks," he said breathlessly.

"What's going on?"

"I'll tell you on the raft."

Sid took the second paddle out from under the bow of the kayak. I was glad I was in back because I could correct his more powerful sweeps just by letting my paddle slice through the water. In no time we were coming around the barge and pulling up against the raft. Sid got out first and tied the kayak to the raft. Then I got out.

"What's up?" I asked.

"Something's going to happen and you have to go along with me when it does. Agreed?"

"Yeah, sure, but—"

"No buts. You're either with me or against me."

"I'm with you, Sid."

"Make sure that you are."

"I am, only what happened?"

Sid looked at me and threw up his arms in a helpless gesture. It was the first time I had ever seen him look overwhelmed by events.

"You did something with the shotgun, didn't you?"

Sid stepped from the raft to the barge. He moved to the far edge of the barge and looked out across the tar pond to the blue water of Sydney Harbour. His face reflected a certain resolve, as if he had finally settled upon a hard course of action.

"What did you do with the shotgun, Sid?"

Before he could answer another voice came over the water.

"*Michael! Come in and pick me up!*"

Sid froze and turned his head toward the CN shore.

"*Michael!*" the voice called again.

"It's Alex. I'll go get him," I said as I moved toward the kayak.

"No, wait." Sid held my arm and listened.

"*Sid! Come in and pick me up! I'm alone!*"

"We have to get out of here," Sid said. He knew what Alex really meant. Sid went into the cabin and brought out our two life jackets. He put one on and threw the other to me. As soon as I saw the jackets I knew that we were going out into the harbour.

"Get in the kayak," Sid ordered. I got in the second position and Sid jumped in the front. We pushed off from the raft and made a slow turn toward Battery Point. Sid was a powerhouse. After only a few strokes we had a little wave and a wash coming off each side of the bow.

"*Michael! Where are you going?*" Alex shouted from the shore.

"Sid, where are we going?" I asked.

"Shut up and keep paddling."

"*Michael!*" Alex shouted again.

I could see somebody in a light shirt on the CN dock. I assumed it was Alex. The figure kept pace with us as we made for Battery Point, which we would have to pass before we got out into the harbour. I looked at the point and saw other people waiting. I saw a white police cruiser. An officer stood in front of the cruiser with a bullhorn.

"Bring your craft to shore," he ordered.

"Sid, for Chrissake!" I pleaded.

"For the last time—" Sid warned me.

"*Bring your craft to shore,*" the voice repeated.

I shut my mouth and paddled. The little knot of people on the shore was directly off us on the port side. We were moving fast and almost out of the oily black tar pond water.

"*Sidney, come back here.*" It was our father's voice on the bullhorn. I looked over and sure enough, Rory was standing on Battery Point with two police officers and Alex. He was the biggest figure on the point. Sid stopped paddling and looked over.

"*Don't make things worse,*" our father called out.

"Will you listen to him," Sid said, more to himself than to me.

Sid had never disobeyed our father so blatantly. He resumed paddling and so did I. We had crossed over the tar pond divide and were now in harbour water. The clearer water was quicker than the tar pond water and it tended to splash. We were also out of the lee of Slag Mountain now, and the ocean wind came around the deepwater pier at the steel plant and blew the bullhorned words back to shore. Only a few phrases reached us now.

"*... talk about this ...*"

"*... best for everyone ...*"

"*... don't blame you ...*"

We were soon completely out of bullhorn range. I watched as everyone on Battery Point got into the cruiser, which drove quickly up the B&D Cement factory's shoreline road.

"We'll go to the inner automatic buoy," Sid said. "That's about halfway across the harbour."

"We can have a rest there, too," I said.

The blue expanse of harbour stretched away for miles

to Westmount and we could see there the black hull and white superstructure of the *Cape Breton Miner*. It looked very small from our position.

As we drew away from the shore in our little canvas kayak, I had a sudden fright of the deep. I watched as the bottom sank away from us. At one hundred feet from shore, I was just able to make out rocks on the bottom. At two hundred feet from shore, the bottom became an almost indistinguishable darkness. At about two hundred and fifty feet from shore, there seemed to be no bottom at all. There was only the dull blue rolling sea and a grey overcast sky. There was only me and Sid, no one else.

I felt my paddle hit something and quickly pulled it from the water.

"What was *that*?" I shrieked.

"What was what?"

"I hit something with my paddle!" I said. I tried to control the fear in my voice.

"You did not," Sid said. "It's over fifty feet deep out here."

"*I hit something with my paddle!*" I insisted. I was freaking out. I thought it was a shark or a whale or something that would wreck us.

"It was probably the side of the kayak," Sid said, trying to calm me. We were starting to drift and Sid didn't want us to get broadside to the waves. He put his paddle in the water and hit something.

"You're right," he said.

"See?"

He put his paddle carefully back into the water and tapped something solid. I looked into the waves and scrutinized the dim rocks that loomed just below the surface. We were floating on top of a long line of submerged boulders, with maybe a foot between us and them.

"It's the old jetty," Sid told me.

I remembered walking out on it once. It had been covered with seaweed and gull droppings and was dangerous to walk on. It was always hidden at high tide. The best thing about it had been seeing how the boulders disappeared into deep water. Now, it was a submerged sentinel at the mouth of the tar pond, warning us back from the clear water—or a rocky finger pointing us toward Westmount. I didn't think of such poetic things at the time. But I have gone over that voyage across Sydney Harbour with Sid a thousand times, and I always think about us floating on top of that submerged ridge when we thought we had fifty feet of water below us.

We paddled backwards off the ridge and followed alongside until we came to its end. Sid corrected our position in relation to the sea swells, as he did a hundred times during that trip, easily, automatically, instinctively. When I think of it, we could have been swamped a dozen times crossing the harbour had Sid lapsed once with his corrections.

"Do you think the cops have a boat?"

"We'll be across the harbour by the time they launch it," Sid told me.

"I'm not so sure," I said. Westmount was a long way away.

We kept the kayak on an angle to the waves in order to ride up a crest and down a trough without putting the bow under. This meant we didn't travel in a straight line and getting to the buoy took a lot longer than we'd expected. The waves, too, were bigger the farther out we got. They were coming straight in from the Atlantic. We had a lot of water in the bottom of the kayak. My butt was soaked. The Westmount horizon kept appearing and disappearing as we rode up the face of a wave and down into its trough. Sid and I paddled without talking. The life jackets were heavy and bulky and uncomfortable. All I thought about was the inner automatic buoy. The closer we got to the steel buoy, however, the more obvious it was that we could go nowhere near it. As the ocean swells passed it by, the buoy plunged up and down in the water so violently that I was worried about being drawn toward it and destroyed.

"Let's just keep going," Sid said.

We didn't have much choice. We shouldn't have come out into the harbour in this found canvas boat, this little handmade kayak with its fibreglass paint cracking on top and its nose snubbed from so many deliberate head-ons. But we couldn't go back now. We were halfway there. I paddled until I became accustomed to the pain in my shoulders and until the blisters forming on the palms of my hands became a dull burning. I looked back at the Sydney shore and saw the huge yellow sign built on a high point just below the oil company storage tanks. It said "–ABLE DO NOT ANCHOR." I happened to know that Colin Crawley had stolen the C. It was nailed to the wall of his bedroom.

We had good luck at the halfway point. The wind turned around and started running before us and the waves carried us along in a most pleasing surf. You could feel the kayak surging along on the top of a wave and then settling down into the back of the wave. When a wave lifted the kayak, my guts were lifted, too. And when the kayak settled in the trough of a wave, my stomach settled with it. The boat was my body, the paddle was my arm. I don't know if Sid felt the same way, but it seemed that the rhythm of the waves urged on our effort, and our effort encouraged the rhythm of the waves.

We went on like this, without speaking, until the detail of the Westmount shore became clearer. The industrial park ran from the warehouses on top of the hill, where I had seen the imported sheep, right down along a wide paved road to the deepwater pier, where the *Cape Breton Miner* was tied up. We came alongside the giant bulk carrier. There was no sign of life on her. The black hull was bubbled and blistered and the huge white superstructure had streaks of brown rust running down from the windows of the bridge. The pier was built in the form of a "U," which made a shallow enclosure for a small Coast Guard ship.

Wilderness came down to the water's edge on either side of the industrial park. We paddled past the bulk carrier and saw that the shore farther on formed a small bay. This area of the shore was called Westmount Gardens, but no one could plant any sort of garden here. Guaranteed. The only way to move around this coastal zone was by boat. We followed the shore for a considerable distance, then passed through a screen of elm and weeping willow trees, their arms hanging down, their leaves trailing in the water. A hidden estuary lay behind this leafy barrier. I'd never seen anything like it before.

Giant trees on the river banks loomed over us, their intertwined roots jealously holding the earth against the action of the current. An oppressive mist covered the green hills, which rolled toward us into small knolls and vales down through which feeder creeks meandered, the sun flashing silver upon them as we silently glided past. I put my hands into the fresh water and washed the salt from my blisters. I could see little fish swimming along with us as we made our way upstream. Pink and white mallow flowers choked the banks and purple thistles bloomed farther on up the slopes. I had heard that thistle was nearly impossible to get rid of once it had taken root. Thickets of speckled alders and wild cherries were filled with birds that made a racket with our approach. They chattered and chirped and it seemed that the estuary was noise-filled for the entire time we were there. I swatted at a hummingbird, mistaking it for an oversized wasp. Dragonflies were buzzing around in squadrons looking for places to land. The smell of the green turf embankments crowded with flowers gave me the same nauseous sensation as does a woman wearing too much perfume. And you hardly knew where to look, the colours were so confused and haphazard—gaudy.

The estuary narrowed as we followed it farther inland. Razor grasses crowded us in places, but the channel itself remained deep and the surface a liquid mirror to a clear blue sky. I saw more fish under the bank, swishing their tails every now and then. Frog eyes watched us. Skater insects raced upstream before us, and slimy-looking pollywogs wriggled around the submerged roots of the razor grasses. I realized that this was probably what Muggah's Creek had looked like one hundred years ago, before the steel plant had turned it into the tar ponds.

"Feel like a swim, Mike?" Sid asked.

"Probably leeches in the water," I said.

The towering elm trees occasionally made dappled patterns on the surface of the water that hurt my eyes. The haze became thicker and the humidity was becoming uncomfortable. A great blue heron that had been fishing in the water saw us coming and slowly took off, long before we got anywhere near him. That set the other birds chattering and screeching and they wouldn't shut up.

The river suddenly opened up to a small beach, which we naturally headed for. The kayak made a gravelly sound as it ran aground, the pebbles turning over like ball bearings under our weight. We took off our cumbersome life jackets. Sid threw his back in the kayak. The first thing we both did was relieve ourselves. I immediately felt better as I watched the current carry the bubbles downstream.

"Look there," Sid said. He pointed to a punt that had been hauled up on shore. A fallen willow lay between us and the punt.

"Let's take a look," I said.

Maybe salvage rights could make it ours, I thought.

I climbed around the willow and beheld the punt. It was a nice one, painted white. It had three seats, and cushions on all of them. It would be perfect for the tar pond. But it was clearly not lost because it was tied to a stump and a rope was neatly coiled in the front under the seat. I recognized, too, the specialized wrappers for rolls of film which were discarded in the bottom of the boat.

"*Psssst*—!"

A long grassy stretch leading off into the glen had been trampled down. Sid had followed the trail to the little knoll from which he was now signalling. I left the punt and crept up to join him. He gestured to me to be quiet and he pointed to something in the depression beyond the knoll. When I reached him, he pulled me down on my belly and we both rose together slowly, our eyes breaching the horizon, our faces gawking at an incredible scene below.

A checkered picnic cloth had been spread out on the grass. To one side were china cups, silver spoons, half-eaten sandwiches, and a teapot inside a basket. On the picnic cloth were three young women. They didn't have a stitch of clothing on, not one stitch. They were posing in some way, their heads tilted, their hips curved, and their long hair tousled over their shoulders. One of the girls had light yellow hair. A man was setting up a camera on a tripod. Another man with a beard rested with the girls, his elbow bent in the grass. He seemed to be giving them directions. There was a large picture book open in front of him. He looked from the girls to the book and back again several times. Both men were fully clothed, in fancy, dark old-fashioned vests and jackets. A top hat lay in the grass.

"Move more into the shade, Amaryllis," the bearded man said.

The girls squeezed together more and resumed their poses.

"Is that better, Marlow?" the girl with light hair said.

The bearded man looked down at the book and up at the girls again. He held the book up for the photographer, who looked at the picture and then back to the girls. They seemed to be trying to reproduce a painting in the book.

"Perfect, girls," the photographer said. "Absolutely perfect."

Marlow put the book aside and posed himself. The photographer pressed the shutter. Sid slid away from the crest of the hill and pulled on my shoe. We left them to their luncheon on the grass and scurried down to the beach.

"Let's get out of here," I said. I expected the two men to come crashing along the path any moment, cursing us. The whole place gave me the creeps.

I hurriedly pushed the kayak out into the water and made it parallel with the shore. I jumped in and looked around for Sid. He had pushed the punt out into the stream and was deliberately leaning all his weight on one side until water slipped over the gunwale and began to fill the boat.

"What the hell are you doing?" I whispered. Sid had never done anything like this in his life. He was still in his church clothes.

The little boat filled quickly. Candy-bar wrappers floated out from under the seats along with the film wrappers as the hull became level with the water. Sid stood on the stern of the sunken punt and stepped into the deepest part of the channel. He went in right over his head and popped up a moment later.

"Whoa," he said. "Water's cold."

The submerged punt started to drift downstream toward the mouth of the estuary but was stopped by its tether. When Sid saw this, he started to swim toward the shore to untie the rope.

"Get the hell into the kayak and let's get out of here!" I hissed under my breath.

Sid paused in midstream.

"Come on!"

But Sid stopped cold and looked at me. I thought something had grabbed him or he had caught his foot because he had a look of distress on his face, as if he was going to cry. But he didn't cry. I wish he had. He screamed at the top of his lungs, a long, agonizing scream confused with anger, pain, and protest.

The echo rang all through the estuary.

In a moment I saw Marlow's bearded face appear over the crest of the hill. Behind him ran the photographer and the three naked girls. I couldn't believe it. The girls hadn't bothered to put on any clothes.

"Here they come," I told Sid.

"Let's motor," he said.

I paddled the kayak farther back into the channel and Sid swam up beside it. Marlow saw us now. His face was full of concern.

"Are you boys all right?" he shouted.

I sank my paddle deep into the water and pulled. On the other side, Sid kicked his feet and between us we propelled the kayak deeper into the channel where we caught the current. Sid scrambled into his front seat position and almost capsized us. I had to paddle quickly from one side and then the other to keep the kayak stable. The near-capsize triggered us both unexpectedly into uncontrollable laughter.

I looked back and saw the photographer with his hands on his hips considering the vandalized punt. Marlow gazed at us from the hilltop, using a hand to shade his eyes. The three girls had come down to the beach where we had just been. The two dark-haired girls walked into the stream up to their thighs and dove into the cold water without hesitation. When they surfaced, they were halfway between the kayak and the beach. Only the tops of their heads appeared out of the water. The light-haired girl stood on the beach and stared at us. In her hand she idly swung the life jacket that I had forgotten. She was still looking at us when we passed through the screen of weeping willows that led to Sydney Harbour.

It was on the way back to Sydney when it happened. The waves were up when we got out into the harbour. The tide was running one way and the wind the other and the chop was coming right into the kayak.

"Put your life jacket on," Sid said.

"I don't have one," I confessed. "I forgot it back there."

Sid flung his life jacket to me and I put it on. There was

no sense arguing with him. He was my big brother. We got as far as the inner automatic buoy before the kayak capsized. It didn't capsize so much as it went into a wave and didn't come out of it. And the way we had cut the kayak to make it seat two people allowed the water to come right in. I remember the water coming right in, swirling around Sid's hips and then his chest and then his shoulders like some sort of silver coat he was putting on, and the kayak just going straight down like a lead weight.

When the water had almost engulfed Sid and began threatening me, all I did was step out of the boat and I was free of it. And maybe Sid managed to do that, too, once he was fully underwater. Maybe he did. When I reached the steel tower of the buoy, I thought I saw an object in the water moving toward the Westmount shore. I'm not just making that up. Sid was a very powerful swimmer and we weren't so far from shore that he couldn't have swum back. People say that I imagined I saw something moving toward the shore because I wanted Sid to have survived, but they weren't there and they don't know Sid. Leaving his family behind is just the sort of thing he would do once he resolved to do it. I have learned to never underestimate someone's first principles.

I hope that it was Sid that I saw swimming for shore. I sincerely hope that it was, because when I stepped out of the kayak, Sid's legs were still under the front part of the canvas, and just for an instant he looked as if he had decided that the best way to continue the journey was underwater. He kept going straight down, like a weighted line, until the blue water of Sydney harbour closed over his head. That was the last time I saw my big brother. Such are the perils of the sea.

I FOUND OUT LATER THAT SID HADN'T GONE TO MASS at all that last Sunday morning. Instead, he had gone around to the back of the apartment building where our father was staying. Sid had the shotgun with him. The white Camero was parked under the bedroom window. I guess Sid just kept loading and firing, loading and firing. The buckshot smashed every window, shredded the upholstery, destroyed the console, took parts of the steering wheel away, punctured the radiator and the gas tank, pockmarked the panelling, and burst all four tires. Some people in the building mistook the noise for thunder. It was Sid's cicada song.

The end of the raft came naturally enough several weeks after Sid's funeral. A storm tore it from its moorings on the barge and drove it up on the CN shore. It remained there, in full gaze of the CN employees, for a week. But the Canadian National Railway employees are the greatest. The railmen gave us all sorts of advice and made all kinds of suggestions on how to refloat the raft. One CN employee even tried to push it back into the water with his backhoe, but the machine's big tires spun ineffectually in the loose landfill and the raft did not budge an inch. A second storm whisked the raft from the CN shore and drove it so far behind a little island on the steel-plant side of the tar pond that it was impossible to reclaim. I know it sits there still, in the shadow of Slag Mountain, finally imprisoned by the forces of industrial authority and half-buried under the onslaught of slag.

I'VE BEEN DREAMING OF SID A LOT LATELY. I'M ON A little sailboat with him and we finally reach Sydney. We tie up to the big opera house that looks like a regatta in the harbour and we listen to Australians sing "Waltzing

Matilda" and "Watch Me Wallabies Feed, Mate." We see kangaroos and platypuses and climb that huge rock that's plunked in the middle of nowhere. And they treat us real well in Sydney because we're from Sydney, too. They feed us acorn bread with butter and we eat as many lamb chops with potatoes and gravy as we want and we never get sick. We sing songs and play flutes under billabong trees as sheep graze in shady meadows nibbling the myrtle grass that grows along the banks of rivers.

And Sid and I just stand there shoulder to shoulder and drink the whole thing in.

And because the people of Sydney, Australia, live in the biggest Sydney in the world, they'll look out for all the people who come from the smaller Sydneys, for the reason that we are just their little brothers and they are morally obligated to look out for us. They would look out for us anyway, without being forced to, because it is my understanding that Australians are big friendly people just like us. And you don't have to force them to be friendly, they just are, just like islanders everywhere.

\\ψ(

A NOTE ON THE TYPE

Dante was designed by Giovanni Mandersteig (1892–1977) and cut by Charles Malin (1883–1955), a talented Parisian punchcutter, in 1954. Originally a private foundry type for the Officina Bodoni at Verona, Dante was later released by The Monotype Corporation, for machine composition in 1957 and in digital form in the early 1990s. The letterforms of Mandersteig's Dante were greatly influenced by his study of types by the fifteenth-century Italian punchcutter Francesco Griffo. Other interpertations of Griffo's types include the roman letters of Bembo and Poliphilus and Mandersteig's Griffo. The version of Dante used here has been slightly modified to better reflect Mandersteig's letterforms.   A. S.

Text copyright © Jonathan Campbell, 2004
Illustration copyright © L. C. Campbell, 2004

All rights reserved. No part of this publication may be reproduced in any form without the prior written consent of the publisher. Any requests for the photocopying of any part of this book should be directed in writing to the Access Copyright (The Canadian Copyright Licensing Agency).

The quotation from Peter V. Marinelli's *Pastoral* (London: Methuen, 1971) is reproduced with permission.

The characters and events of this book are fictitious. Resemblance to actual events or persons, living or dead, is entirely coincidental.

Typeset in Dante by Andrew Steeves, printed offset on Zephyr laid paper and Smyth-sewn at Gaspereau Press.

Gaspereau Press acknowledges the support of the Canada Council for the Arts and the Nova Scotia Department of Tourism & Culture.

2 4 6 8 9 7 5 3 1

National Library of Canada Cataloguing in Publication

Campbell, Jonathan, 1961–
Tarcadia / Jonathan Campbell.

ISBN 1-894031-94-6
I. Title.

PS8605.A547T37 2004   C813'.6
C2004-902116-8

GASPEREAU PRESS ❧ PRINTERS & PUBLISHERS
47 CHURCH AVENUE, KENTVILLE
NOVA SCOTIA, CANADA B4N 2M7